The Price of Freedom

By Donna Every

The Price of Freedom
Copyright © 2013 by Donna Every. All rights reserved.

This book is a work of fiction. Names, characters, places and incidents are either products of the author's imagination or are used fictitiously.

Cover design © 2013 by Simone Davis. All rights reserved.
Cover photography by Andre Williams
Model: Sarah Lambert

ISBN-13: 9781494204945
ISBN-10: 1494204940

Dedication

This book is dedicated to my dad who died before it was finished.
He was my biggest salesman and greatest supporter.
May he rest in peace.

Acknowledgements

I would like to acknowledge all the people who helped to make this book a reality.

Morris Greenidge, noted Barbadian historian, who shared his great knowledge of Barbados' history with me. Thanks also to Penny Hynam who loaned me books from her substantial library and did a wonderful job of editing the manuscript. I would like to thank those who helped to create the beautiful cover: Andre William, the photographer, Sarah Lambert, the cover model and Simone Davis the designer. Thanks also to my dear friend Hudson Husbands who loaned me his copy of Richard Ligon's *"The True and Exact History of the island of Barbadoes 1657"* which I drew on heavily. And last but not least, my wonderful husband, Stephen who cooked many meals while I wrote and my friends Alastair Dent, Rachel Read, Maureen Earle and Kashka Haynes who read the manuscript and gave me feedback.

Chapter One

June 1694
The Acreage Plantation, Barbados

Deborah practically ran from the dining room in her haste to escape William's smoldering gaze that burned into her more hotly with each course. Her heart pummeled her ribs as fear and anger battled for supremacy and she fled out to the kitchen where she could have a brief respite until it was time to serve the next course.

The plain servant's dress she wore did nothing to deter him. She had felt him mentally stripping it from her vulnerable body and knew she was as powerless to stop his thoughts as she would be to stop him when he chose to act.

She was a chattel in his father's house and if he wanted her there was nothing she could do about it, short of running away. But she had seen what happened to those that ran away. Besides she couldn't leave her mother and where would they go anyway? How would they survive? So she would have to stay and endure; at least for now. They may own her body but they would never own her soul.

The Edwards were hosting a dinner party, plantation style, and the five of them were joined by a family from a neighboring plantation with some visiting relatives from England. The long mahogany table could easily seat eighteen but tonight there were just fourteen at dinner and the amount of food she and Cassie, the other house slave, had served could have surely fed the entire slave population of The Acreage, if they were ever so fortunate to taste the delicacies that were presented tonight.

They had already brought in beef, stewed chicken and a leg of pork, followed by pickled oysters, anchovies, caviar and olives, potato pudding, cassava cakes and all sorts of vegetables accompanied by vast quantities of wine and brandy for the men and non-alcoholic drinks for the ladies.

Deborah took several breaths to compose herself before heading to the small table in the corner where the house slaves were eating their corn soup. Cassie had said that she would wait by the dining room so that she could let Deborah know when it was time for the last course which was dessert, so she folded her arms on the table to create a pillow for her head and lay down.

"Deborah, what is wrong with you child?" her mother asked from across the table.

"Nothing. I'm just tired," she answered raising her head slightly. The last thing she wanted was to add to her mother's burdens.

Sarah, her mother, was a mulatto whose light brown skin and curly hair were a testimony of the fate that many African slave women suffered at the hands of a white overseer or master. At thirty-four she was still very beautiful and it was well known that she had commanded the high price of £50 when the master bought her from another plantation seventeen years ago, to help his wife with the children.

William had been four, Mary two and Rachel had just been born. After they had grown up, Sarah was given the responsibility for doing the laundry, the ironing and sewing for the household. Deborah saw genuine tiredness on her mother's face and felt justified for the lie she'd told.

She knew that the mistress made her mother's life difficult since it was no secret in the household that she was the master's favorite.

Her own fair skin paled as her thoughts led her back to William and it was only the attractive tinge of olive that saved her face from looking chalky. The green eyes that darkened with renewed anger and the stubborn chin which she now lifted, gave her a greater resemblance to the master than his two daughters, a fact that was a source of consternation to the mistress. William on the other hand, favored his father with a ruggedly handsome face and thick dark brown hair but cold flat eyes.

"Deborah, they're ready for the next course," Cassie announced, bringing in empty plates on a trolley.

She reluctantly got to her feet and moved to load another trolley with plates of custard, stewed guava and cheese cake that the cook had put out.

Her mother rose and came behind her, saying quietly: "I know that William has been bothering you but don't worry, I'm going talk to the master when he sends for me."

Deborah nodded without answering. She didn't know what talking to the master would do. She knew that if William wanted her he would have her. After all, he always got what he wanted.

She served the master first and she and Cassie moved down opposite sides of the table. On her side were the girls, who were separated by two of their girlfriends and strategically seated across the table from the younger male visitors. They favored their mother with roundish faces, blue eyes and dark blonde hair which they wore high up on their heads in elaborate styles with tendrils teasing their cheeks. Who would believe that she had played and learned how to read and write with them? Now that they were nineteen and seventeen and she was sixteen, she was no longer a playmate, she was their slave.

"What's that Deborah?" William asked from the foot of the table, drawing her attention. As if he couldn't see, she thought angrily. "It looks tempting," he added with a falsely innocent look.

"Custard, stewed guava and cheese cake," she answered shortly, dropping a plate in front of him. Her attitude could have earned her a slap but he just smiled and replied: "My favorites. I can hardly wait to taste them," he added softly.

His cold green eyes slid to her bosom leaving her in no doubt that he didn't mean the dessert. She turned away abruptly as fear and anger battled in her. He had been content to stalk her before, but she could tell that he was getting ready for the kill.

William wanted Deborah. Every time she served dinner, her graceful movements enticed him and her long elegant neck seemed to beckon him to taste it. He wasn't even deterred by her off-putting manner. If anything it was a challenge for him and he needed some kind of challenge in his life lest he died of boredom. Although it was fun to play with her he didn't intend to wait much longer.

He couldn't remember ever being denied anything in his life. As the first born and only son, his mother lavished her attention on him and gave him whatever he wanted. He hardly ever saw his father when he was growing up since he was more focused on bringing the plantation back to profitability, than on his children or his wife for that matter.

That didn't stop him from finding time to enjoy the beautiful slave women that his plantation was famous for, William thought resentfully. After Sarah had been there for a while the other house slaves started calling her Mistress Sarah but he didn't understand why, until he got older and realized that she was his father's mistress and therefore enjoyed an elevated status among them.

His father was therefore in no position to tell him anything when he started to follow in his footsteps with his own enjoyment of the slave girls on the plantation.

He resented the fact that his father didn't bother to hide his preference for slave women, and Sarah in particular, and it angered him to see the humiliation his mother suffered as a result.

He couldn't do anything about that, after all his father was lord and master of the plantation for now, but he would extract his revenge on Deborah. He knew that her mother protected her and used her influence with his father to prevent her from being sold or offered to any of the visitors who often stayed at the plantation. That was fine with him though because, as far as he was concerned, she was just saving her precious daughter for him.

"I'd like to get my hands on that one." A voice interrupted his thoughts. His longtime friend Henry Bowyer who lived on the neighboring plantation, leaned over and whispered in his ear as Deborah left the room.

"Not before me, my friend."

"You mean to say you haven't sampled it yet? That's not like you," he teased.

"I haven't been able to get her alone. The mother watches her like a hawk and my father favors her, so it hasn't been easy."

"Next time he's off the plantation why don't you pretend to be sick and ask for her to bring your dinner to your room?"

"Brilliant!" praised William, smiling slowly. The thought made him shift in his chair with anticipation. "Yes. That's what I'll do."

"Since it was my idea, I want all the details."

William began to feel much better. From the time Deborah had turned sixteen, he'd given himself permission to have her; not that he really needed to wait until she was sixteen, but it gave him something to look forward to.

He and Henry had taken to spending a weekend in Town from time to time to relieve their boredom. Between drinking and gambling in the taverns and patronizing the best brothels, they usually came home with barely two shillings to rub together.

It would be at least two months before they would be able to enjoy another weekend so he had to create some form of entertainment for himself and he couldn't think of anything more entertaining than overcoming Deborah's resistance.

Four weeks earlier

"Wake up, wake up, Deborah," urged her mother shaking her shoulder.

Deborah cracked one eye open and saw through the tiny window that it was still dark outside and turned over to get a few more minutes of sleep. The pallet she was lying on was not the most comfortable, but at least it was warmer than the chilliness of the morning outside of the hut where she slept.

"Wake up!" her mother repeated. "It's your birthday! You're sixteen today," she added excitedly.

That roused Deborah from her sleep but no excitement filled her at the thought of turning sixteen, instead an uncharacteristic hopelessness came over her until she ruthlessly pushed it aside and made way for the customary resilience to rise up in her, giving her the strength to face another day.

"So what?" she asked her mother huskily, her voice rough with sleep. "All it means is that I've been a slave for sixteen years!"

She pushed the thin sheet off her shapely body and sat up, rubbing her eyes. She felt bad the moment the words left her mouth as she saw her mother's excited face fall but she found it hard to apologize for saying what she meant.

"I have something for you," her mother said quietly, ignoring her outburst. After all, she couldn't argue or reason with the truth. "The master gave me some material he bought from town and I made this for you."

With that she held out a beautiful dress of green satin enhanced by an overskirt of the palest cream with the same material trimming the sleeves. Around the modest neckline tiny flowers were beautifully embroidered in the same cream color. It looked as fashionable as any dress a free woman would wear.

"Thank you, mama. It is beautiful. When did you make it?" She softened her voice. What was the point of upsetting her mother; it wasn't her fault that they were slaves.

"I worked on it after you went to sleep at night." Deborah was touched by the effort her mother had gone to so she held back the words that were on her tongue to ask where she would wear it.

"I'll put it in the trunk that the master gave me," Deborah said getting up.

"I warmed up some water in the front room for you," her mother said, making her way through the partition to the front of the hut that she and Deborah shared. Deborah wondered how long she had been up since she was dressed for the day and her hair was already covered by its customary handkerchief.

The cocks began to crow signaling that dawn was approaching. Since she had to help get breakfast for the family she washed quickly, while her mother made her way to the big house, pulled on a drab brown dress and cleaned her teeth with a chew stick which made her teeth white and her breath fresh.

Efficiently unraveling her long plait which fell past her shoulders, she pulled a brush hastily through the soft brown waves and plaited it again, piling it on her head and wrapping it in a large handkerchief before heading to the kitchen to help with the breakfast.

"Good morning, Master Thomas," said Deborah, putting his plate of eggs, fried pork and fried plantain in front of him.

"Good morning Deborah," he answered with a warm smile. "Happy birthday," he said handing her a small beaded purse that felt quite heavy.

"Thank you, Master," she said, slipping the gift into her pocket to examine later. Deborah was surprised that he had remembered her birthday, but maybe her mother had told him. In any case the birth of all slaves on the plantation were recorded so he may have come across it as he was adding in the new one that had been born that week.

"Your mother told me she made a dress for your birthday with some material that I gave her. Did you like it?"

"Yes, master. Thank you." Deborah was surprised that he and her mother talked about such things. She had not thought that they talked at all.

Thomas Edwards was a tall, handsome man in his early fifties with short thick hair almost the same brown as Deborah's, although it was now sprinkled with grey. He was still very fit and trim from his active involvement on the plantation. It was one of the largest in Barbados covering over 500 acres, of which more than half was planted with the precious Muscovado sugar that had made the island rich. His father had visited Barbados and purchased the plantation in the 50's and returned to England, appointing a manager to run it.

For several years it appeared to be doing well but within twenty years the plantation was struggling under a heavy burden of debt and on his father's death he had moved to Barbados to run it himself. It was then he discovered that the manager had mismanaged the property and had absconded with much of the profits.

He had to sell off most of the slaves and servants and start afresh, running the plantation with a minimal amount of labor until it began to prosper again and he was able to increase his slaveholding and now had two overseers to help him. To diversify his investments he had invested in a ship with two other planters and he had recently started distilling rum.

William came in a few minutes later, followed by the mistress and the two girls. Deborah was surprised to see the women at breakfast so early. They were dressed in fancy clothes so she assumed they were going out.

Looking up as the women came in, Thomas absently noted that they were dressed attractively for the day but they paled in comparison to Deborah, with her beautiful olive skin and exotic looks.

"I will let the cook know that you're ready for breakfast," offered Deborah heading out to the kitchen and giving William a wide berth. His eyes followed her as she left the room.

"I hope you haven't forgotten that we had planned to go into Town today," Elizabeth said to her husband taking her place at the table. "We will take Cassie and Jethro."

"This is not the best time to take staff into town. You know that we're in the midst of harvest. You should take Deborah instead. It's her birthday."

"It is? Then the last thing she would want to be doing on her birthday is traipsing all through Town carrying parcels for us," said the mistress dismissively as Deborah returned carrying three plates on a tray.

"I didn't know it was your birthday," said William lazily, looking her up and down. She quickly looked at the master who must have mentioned it to them but he was eating his breakfast.

"Happy birthday, Deborah," said the girls. "We'll get you something in town."

"Thank you." She noticed that the mistress seemed to begrudge offering her even a birthday greeting and had started on her breakfast without comment.

"How old are you now?" William asked, as if he didn't know that she was a year younger than Rachel.

"Sixteen," she answered shortly.

"You're all grown up." He smiled in a satisfied sort of way, which made her skin crawl. His father gave him a hard look which he ignored. William didn't care how he looked at him; nothing would stop him from sampling the delectable slave girl who was now serving him.

Chapter Two

July 1694

D eborah was surprised to see that only the ladies of
the house were at dinner. She and Cassie were instructed to put the dishes on the table so that they could
serve themselves and informed that the master had
gone to Town on business and was spending the night
there. She assumed that William had gone with him
and she was relieved that she would have peace tonight
from his prying eyes.

Returning from the kitchen with a light step, carrying a platter of baked chicken and one of cassava cakes,
she set them on the table with the other dishes and
turned to go.

"Enjoy the meal, mistress," she offered generously.

"Thank you Deborah. William is not feeling well
this evening. Make one of your teas for headache and
take it and his dinner to his room for him," Elizabeth
instructed her.

Deborah often used plants that she grew or that were
bought in Town to treat minor illnesses. She'd never had
to treat William for any illness. He was never sick. It was

clearly a way to get her alone. Didn't his mother realize that? Perhaps she knew what he planned and didn't care; after all William always got what he wanted and he wanted her.

He was obviously tired of playing with her and was ready to taste "the dessert", as he had said at dinner a few weeks ago.

"I can take it, mistress," offered Cassie. She knew that William had his eyes on Deborah and wanted to protect her. She had experienced what it was to lose her innocence, having been violated by another master when she was just fifteen.

"No. He asked specifically for Deborah," Elizabeth stated and that was that. She didn't expect any further discussion.

"Yes, ma'am," agreed Cassie casting a sympathetic glance at Deborah. Deborah's silence and the narrowing of her eyes, spoke loudly of her rebellion at the idea.

Returning to the kitchen on leaden feet she asked the sweating cook to prepare a tray for William while she got the leaves to make the tea. She knew that he didn't really have a headache but she would play along. She looked around for her mother, and was relieved to see that she was not there; she was probably still ironing the clothes that had been washed that day. At least she would be spared the anguish of knowing where she was going.

Heart beating like one of the drums that were now forbidden to the slaves, she took the tray and made her way up the stairs to his room which was at the far end of the hall.

Balancing it in one hand, she knocked and heard him command her to come in. Her hand shook on the knob as she opened the door. She hated herself for that show of weakness.

"Deborah, what took you so long? I've been waiting for you." He certainly didn't look sick to her as he sat up in his four poster bed with his bare feet crossed at the ankles, wearing a robe.

"Bring the tray over here and close the door behind you." She hesitated a few seconds as she deliberated on whether or not to obey him. Calculating the distance between the bed and the door she knew that if she took the tray she couldn't get away before he got to her.

"I'm waiting," he added, "and I don't like to wait."

Her breathing rapidly increased as panic began to overtake her. She knew that unless some miracle happened he would have her and there was nothing she could do to stop him.

Moving like molasses she inched toward the bedside table, keeping him in her sight through the corner of her eye and holding the tray in front of her protectively as if it could be any defense against him.

She put down the tray and turned quickly towards the door. She was halfway across the room and to freedom when she felt, more than saw, the movement as William sprang from the bed and caught her around her waist, dragging her back against him with her head against his shoulder.

She stiffened up like a corpse as she felt his arousal.

"You didn't really think I would let you go, did you?" he taunted softly.

He pulled the handkerchief off her head and her long plait cascaded over the front of one shoulder to her bosom.

"Undo it!" He commanded. She hesitated and his hand tightened warningly around her waist until she complied with shaking hands.

Pushing the soft waves aside, he kissed her neck and slipped his hand into the neckline of her dress. She trembled in fright and could hear her teeth start to chatter.

"Beautiful," he praised. "And mine to do with as I please."

"P...please, William." She hated herself for begging. "Let me go."

"That's Master William to you. Let you go?" he scoffed. "Why would I do that when I've waited for this for weeks?" He laughed as he carried her over to the bed and dropped her onto it. Some distant part of her mind briefly noticed the softness of the mattress that contrasted with the hard pallet that she slept on.

She immediately tried to scramble off the other side but he caught her by one foot and dragged her back. As she struggled to break free he held her with one hand and pulled back the other to strike her. Deborah twisted her head away to protect her face as she braced herself for the blow, but it never came. Instead he tossed her back on the bed and threw himself on top of her, covering her mouth with his hand to silence her as she opened her mouth to scream.

She pushed at his shoulders and tried to buck him off but he was much stronger than she was. He rolled slightly to the side so that he could pull her skirt up to her waist baring her before quickly pinning her thrashing her legs down with one of his.

"Don't do this!" she cried wrenching her mouth from beneath his hand. "This is wrong! I'm your sister!"

"You're not my sister. You're my slave," he taunted, pulling apart his robe. He wasted no time with preliminaries and she soon felt pain rip through her body as he tore her innocence from her and changed her life forever.

Silent tears ran down her face even as anger and hatred took root, hardening her heart and she swore to herself that she would die before she let another man violate her again.

Sarah finished the ironing and came back to the kitchen.

"Wuhloss, I glad to get through that pile of clothes," she said tiredly. She was greeted with silence and the awkward shuffling of the house slaves.

"Something happened?" she asked as she felt a prickle of alarm.

"The mistress said that Master William was sick and he asked for Deborah to bring a tray to his room," Cassie answered. "She didn't come back down," she added quietly.

Sarah bent over, wrapping her hands around her waist, as grief and anger swept through her with the force of a hurricane. She knew, without anyone telling her, what that meant. Hatred rose up in her for William for stealing her child's innocence and for the very life that they had been born into. She hated that it made her powerless to protect her child.

She put a hand over her mouth to hold back the wail that was rising in her throat and ran out to their hut where she found Deborah lying on her pallet with her back to the door and her knees drawn up to her chest.

"Deborah?" Sarah said quietly, sitting down next to her and gently touching her shoulder. Deborah turned over and Sarah briefly saw her face that was red from shame and from crying, before she threw herself into her arms and began to weep afresh.

"I'm so sorry child. So sorry that this happened. I'm going to talk to Master Thomas when he comes home tomorrow and tell him what that boy did to you." She stroked Deborah's hair comfortingly, even as tears streamed from her own eyes.

"I told him that I was his sister but he wouldn't listen!" Deborah cried. "I hate him so much I could kill him!"

"Sh, don't let anybody hear you saying that girl! Don't worry, I will talk to Master Thomas. I will talk to Master Thomas."

Deborah let her go on, but she really didn't hold out any hope. It was going to be up to her to do something because she couldn't live this way anymore. She was the master's property! He could leave her in his will to William; he could sell her if he wanted to; his family could do whatever they wanted to her because they owned her. How could that be right? She was a person.

She had a soul and her soul cried out for freedom, whatever the cost.

Thomas sat at his desk and opened a ledger. He and one of the overseers had left Town at nine that morning and had just got back to the plantation with five new slaves. Jethro, the carpenter who also helped around the house, had driven the cart, but he was tired from the long, bumpy drive and he didn't feel like dealing with the books but he had to make a record of the new slaves they had just bought.

The door flew open with force, bringing his head up sharply to reprimand whoever had dared to come into his office without permission. When he saw that the uninvited visitor was a very distraught Sarah, he held his peace.

"What's happened Sarah?" he asked getting out of his chair and coming around to grasp her shoulders. "Has something happened to Deborah?"

"Yes, something happened to Deborah! William raped her last night. He waited until you had left the plantation and told the mistress he was sick and he wanted Deborah to bring a tray to his room and he raped my child." She began to weep.

Thomas fought against the rage that rose up in him. He had warned William not two weeks ago to stay away from Deborah and he couldn't believe that he had blatantly ignored his orders. The boy had gone too far. He was putting him on the next boat to England. Perhaps he would learn some civilized behavior from his English kin.

"I will deal with William. There is a boat sailing to England in the next few days. I'm going to make sure that he's on it. A few years in England may do him good."

"You would do that Master Thomas? Oh, thank you, thank you. Deborah will be so glad to hear that."

Thomas nodded, distractedly. Telling Sarah was the easy part. Dealing with William and Elizabeth wouldn't be that easy.

When Sarah left, Thomas returned to his leather chair and sank down into it, holding his head in his hands. When his son should be looking to get more involved in the plantation, all he was doing was wasting his life away.

When he was in town he had found out the extent to which William had been drinking and gambling. He owed some of the tavern owners a lot of money. This was the last straw. He wasn't working so hard for William to gamble away everything and now he had dared to violate Deborah although he had been warned to stay away from her.

He pulled out a piece of parchment and dipped his quill in ink and began a letter to his uncle in England. Unfortunately the only notice his uncle would have that William was coming was when he was presented the letter by William himself. He only hoped that he wouldn't put him on the next boat back.

Looking out the window, he saw William riding into the yard and shouted through the window for him to come into the office.

Belligerence was like a cloak on William as he walked through the door.

"You wanted me?"

"Why the hell did you take Deborah to your bed last night? You could have had your pick of any of the other slave girls!" Thomas didn't waste time in getting to the point.

"Why should you care? Were you saving her for yourself?" His son sneered. In two seconds his father was on his feet and had delivered a blow to his insolent face. For a moment, William looked as if he would strike him in return but he managed to restrain himself.

"I don't sleep with my offspring," Thomas snarled. "And neither should you."

"She's just a slave." He defended.

"I've had enough of your behavior! I'm sending you to England for a few years. I hope that you come back more civilized. There is a boat leaving in a few days and you can travel on that. Until then don't let me hear of this happening again. Do you understand me? I hope to God she's not pregnant."

"You're sending me to England? Over a slave?"

"This is about more than a slave. I hadn't been to Town in over three months and as soon as I arrived in town more than one merchant were waiting to present me with IOUs for your gambling and drinking. I didn't build this plantation back up for you to gamble away."

"You can spend a few years in England getting some education so that you'll have some use when you come back. Go and break the news to your mother and start packing."

William was speechless. He couldn't believe that his father was serious but he had never seen that particular implacable look on his face. He turned and walked out without uttering another word. This wasn't the end of the story; he would write the ending, not have it dictated to him.

Thomas had just finished the letter to his uncle and he felt that he was doing the right thing for William. He admitted to himself that as a father he had not been a good example so he really couldn't expect any better of his son. He was hopeful that the years in England, away from colonial life, would mature him and make him into a good man.

He was just about to seal the letter when the door was thrown open for the second time that day and this time his wife stormed in.

"What is the meaning of this?" he demanded.

"I should be asking you that! William tells me you're sending him to England in a few days. You can't be serious!"

"Believe me I'm very serious and unless you want to be on the boat with him, madam, I would suggest you adopt a more respectful tone."

Elizabeth bit back a reply and asked in a more reasonable tone, "What's brought this on so suddenly?"

"As if you don't know. What did you think would happen when you made Deborah take a tray to his room last night?"

"What of it? That's what you use them for isn't it? Is she more to you than your own son?"

Thomas fell silent. He had no defense for that. Elizabeth was right. His own behavior had taught his son well.

"That's only part of it. He's been drinking and gambling in town and piling up a lot of debts. If some disease doesn't kill him from sleeping about with whores in Town then one of the merchants might. I think it's best for him to spend a few years in England. I'm sure he'll be the better for it."

"And what of you?" she asked bitterly, tears filling her eyes, "Is there anything that would make you the better for it?" With that she ran out, heading blindly for her room.

Elizabeth was relieved to reach her room without running into anyone. She tried to remember the last time Thomas had shared it with her and could not. His room was separated from hers by a dressing room and although the walls were fairly thick she could hear the muffled sounds coming from his room on the nights he sent for Sarah. It was beyond humiliating.

She had loved him as a young girl and was delighted when her father had arranged for them to marry. The thought of coming out to Barbados with him and starting a new life in the colonies was exciting. It had not been easy at first, as he rebuilt the plantation, but she hardly complained.

As sugar became like gold in Barbados and they repaid their debts and began to prosper, Thomas was able to take on overseers and to increase his slave-holding again and then he had bought Sarah to help with the children. She had taken one look at the beautiful mulatto woman and knew the real reason Thomas had purchased her for the exorbitant sum of £50, as she had discovered by looking through the books in his office.

She knew that Sarah wasn't the first Thomas had bedded but she couldn't help but notice the way he looked at her and it pained her to admit that he had never looked at her with the stark desire that she saw in his eyes as they followed the slave woman when he was unaware that she was watching him.

When she discovered that Sarah was pregnant just a year after she came, it was almost more than she could bear. The child had looked like Thomas from early and she felt as if she was the laughing stock of the island when neighbors came to visit even though they never openly remarked on the resemblance.

She was not the only one that had to deal with this kind of humiliation; it was common for many of the planters' wives in Barbados, but she had feelings and she was not going to let him humiliate her this way anymore. She couldn't believe that he would take the side of those slave women over her son. She hoped that one day he would suffer for this as she had suffered.

The tension in the house at dinner permeated the kitchen where the house slaves gathered quietly to eat their meal. Deborah reluctantly joined them at Sarah's urging, only because she had only eaten a little porridge that morning in their hut and she was starving. She avoided the sympathetic gazes of the other slaves and kept her head down as she ate.

Finally breaking the silence Cassie said, "Deborah, you don't have nothing to be shame about. The shame is William's not yours and we know how you feel because it happen to us too." Tears pricked Deborah's eyes at her words of sympathy and she nodded silently, too overcome with emotion to speak, but the truth of Cassie's words enabled her to lift her head. Sarah sent a silent look of thanks to Cassie.

Jethro came in after closing up the house. He had driven the master to Town the day before and had spent the night but had heard the news when he came back. He was almost as distraught as Sarah since he had deep feelings for her and looked on Deborah as a daughter but since Sarah belonged to the master he knew he would never be able to marry her as he desired.

He was a tall, well built, handsome man with ebony skin. He had lived on the plantation all his life and had been just a teenager when the master had come to Barbados. He was now forty and once the master had discovered that he was a gifted carpenter he had taken him from the fields.

He now pulled up a chair at the table and looked around furtively before announcing to the women that he had been to a secret Quaker meeting in town the night before.

"The Quakers used to live in Barbados years ago and they would speak out about how bad the masters treated their slaves. All of a sudden they stopped them from holding meetings and they made their lives so miserable that most of them left the island and went to America. They only have a few left back but they don't hold big meetings now. But every now and then they would have a small one at a house," Jethro explained.

"They said God loved the world so much that he sent Jesus to set us free," he told them. All the slaves sat up attentively at that.

"Who is this Jesus? He goin' lead a revolt?" Cassie asked. The last one had been four years earlier but it had failed.

"No," Jethro explained patiently. "Jesus is God's son. They say that if we sin we are slaves to sin so Jesus come to set us free from sin. From doing wrong things."

"It's the masters that doing wrong things," Cassie insisted. "Look what Master William do to Deborah last night."

"All of us is do wrong things."

"So if we keep doing wrong things we will be slaves?" Hattie, one of the newer slaves, asked.

"Slaves to sin," repeated Jethro.

"So how is Jesus supposed to set us free from sin?" Asked Deborah joining in the conversation.

"By dying for our sins."

"So how that could help us?" Cassie asked.

"By coming back to life. That is how he able to save us." The slaves could not understand this and Jethro could not explain it so they were confused.

"All I know is that if you believe he died for your sins you will be free."

"But we won't be free from slavery, so as Cassie said, how does that help us?" Deborah pointed out bitterly. Jethro had no answer.

Deborah had heard about God when the children's tutor had taught them but he never really talked about Jesus or him dying for their sins. Anyway how important was being free from sin when she was still a slave? If he could free her from slavery that was one thing but if he couldn't or wouldn't, why would she need him? She would just have to find a way to do it herself.

Chapter Three

October 1695
Charles Town, Carolina

Richard Fairfax was going over the manifest for their next shipment to England. He noted that an increasing percentage of the cargo was rice and his instincts told him that this was the way of the future for Carolina and they needed to be a part of it. Convincing his father of that was another matter.

"Father, although our business is doing fairly well, mainly through our exports, we can't compete with the goods that the pirates sell at a fraction of the price here in Carolina. And we still have the French war ships to worry about in the Caribbean Sea, so I think it is important for us to diversify. We should invest in a plantation and start to cultivate rice. That way, rather than shipping other people's rice we will be shipping our own as well. Some of the other planters are already way ahead and have been paying their taxes with rice for the last four years. It is clear that rice is the way of the future."

"What do we know about growing rice? We know how to fill ships with cargo and get the best price for it and we've done exceedingly well at that."

"I'm not disputing that but rice will be to Carolina what sugar is to Barbados. That's why we should invest in it. We can get slaves from West Africa to work on the plantation. They are being brought from there particularly because they know how to grow rice."

"Then we'll be relying totally on them. How do we know they won't try to deliberately ruin the crops?"

"Why would they?" Richard asked in exasperation as he ran a hand through his long, dark hair impatiently. At twenty-four years old he had been involved in his father's business for eight years, except for the two that he had spent in England and even then he had been learning different aspects of business.

James Fairfax, at fifty-two was set in his ways and was resistant to change. He had said that he was ready to turn the business over to Richard but he still seemed very reluctant to do so. Their constant battles were a source of frustration to Richard and he wondered why he had been sent to England to study if every suggestion he made was met with resistance.

His younger brother Charles, Richard noted, was at least using his training, as he had been taught how to keep the books and deal with the paperwork. He preferred to spend his time sourcing profitable cargo for their ships and often worked alongside the crew helping to load the cargo, which was evidenced by his well muscled body and work roughened hands.

"Look, Benjamin Carlisle and I have been talking. Since his illness, he's not up to running his plantation anymore and since he has no sons, we agreed that it would make sense for you and Ann to marry. You could talk to him about converting his plantation into rice production rather than starting fresh."

Richard thought about that for a moment. The Carlisles, who had come to Carolina from England a few years after his father, owned a plantation in the Low country as well as a house in town. Their only son had died in childhood and they had two daughters, of which Ann was the elder.

He had no objection to Ann as such. She was quite an attractive girl and he knew that she had been smitten with him for years. If he married her he could run the plantation without having to buy land and he could instead take the money and invest it in clearing the property to plant rice and buy slaves. He knew that he could make it successful and show his father that he was right about rice.

Richard smiled. "That would be good," he agreed. "I could invest the money into converting the plantation if he agrees. I'll ask her father permission to court her right away and I'm sure that we will be able to announce our engagement by Christmas."

"Good man," his father praised, slapping him on the shoulder.

Richard was anxious to talk to Ben Carlisle as soon as possible. Since he was no longer able to run the plantation himself he would probably allow him to implement whatever changes he wanted, especially since he was willing to invest in it.

His juices began to flow in anticipation. He needed to learn about using Africans for labor, and although many planters used them in Carolina, including Ben, he preferred to go to where they had been using slaves for decades: Barbados.

Richard's father, his father's sister Elizabeth and her husband Thomas had travelled to Barbados together, where Thomas took over the running of his father's large sugar plantation which had been mismanaged for years. However land was by then becoming very scarce and his father, James, had been unable to secure a sizeable portion and had decided to go on to Carolina with a group of Barbadian Adventurers to help with the colonization.

Land was plentiful in Carolina but was being distributed based on the number of family members and slaves or servants owned or brought into the colony. Having no slaves of his own, and seeing an opportunity to ship goods between England, Barbados and Carolina, James had bought two sloops with his money, hired some able sea men and began to trade. He sent for his fiancée, Mary, from England and they had married early in 1671 and had Richard later the same year.

The first Navigation Act which legislated that produce from the colonies could only be shipped to England in vessels owned by English or colonists boosted their revenue considerably in the early days and they were able to expand to their current fleet of five ships which traded not only with England but with several of the islands, primarily Barbados which was like Carolina's mother land.

They had an agent in Barbados whose job was to ship sugar and rum to Carolina and handle the lumber, pipe staves, pitch, tar, beef and corn that they exported to Barbados. However Richard had been somewhat dissatisfied with the agent's performance for several months now and would use the opportunity to meet with him while he was in Barbados.

It would probably be more beneficial to go in the first months of the New Year. That would give him time to begin courting Ann and get his future father-in-law to agree to his suggestion before he left for Barbados. If he stayed there at least three months he should be able to see the canes harvested and processed into sugar as well.

For the first time in a long while he began to feel excited. He would talk to Ben Carlisle that very day. He would keep his plan to go to Barbados quiet until next year to avoid any opposition to the plan. His aunt told his mother, who she corresponded with, that they were welcome to visit any time and he would certainly take her up on the offer. It was shameful that they had boats which sailed to and from Barbados frequently and they had never taken the time to visit the island.

Richard replaced the quill in the inkwell on his desk, glad that the chore had been completed. Letter writing and record keeping were a bane to him so he preferred to leave them to his brother Charles; however this was one that he had to deal with himself. He waited a minute for the last of the ink to dry and then read back the letter.

February 7, 1696
Charles Town, Carolina

Dear Uncle Thomas

I hope that this letter finds you in good health. I was just remarking to myself that although our ships frequently sail to Barbados, I have never accompanied one to visit you, to my shame. However mother often speaks of you and my aunt, and shares news of your life in Barbados from the letters that my aunt sends. She longs to see you both and hopes to visit you someday soon. My sister Charlotte will be getting married soon so perhaps my parents will visit you after the wedding.

My father has said that he plans to hand the running of the business over to me. Currently I oversee the operations while Charles is responsible for the administration. However I have entered into an arrangement to marry a young lady whose father owns a plantation in the Low country. He is no longer able to run it and intends to turn it over to me after the marriage. I am keen to convert it to rice production and will need to import slaves, primarily from West Africa, for labor.

Since you have used Africans on your plantation for many years, I desire to seek your advice on their use and to learn all that I can from you. I have given it much thought and I believe that I would best be served by a visit to Barbados. I therefore seek to impose upon your hospitality for about three months to observe your use of Africans in the production of sugar, as well as your upkeep of them to maximize the return on your investment, so that I can successfully implement the same upon my return to Carolina.

Mother has said that you and my aunt have extended an open invitation to visit Barbados at any time, so I will put my affairs in order here and set sail by the end of the month and should reach Barbados by the middle of March, barring any unforeseen circumstances.

I am looking forward to meeting you and my aunt and of course my cousins, Mary and Rachel. Mother tells me that William is still in England so it will please me greatly to help you on the plantation in his absence. Mother will no doubt be sending several gifts for the family and I will bring you some of Carolina's best tobacco.

Your faithful nephew
Richard Fairfax

Satisfied, he folded the letter, sealed it with some wax and called a servant to arrange to have it taken down to their next boat sailing for Barbados together with the one his mother had written.

"I saw Jackson heading down to the harbor with letters," said Charles coming into the small office a short while later.

"Yes, I've finally written to our uncle to let him know that I'm coming to Barbados. I couldn't put it off any longer."

"So when are you planning to sail?"

"At the end of the month. Father will no doubt take over my job, so everything will be fine."

"I'm not worried," assured Charles. "How is Ann taking the news?"

"I haven't had the opportunity to mention it to Ann as yet."

Charles sputtered, "Not had the opportunity? Richard you've been thinking about this for over a month! Don't you think you should have mentioned it to your fiancée by now?"

Richard shrugged. "I didn't want to bring it up until I had actually sent the letter to our uncle." Charles snorted at the poor excuse.

The truth was that Richard didn't want to deal with his fiancée's whining so he had delayed telling her as long as possible.

It hadn't been that much of a difficulty to convince Ann to marry him, since she had made no secret of the fact that she had set her heart on him from the time she was a young girl of fourteen to his eighteen and she always got what she set her heart on. They had officially become engaged on Christmas Eve the year before, on her twentieth birthday.

"I don't know why you treat Ann so abominably," protested Charles. "She's a beautiful girl, inside and out. She's too good for the likes of you."

"Then why don't you marry her?" Richard challenged. He knew that Charles admired Ann and if it wasn't for the plantation at stake, he would be the first to encourage a marriage between them, but fortunately Ann was besotted with him. To be honest he really didn't know why; he offered her no encouragement.

Charles scowled at him in reply and took out a ledger and started to work.

Ann was a pleasant girl, if somewhat spoiled, but she certainly didn't stir him to passion. Her glossy reddish brown hair and turquoise eyes were attractive, but her inane conversation was a source of aggravation for him. She seemed to have no interest in anything beyond the next new dress she would get from England or the next party she was going to.

After being with her for any length of time, Richard was sorely in need of the relief he got from visiting his mistress, Anise, a French woman whose family had moved to Charles Town in the late 80's to escape the persecution of the Huguenots in France. She obviously no longer followed their faith and apart from her other talents, she could at least provide him with good conversation or quietude, depending on his mood.

It was a pity he couldn't marry her, but since her father did not own a plantation, what would be the point. Just as well that he was ruled by his head and not his heart. That was not to say that his heart was involved where Anise was concerned; no it was definitely something else that made him seek her out regularly. Realizing that he'd been so busy he hadn't seen her for more than a week, he picked up his hat and headed for the door, telling Charles that he was going out.

"Where are you off to?" Charles called after him.

"To see Anise. I haven't seen her for nearly two weeks."

"You're incorrigible!"

"Women love incorrigible men," said Richard with a smile.

"Richard, I have missed you, chéri," declared Anise with a pout, her French accent distorting the English words in the way that Richard loved.

"Why have you not come to see me recently?" she demanded with her hands on her hips. Her black hair was piled in an elaborate style high on her head and her sparkling blue eyes challenged him. As beautiful as her face was, his eyes couldn't help their downward trek to her magnificent bosom that threatened to spill over the low neckline of her satin gown.

"I was busy Anise." He reluctantly pulled his gaze back to hers. "I've been putting things in place so that I can visit my uncle's plantation in Barbados at the end of the month."

"You're going to Barbados? Take me with you. I will keep you company on that long journey." She purred, drawing closer.

"Tempting, my love, but I don't think my aunt would approve of me bringing my mistress to stay at her house, especially when she knows that I'm engaged."

"I can't believe you are going to marry that girl, Richard. I have seen her in town and I don't know what you are thinking. She seems attractive enough but I can't imagine she will satisfy you." She stepped back from him.

"Darling, that's why I have you. I'm thinking how profitable her father's plantation will be when I convert it to rice. She's the older of two girls, you know, and her brother died in childhood, so her daddy wants to make sure there will be someone to run the plantation when he passes on."

"That's what I like about you, Richard. You don't pretend to be anything other than what you are; an opportunist."

"It takes one to know one, my love," he returned, taking the pins from her hair so that it fell down her back. He ran his fingers through the thick tresses, drawing her closer. "As much as I love to converse with you, I didn't come for conversation today. It's been almost two weeks since I saw you."

"And whose fault is that, chéri?"

"I confess that the fault is mine, but I intend to make up for my absence," he promised nibbling her neck.

"I look forward to that," she laughed throatily as she threw back her head to give him better access.

Pausing to unbutton her gown he encountered her tightly laced up stays. "Why do you women wear these contraptions?" he complained in frustration.

"If I had known you were coming today I wouldn't have bothered to put it on." He impatiently undid the laces and was rewarded by Anise taking a deep breath as she was freed from the instrument of torture.

"What a relief! That feels wonderful," she sighed blissfully.

"That's nothing compared to how wonderful you'll feel in a few minutes," he promised pushing the gown to the floor. Swinging her up into his arms he headed for her room in haste.

"How long will you be in Barbados?" asked Anise much later as she lay with her head on his chest.

"About three months."

"Three months! What will I do without you?"

"I'm sure you have plenty of admirers to keep you company while I am away." Richard was under no illusions that Anise would spend the time pining for him. She was too resourceful for that.

"What will you do in Barbados?"

"Learn how they use African slaves to help produce the sugar on the plantation. I want to accompany my uncle to a slave market to see how he selects slaves, what he looks for, how much he pays for them and how he upkeeps them. Things like that."

"You will be using Africans on the plantation then?"

"Yes, everyone else is. Apparently the ones from the West are very knowledgeable about cultivating rice."

"You're a good business man, Richard. I have no doubt you will be very successful. But I will miss you, chéri,"

Richard absently played with her hair as he replied "I'll miss you too."

"Will you be getting married when you come back?"

"Yes. I'll probably be married by the end of the year if not before."

"Will you continue to visit me when you're married?"

"Why would that change?"

"I don't know, you may fall passionately in love with your wife and become faithful."

Richard laughed quietly at the thought. "I don't think I have it in me to fall passionately in love, darling. I'm far too practical. But you certainly arouse the passion in me." With that he proceeded to show her just how much.

Chapter Four

Richard pulled on his black breeches, buttoned up his soft white linen shirt and sat on the side of his massive bed to put on his stockings and buckle his black shoes which had been polished to a high sheen by one of the servants. He donned a buff colored waistcoat and shrugged into a black jacket before heading downstairs to pick up his warm black coat from the coat hanger by the door.

He was escorting Ann to a party at the Berkeley's Charles Town house. The Berkeleys were a prominent family who owned a large plantation along the Ashley River but like so many of the elite, including the Carlisles, they kept a second property in town which they resided in during the winter.

In his opinion, the only good thing about this party was that it would give him the chance to talk to some of the planters who had already started to grow rice and find out how they were faring. Based on the quantities that they were shipping out, they seemed to be doing very well.

He met Charles at the bottom of the stairs and they went out to the coach where their servant, Jackson was sitting with the reins in hand.

"How was Anise?" Charles asked sarcastically.

"Happy to see me," replied Richard with a contented smile.

"I don't know how you can bed your mistress at four and take your fiancée to a party at seven without a twinge of conscience," Charles remarked.

"What has one to do with the other?" Richard asked, totally unconcerned.

Charles made a noise of disgust. "Ann deserves better than you."

"I believe you made that point today already," he agreed, "but our marriage will help the fortunes of both families."

"There's more to life than fortune, you know."

"Oh? Like what?"

"Well... there's love." Charles braced himself for Richard's scornful reply and he was not disappointed.

"Love?" Richard scoffed. "Spoken like a true romantic. Will love help to put food on the table, shelter over your head, clothes on your back? Give you respect among your peers?"

"There's no talking to you." Charles ended the conversation by looking out the window. He fervently hoped that one day Richard would be forced to eat his words.

"Here we are," announced Richard as the carriage drew to a halt in front of the Carlisle's town house. He alighted and disappeared into the house when the door was opened by a servant.

He returned in a few minutes with Ann who, in Charles's opinion, looked magnificent in a turquoise satin gown that matched her eyes and was a perfect foil for her auburn hair, and a long, warm looking cloak over her dress.

She was clinging to Richard's arm, gazing adoringly up at him and chatting away, while he looked slightly bored as he listened to her. Charles was once again angered by his brother's treatment of Ann; he would never treat her so shabbily if she was his.

"Hello Charles," she said and offered her hand for him to assist her into the carriage. She settled herself across from him as Richard got in next to her.

Charles was struck by the daintiness of her hand in his as he helped her up.

"Hello, Ann. You look beautiful tonight."

"Thank you. I just got this dress from France," she added. Richard almost rolled his eyes but caught himself in time.

"I'm looking forward to this party very much. The Berkeleys throw the best parties," she gushed.

"I hope you will save a dance for me," Charles said.

"If Richard consents," she said coyly, eyeing him as he gazed out the window.

"I'm sure Richard will be fine with it, won't you Richard?" Charles challenged.

"Hmm, of course," he said distractedly. He'd been listening to the conversation with one ear since his thoughts were on the trip that he would take to Barbados. He supposed now was as good time as any to break the news to Ann.

"By the way Ann, I'm going to Barbados at the end of the month."

Charles was dumbfounded. He couldn't believe that Richard would choose to break the news to Ann in this fashion.

"What!" Ann exclaimed in dismay. "Barbados? What are you going there for?"

"I'm going to visit my uncle's plantation to learn from him."

"Why do you need to go to Barbados for that? We have a plantation. How long will you be gone?"

"About three months." He answered her last question.

"Three months?" She whined. Richard was becoming impatient with her questions.

"We can talk about this later, Ann," Richard said abruptly, closing the conversation. Ann hung her head and Charles glimpsed tears on her lashes. He desperately wanted to comfort her and smash Richard's face at the same time.

"Don't let this ruin the evening," Charles said trying to lighten the atmosphere and was rewarded by a brave but tremulous smile from Ann.

"You're right Charles. You always cheer me up," she added pointedly.

"It gives me pleasure to see you happy, Ann."

"That's very sweet," Richard said drily, "but I encourage you to find your own fiancée and make her happy."

Ann's smile widened, thinking that Richard was being possessive but Charles knew exactly why Richard was warning him off. His sights were set on running her daddy's plantation.

Peter and Caroline Berkeley stood in the hallway of their town house, to welcome their guests. It was not as grand as their Ashley River property but was still fairly impressive.

"Good to see you, Richard, Charles," said Peter shaking their hands. "And Ann you look as beautiful as ever."

"Thank you Mr. Berkeley. My parents send their apologies that they were unable to come since my mother is feeling poorly."

"I do hope she feels better soon," sympathized Caroline as she kissed Ann.

"Thank you."

"Your parents and sister arrived a little while ago," she advised the brothers.

"Thank you, ma'am," they said. They had left in another carriage before them since they would not all have been able to fit into one.

Richard offered his arm to Ann and Charles was left to follow behind.

The room was brightly lit by massive chandeliers bearing scores of candles. Sheer white panels of cloth were draped across the ceiling, a safe distance from the chandeliers, giving the impression of clouds floating overhead.

"This is so beautiful!" exclaimed Ann excitedly.

"Yes, it is," agreed Charles coming to stand next to them.

Richard surveyed the room from his considerable height and spotted his father speaking to a group of planters close to the bar. The room was full of the crème de la crème of the Charles Town society and its environs.

"Ann, so wonderful to see you," his mother greeted her with a hug. "How are you, dear? You look lovely."

"Thank you, Mrs. Fairfax," she responded with a smile. "I am well."

"Charles, darling we really have to find you a nice girl like Ann, although they are in such short supply," said his mother to his embarrassment.

"Mother, I can find my own girl. I'm in no hurry to settle down."

"My dear I know you are only twenty-two, but it doesn't hurt to keep your eyes open. Look, there's Charlotte and Albert with Julia Drayton and some other young people. Ann, be a dear and take Charles over there. I'd like to have a word with Richard."

"I'd be happy to," said Ann and practically dragged the reluctant Charles to accompany her to visit with the group.

She waited until Ann and Charles were well away before she turned back to Richard and demanded, "What is this I'm hearing about you and a French mistress?"

"Depends on what you're hearing, mother."

"Don't be difficult, Richard."

"Sorry mother, I wasn't trying to be difficult. I was simply trying to ascertain what you were referring to specifically."

"So you don't deny that you are seeing a French woman?"

"Mother, I don't think this is something I should be discussing with you. And could we not have discussed this at home?"

"Don't patronize me Richard; I am not innocent of these things. However since I arrived, more than one of my friends has mentioned that they have seen you leaving the house of a French woman in town, although you are now engaged to Ann and it is of great concern to me."

Richard sighed. He really wasn't in the mood to have this discussion with his mother and he would not allow her to dictate his life.

"Anise is merely a diversion, mother, nothing more. Besides I knew her before I became engaged to Ann."

"Well I hope you plan to put an end to that diversion immediately," she said. "It is shameful! And as your fiancée, Ann deserves your respect."

"Yes, mother," he agreed in a conciliatory tone. "I see father talking to some planters, would you excuse me while I go and join him?"

"Certainly," his mother said tight-lipped. She knew that Richard had totally disregarded what she said and would do exactly as he pleased.

"Good night gentlemen. Good to see you." He was greeted warmly by the older men, who liked him and had great respect for his business acumen.

"Your father tells us that you're planning to visit Barbados," said one of the planters.

"Yes, I sent a letter to my uncle only today advising him of my visit. I'm going to observe how he runs his plantation."

"Their plantation system has done the island well and Carolina too. Barbados exports more than twice all the other islands put together."

"Yes, that Muscovado sugar isn't called white gold for nothing," remarked another planter.

"You will surely enjoy Barbados, my boy. I visited the island a few years ago," reminisced a neighboring planter, "and I found the plantation owners to be very hospitable. So hospitable in fact that I was offered the use of a beautiful mulatto house slave for the duration of my visit."

"I'm sure my uncle would never do such a thing," assured Richard. "Besides, I'm an engaged man."

"Speaking of which, where is your lovely fiancée?" asked his father.

"She is here somewhere. I'm sure that Charles is taking care of her."

"Well, don't you think that you should be the one doing that?" his father asked pointedly.

"Most assuredly," agreed Richard. "Please excuse me gentlemen." He would have to speak to them about cultivating rice later, after he had done his duty.

Richard looked around the room and saw Ann and Charles speaking with a group of young men and women.

"Good evening," greeted Richard, "I've come to claim my fiancée for a dance. Please excuse us."

Ann was delighted that Richard had come for a dance. She hoped that it would be a slow one but when they reached the dance floor, the musicians were playing some lively songs. Richard was a surprisingly good dancer, having been formally taught when he was in England. They danced several rounds until Richard led her off the dance floor, satisfied that he had done his duty.

"Thank you, miss," he flirted, bringing her hand to his lips. Ann shivered as his lips touched the back of her bare hand

"You're welcome, sir" she flirted in return.

"Allow me to get you a drink, my dear." Richard was at his most charming and Ann beamed happily. He escorted her to the table where the drinks were being served and got her some punch and some French brandy for himself.

"May I borrow your fiancée for the next dance?" Charles asked joining them.

"Be my guest, as long as you return her." Ann smiled at his possessiveness as Charles led her to the dance floor.

"Well, I'm glad to see Ann looking happy," remarked his mother appearing next to him.

"And why wouldn't she?" Richard asked rhetorically. "She's engaged to a very charming fellow."

His mother rolled her eyes, not at all fooled by his charm. "When he wants to be."

Charles came back after one dance and returned Ann to her fiancé's arm.

"You look quite flushed, my dear," remarked Richard, "would you like to take a turn on the terrace to cool off? I hope it's not too cold."

"That sounds lovely," Ann agreed and Richard excused them and headed for the terrace, leaving his mother smiling approvingly after them while Charles' eyes followed enviously.

The terrace was refreshing after the heat of the ball-room with a bit of a chill in the air. Ann shivered slightly and rubbed her hands up and down her arms.

"Come closer, so that I can warm you," invited Richard, drawing her into his arms and deeper into the shadows. Ann snuggled contentedly in his warm embrace. Richard felt her curves pressed against him, or as much as the ball gown would allow anyway and found it quite pleasant.

"Is that better?" he asked pulling back from her slightly.

"Yes, thank you." Her eyes hungrily watched his mouth as he spoke and she unconsciously licked her lips in invitation.

Richard obligingly bent his head and softly kissed her moist lips. They had exchanged fairly chaste kisses before but this time Richard deepened the kiss to test Ann's response. She responded with an unexpected display of eagerness causing his body to stir of its own volition.

Perhaps it was the knowledge that he was leaving soon that prompted her response or maybe she had been waiting for him to increase the intimacy of their kisses. He smiled to himself as he realized that though Ann may not stir him to great passion, bedding her might be more interesting than he had anticipated if she showed as much eagerness in the bedroom.

She wound her arms around his neck and pressed her body against his, swept away by the unfamiliar sensations that he was arousing in her. Only the sound of another couple entering the terrace caused her to break the kiss and hide her face against chest, breathing heavily. Richard smiled against her hair, pleasantly surprised by her response.

"Do you really have to go to Barbados?" She asked breathlessly pulling back from him. She was now even more eager to marry him than before.

"Yes. There's much for me to learn there to make your plantation more profitable."

"I will miss you so."

"The time will pass quickly and before you know it I will be back home."

"I'm afraid that you will fall in love with the daughter of some plantation owner and want to stay there," she confessed worriedly.

Richard laughed softly. "Not likely, my dear. There's too much here for me to give up," he added caressing her cheek. Ann leaned into his hand with a sigh, reassured by his words.

"I would give up everything for love," she declared romantically.

Richard gently kissed her lips and allowed her to believe that he agreed, but he knew that there were some things that he wouldn't give up, even for love.

Three weeks later

Richard watched as the last of his trunks was loaded onto their ship, the Adventurer. She was a beautiful schooner, long and elegant, freshly painted in blue and white, with bright white sails that had recently been replaced.

The boat was a hive of activity, with the sailors scampering about in response to the captain's shouted orders. In quick time the sails were unfurled in anticipation of her departure and the captain shouted "All aboard!" although it was only Richard waiting to get on.

The whole family, as well as Ann, had come to see him off. He turned to hug his mother and his sister who were teary eyed as if he were going off to war instead of a trip to Barbados.

"Give my regards to Elizabeth and Thomas. And kiss the girls for me. I hope they like their gifts."

"I'm sure they will, mother. Now look after Ann for me while I'm gone." His mother gave a tearful smile in response.

"I'll be back in time for your wedding," he promised his sister Charlotte.

"You better be, because we're not waiting any longer than we have to." She and her fiancé Albert, who was his good friend, were very much in love and eager to get married and Richard was happy for them.

"Now Charles, let me hear that you're engaged when I get back," he teased. "And to your own fiancée," he added for his ears only. Charles flushed guiltily.

He shook hands with his father who said, "Now don't worry about things here. I was running this business before you were born. You just enjoy your time in Barbados, learn as much as you can and spend some time with our man there. And give my love to my dear sister."

"I will, sir."

The family moved away to give him and Ann a little privacy, as much as could be had on the busy dock.

The tears she had been holding back now spilled from her eyes.

"Shhh. Don't cry love. I'll be back before you have time to miss me." He wiped her eyes with his handkerchief.

"I already miss you! Remember what I said and don't go falling in love with any beautiful Barbadian girls," she warned half-jokingly.

"Not likely, sweetheart," he assured her. "Not when I have my own beauty here in Carolina." He gave her a long kiss and gently pushed her in the direction of his family.

He waved briefly to them before turning to walk across the shaky gangplank. As he stepped on board and gave them a final wave the sails were slowly raised and the boat began to move away from the dock. A great sense of freedom and adventure came over him and an eager anticipation for the visit to Barbados.

Chapter Five

March 2, 1696
The Acreage Plantation, Barbados

D eborah ran from the yard to her favorite spot on the plantation, as anger and despair welled up in her, almost suffocating in their intensity. She had discovered the grove of trees that overlooked the East Coast of the island years ago and the vista had been a balm to her soul on many occasions. From this vantage point she could see the lush vegetation of the eastern part of the island with deep aquamarine waves as a backdrop and the scenery usually calmed her.

Today she struggled to find peace as the agonized cries of a mother and daughter still rang in her ears. The girl, probably no more than fourteen, had been sold to another plantation to help the mistress. She had been dragged away, screaming for her mother who fought in vain against the restraining arms of her husband, as he watched stoically while their only child was wrenched from their lives, powerless to help her.

Deborah couldn't believe that Master Thomas could be so cruel as to sell the girl. How could he stand by unemotionally while a family was being torn apart on his orders? This was the same man who sometimes slipped presents to her and her mother and who had sent away his son after he raped her? What was to stop him from selling her? He could just as easily sell any of them.

The harsh reality of the scene she had just witnessed snapped her out of her complacency. She had become almost comfortable in the time that William had been away, only having to deal with the mistress' sharp tongue, for behavior that she called insolent. But life had been fairly uneventful until today.

She should be glad in a way, for it reminded her that she was still a slave and she hadn't made any progress with her plans for freedom. Never again would she forget what she was and what could possibly happen to her. Suppose the master died suddenly and William took over the plantation? She shuddered at the possibility of that happening. She needed her freedom.

The beauty of the landscape tugged on her eyes like a magnet and she couldn't help but admire the magnificent trees with their dense foliage, the contours of the land as it sloped gently towards the coral sand against which powerful waves crashed every few seconds.

The family Bible that the girls' tutor used to read to them said that God had created all the earth and that he created man. She wasn't sure if she believed a Bible which was used to justify slavery as well, but when she looked out at the trees, all so different from each other, the sky and the sea, she knew that there must be a divine being who had created it all.

Jethro had said that God loved the world but she didn't know if that was true. He certainly didn't seem to love slaves. Are you real? She asked silently. Where are you? Where were you when William took my innocence? Where were you when that girl was wrenched from her parents today? Why do you do nothing while we are bought and sold like cattle?

The wind in the trees was her only answer and her soul cried out for answers to the questions that left a gaping hole in her that only the truth could fill.

Pulling herself up from the soft grass, she headed back to the house despondently. There was lunch to be served.

Deborah could hardly bear to look at Master Thomas as she served lunch to the family. She generally liked him, even loved him, but today she couldn't suppress the resentment that rose up in her at the sight of him calmly opening a letter and handing one to the mistress while she and Cassie served the meal. How could he be so unaffected by the agony he had just caused?

"This is from your nephew Richard, Elizabeth," he said reading the letter. "He says that he would like to come and spend three months in Barbados to learn how we use slaves on the plantation to produce sugar since he is planning to invest in a plantation and convert it to rice and plans to use African slaves."

Deborah couldn't help hearing that and took an instant dislike to the unknown man who was talking of using slaves on his plantation in the same way that he would talk about using mules.

"Oh, wonderful!" exclaimed Elizabeth. Deborah had not seen her so lively since William had been sent away. Most days she was very morose but these were punctuated by days where she roused herself enough to be verbally abusive to all the slaves but mainly to Deborah whom she blamed for William's banishment, as she called it.

"We can put him in William's room. I'll have to get one of the girls to get it ready. When will he arrive?"

At the mention of William's room, Deborah tensed. Memories of William trapping her in that room and violently stripping her of her innocence surfaced bringing back feelings of anger, fear and shame.

"He said that he would be leaving at the end of February so he should be here by the middle of the month."

"This is so exciting! Mary says in her letter that he has recently got engaged to the daughter of a plantation owner and that Richard will run it when they get married, which should be towards the end of the year. Charlotte, my niece, will get married when Richard gets back and that will only leave Charles who she is trying to find a nice girl for."

"Richard says that he is looking forward to helping me on the plantation. That would be a welcome change." The veiled criticism of William did not go unnoticed by Elizabeth whose face became bitter and resentful. Her look was lost on Thomas who had folded up his letter and now shifted his attention to the food on his plate.

Cassie and Deborah returned to the kitchen where the house slaves were eating their midday meal of fried plantains and cassava cakes.

"The mistress' nephew coming here for three months," announced Cassie. "The mistress said she going to put him in Master William's room so somebody goin' have to clean it out soon. I ain't seen the mistress so happy since Master William left."

"I wonder if he is as handsome as the master," said Hattie.

"He is the mistress' nephew, not the master's," corrected Cassie.

"That don' mean that he can't be handsome like the master," insisted Hattie.

Hattie was a house slave who had been bought about a year ago to help with the cleaning and serving on occasion. She was an attractive buxom girl of about twenty with smooth brown skin. She made no secret of the fact that she was looking to improve her status and would like to become the master's favorite. Deborah considered her to be no better than a prostitute willing to sell herself for trinkets or a few coins.

She wasn't surprised to hear Hattie wondering about the mistress' nephew. She was probably already thinking about how to get money or gifts from him for her services. Deborah however, didn't care if he was handsome or not; she already disliked the sound of him and she was not looking forward to his visit.

She preferred to stay as far from men as possible, especially white men, and she had no desire to just improve her status, she wanted to be free. She knew that some slaves sold their favors to earn money to buy their freedom, but she would never sell herself in that way.

Tuesday March 20, 1696
Off the coast of Barbados

"Land ho!" The lookout shouted from the crow's nest.

Richard Fairfax peered into the horizon but all he could see was a speck. Eventually it grew until he could make out white sands and lush vegetation as the ship headed towards Carlisle Bay where it would drop anchor.

Leaning against the side of the ship he waited with barely restrained patience as they got closer to the coast of Barbados. After being on the boat for almost three weeks, doing very little, he couldn't wait to get to his uncle's plantation and start working.

The brisk breeze blew his dark hair away from his face and it settled on his broad shoulders as the wind subsided. He squinted his navy blue eyes against the glare of the sun which was now high in the sky.

"Barbados straight ahead, boss," advised the Captain, coming over to have a word with him.

"Will I be able to hire someone to take me to my uncle's plantation?"

"For sure. They're always lackeys around the shore to transport people."

"Thank you, Bostick. I'm looking forward to feeling some firm ground under my feet. I can't say that being cooped up on a boat for weeks is my favorite thing." The captain laughed and went about shouting orders to the crew to prepare to drop the anchor. From there cock-boats would transport them and the cargo to the shore.

Richard gazed towards the island with eager antici-pation. He had heard much about Barbados and he was looking forward to making her acquaintance.

"Your trunks will be unloaded in a few minutes," the captain advised him.

Richard thanked him and climbed down the ladder into the waiting boat which carried him to Barbadian soil.

He was able to hire a carriage to transport him and his trunks to The Acreage with little effort. He decided that he would come another day to meet up with the family agent, but for now he was eager to get to the plantation.

As he passed through the town he was amazed to see how well developed it was with straight, long streets, well-built houses of stone alone or combined with wood and numerous taverns and shops with all kinds of mer-chandise. The island certainly looked prosperous. Then again it had been colonized long before Carolina and was England's wealthiest colony in the West.

He had opted to sit up in the front with the driver so that he could ask questions as they travelled. The driver was a talkative fellow and soon inquired of Richard where he was from and the reason for his visit to Barbados. The island being so small, he knew Thomas

Edwards who, Richard discovered, was one of the very prominent planters in the island.

"The city used to be known as The Bridge up to about 1660 but now it's officially known as St. Michael's Town or people just call it Town. The streets were laid out by a surveyor by the name of James Swan in '57 which accounts for them being so well ordered," his driver told him. "The country is divided into eleven parishes and The Acreage is in St. James, which is on the west and it's high up, so you can probably see the East Coast of the island from some parts of the plantation. We will pass through Jamestown, where the first settlers landed, to get there."

Richard listened attentively to the history lesson and was also brought up to date on the more recent events that had taken place in the island. He caught glimpses of the ocean as they travelled along the road that ran parallel to the coast and he felt strangely at home in the beautiful island with its lush vegetation and colorful wild flowers.

"How long will it take to get there?" he asked. He was already sweltering in the unaccustomed heat.

"About three hours. I can stop in Jamestown so that you can get something to eat and drink if you didn't bring anything with you."

"Thank you. I'd appreciate that. I didn't think to bring anything."

"The roads are better than I expected," he remarked some time later.

"Yes, we've spent a lot of time and money repairing the main roads and keeping them clean. But they're a lot worse after the rainy season."

After about two hours, by which time Richard's throat was parched, the driver pulled into a tavern in Jamestown and said, "You can get something to eat and drink here before we turn inland to the plantation."

An hour later, feeling much refreshed, they continued on their way. The driver soon pointed out St. James parish church which he said was the oldest church on the island.

"The original building was destroyed by a hurricane in 1675 but a few years ago they replaced the wooden building with this stone one. It stands on God's acre, you know." Richard nodded in response, humoring him.

"Do you all have many churches in Carolina?" the driver asked.

"Yes, attending church is quite a social event. People go every Sunday and spend almost the whole day there. There are usually picnics and that kind of thing after the service."

"Here too."

His driver flicked the reins and turned the horse onto a narrower road which was bordered by bushes. Houses became sparse and the vegetation increased, giving much needed shade to the travelers and Richard was happy that the air was also cooler.

"Soon be there now," the driver announced. Richard was looking forward to reaching the plantation. Looking at his pocket watch he saw that it was near five o'clock and they had left Town around one.

"The Acreage begins somewhere around here," he said a few minutes later and Richard could see rows and rows of tall sugar cane plants in the distance. Majestic

Royal palms, lined the road as they got closer to the house, towering over thirty feet in the air.

"Here it is," the driver informed him as the horses strained to go up a slight incline and pulled into the driveway of a beautiful plantation house made of stone and painted in a warm yellow. Upstairs the windows were flanked by moss green shutters and covered by hoods of the same color while downstairs a patio ran the full length of the house with more windows and several pairs of wooden doors thrown open as if in welcome.

Three ladies, who he assumed were his aunt and cousins, were sitting in rocking chairs on the patio with a young slave girl in attendance. On seeing the carriage the older of the ladies hurriedly got up and ran towards the carriage as Richard made his way down from his seat.

"Richard?" she asked excitedly.

"Yes. Aunt Elizabeth?"

"Yes, my dear," she confirmed hugging him tightly. She pulled back, looking quite a way up into his face saying, "You look so much like my dear brother and you're even taller than I remember him being! I'm so glad that you're here. Come in and meet the girls."

She gave instruction to the driver to take the carriage around the back and she told the child to get someone called Jethro to deal with the trunks and to get one of the girls to bring them something to drink.

"These are your cousins Rachel and Mary. Mary is named after your mother. Girls this is your cousin, Richard."

Richard greeted each girl with a brief kiss on their pale cheeks. He noted that they were quite pretty and looked very much like their mother.

"I'm pleased to meet you. I've heard much about all of you from my mother. She's sent you some gifts which I will find when my trunks are unpacked."

"Thank you," they said shyly, eyeing him from beneath long lashes.

"Do come and sit down Richard. You must be exhausted from your journey."

"Yes, it was rather long but I enjoyed it. The driver shared a lot of the history of Barbados with me so now I feel I know the island already."

"I've so looked forward to your coming," she replied. "Oh good, here's Hattie with our drinks."

Richard took the drink that was offered by the brown skinned slave girl who kept her eyes respectfully cast down but he could sense her appraising him from beneath her lashes. He noted that she had beautiful smooth skin and a very nice figure. He wondered if it was true that planters really offered guests the use of their slave girls and thought that he wouldn't mind if she was offered to him.

"Thomas is out on the plantation but he should soon be in and you can meet him at dinner after you freshen up."

"I'm looking forward to both."

From the comfortable rocking chair, he looked around in appreciation. Everywhere there were bursts of color from the tropical flowers, large trees offered shade and in the distance he could see fields of sugar cane and other crops in every direction. Barbados! She was certainly beautiful. He wondered what she had in store for him.

Chapter Six

R ichard felt like a new man as he stepped from the tub of lukewarm water in his bedroom. He had never been so glad to see bath water and was most grateful to his aunt for providing it, especially as the driver had told him that water was a precious commodity in Barbados. The existence of few rivers on the island meant they had to collect rain water in cisterns on the roof and in ponds that most of the plantations created.

His aunt had been delighted to show him around the house once he had relaxed for a bit. He was amazed at the lavish furnishings that adorned the house which were even more impressive than most of the estates he had visited in England and definitely more than their house in Carolina. The mahogany dining room table that could seat eighteen was polished to a high sheen and flanked by oval backed chairs caned for comfort. An elaborate arrangement of white and red lilies in a silver vase held the place of honor in the centre of the table.

A beautifully carved oak sideboard, a clock in a tall case and a Chippendale cabinet filled with silver hugged the walls and the Persian carpets that graced the floors in the sitting room between beautifully styled couches and arm chairs were more luxurious than any he had seen before. He had sincerely complimented his aunt on the loveliness of her home, much to her delight.

His uncle had come in just before the bell rang to announce the end of the day for the slaves and he had taken an immediate liking to the tall, good looking man. From the strength and roughness of the hand that shook his he could tell that, like himself, his uncle was intimately involved in the running of his plantation and was not a gentleman farmer.

He dried himself off with the large towel provided and donned clean clothes that had been unpacked by one of the slaves and draped across the huge four poster bed which was flanked by two sturdy looking bedside tables. He had not had the chance to lie down but he was very much looking forward to testing its comfort. The room was well adorned with a writing desk and chair made of mahogany, a massive oak closet and an elaborately carved chest of drawers with brass handles. A wash stand stood separately but his aunt had told him that there was a bath house and a separate outhouse in the yard.

With the rumbling of his stomach reminding him that it had been several hours since his meal in Jamestown, he quickly headed for the door and made his way down to the dining room. His aunt had said that they usually ate around seven since the slaves' day ended at six and that gave her husband time to ready himself for dinner after he came in.

"Richard, my boy, come and join us," invited his uncle as he entered the room, gesturing to the chair next to him.

"Thank you. Good evening Aunt Elizabeth, Rachel, Mary," he added taking his place. The girls greeted him shyly, obviously still in awe of their tall, good looking cousin.

"You look much refreshed, Richard," observed his aunt.

"Thank you so much for the bath, Aunt. I feel like a new man." She laughed delightedly.

"I look forward to spoiling you while you're here," she promised. "Tomorrow Jethro can show you the bath house and the outhouse."

"That will be fine."

"Now you must be starving. The girls should be in to serve dinner any time now."

As if on cue, another brown skinned slave in a long skirt with a handkerchief on her head came in offering drinks from two jugs, which she said, were mobbie and Beveridge. His aunt explained that mobbie was an alcoholic drink made from sweet potatoes while Beveridge was a refreshing drink made of water, white sugar and the juice of oranges. Not desiring to drink spirits that night, he chose the orange juice drink.

The slave who offered the drinks was not the one who had served his drink earlier; she looked a few years older than her. He noticed that she kept her eyes respectfully lowered even as she greeted them cheerfully and poured their drinks.

"How was the voyage from Carolina, Richard?" asked Thomas.

"It was quite pleasant if rather long as we had to avoid French warships in the Leeward Islands. I couldn't wait to get dry land under my feet again," he admitted.

71

"I know what you mean. At least it's not as bad as travelling to England." Richard agreed readily, having made that trip himself.

"Speaking of England, when is William due to return?" he asked. The answer to his question was interrupted by the loud clatter of the dishes on the trolley that was being pushed into the room.

"Do be careful, Deborah!" scolded his aunt sharply. Richard looked at her in surprise and his eyes sought out the recipient of her sharp tone. Streaks of red appeared on the well sculptured cheekbones of the girl, who was dressed similarly to the first slave, and if he wasn't mistaken, her chin lifted a notch.

At first glance he thought that she was white but then noticed that her complexion had an attractive olive cast to it, however it was her startling resemblance to his aunt's husband that arrested him. He looked at Thomas quickly but discreetly and then looked back at the girl. There was no mistaking it. He glanced at his aunt to find her looking at him with an expression of shame on her face before she looked away and picked up her glass.

"... before next year I would think." Richard only caught the last part of his uncle's sentence as he was still grappling with the blatant evidence of his uncle's infidelity with a slave woman, possibly one of the house slaves.

The girl was now transferring dishes from the trolley to the table. He observed that she had offered no greeting and although she did not make eye contact with any of them, she did not lower her gaze demurely as the others had done.

As she focused on her task, he couldn't help but notice the grace of her movements, the slenderness of her neck and the smoothness of her olive skin. Even with her hair concealed by a handkerchief, she was beautiful, even more beautiful than Anise. The plain garments she was wearing could not disguise her feminine curves and the proud thrust of her breasts. Richard felt a stirring in his body and forced his eyes away from her.

"How did your fiancée bear to part from you?" his aunt asked him. He wondered if she had noticed his interest in the girl and had deliberately asked the question to remind him that he had a fiancée.

Richard smiled, even as his eyes were drawn almost against his will to the girl's retreating backside that swayed gracefully as she walked unhurriedly from the room.

"She made me promise not to fall in love with any beautiful Barbadian women before she would let me get on the boat." His aunt laughed.

"I'm almost sorry that you're already betrothed because I would love to find you a Barbadian girl and keep you here."

"I agree," added his uncle. Richard smiled but the lure of running the Carlisle's plantation was strong.

"I've heard that land is scarce in Barbados anyway, so I doubt that I'd be able to find a plantation to buy if I could afford it and I was inclined to stay."

"You never know," his uncle said enigmatically as he gestured Richard to begin serving himself.

Richard enjoyed the meal immensely, especially after the food he'd endured on the ship for the last three weeks. However he found himself looking forward to the end of the meal and the girl's return to clear the table so he was disappointed when she was replaced by the one who had served him his drink when he arrived. While this one was attractive, for some reason, she certainly didn't stir him as the other one had done.

"Come to my office tomorrow morning after you've had a good rest and we can talk about the plantation and then I'll take you around to see how things work," his uncle invited.

"Thank you. I'm looking forward to that but I must confess that right now I'm longing for a good night's sleep in a real bed even more."

"I'm sure you'll find William's bed very comfortable," his aunt remarked. "If you need anything, please let me know."

"Thank you, Aunt Elizabeth and you Uncle Thomas for your hospitality."

"You are very welcome, Richard. I want you to make yourself at home. What is ours is yours," Thomas added generously.

I wonder if that includes the delectable girl who served dinner, he thought silently.

Deborah escaped to her sanctuary, the kitchen. The mistress' scolding had humiliated her, but she hadn't been able to help the shaking of her hands when she heard the nephew ask when William was coming back.

She had felt his eyes on her, initially out of curiosity she knew, for she had seen the same look on the faces of many visitors when they noticed her resemblance to the master. But as she had put out the dishes, she continued to feel his eyes on her until she left the room. It was only immense self control that enabled her to walk calmly from the room when she had wanted to run from his disturbing gaze.

She took several deep breaths to control the beating of her heart. Not again! She couldn't go back in there tonight. His penetrating gaze disturbed her and she didn't care to find out why. She hoped that he was not like William, but then again they shared the same blood.

"Hattie, would you clear the dishes for me? I'll wash up for you."

"You would do that? Thank you Deborah. I will be able to get an eyeful of the mistress' nephew again. I goin' dream 'bout him tonight," she sighed. Cassie smiled and shook her head indulgently at Hattie.

"The mistress' nephew real handsome, nuh Deborah?" Cassie asked.

"I really didn't notice," she lied.

"You didn't notice?" Cassie replied disbelievingly. "You must be blind then. I know that Hattie not sorry to clear the table for you though."

Although Deborah would never admit it to Cassie, she was honest enough with herself to grudgingly agree that Hattie and Cassie were right; the nephew was very handsome. Not that she cared. As long as he kept his distance from her she would be happy.

"I better go and carry out this desert quick. Poor man must be tired enough after travelling all the way from Town today," said Cassie carrying a tray with plates of dessert out of the kitchen.

That reminded Deborah that the mistress had said he had a fiancée in Carolina. Good. Maybe he would keep his hands to himself. Then again, the master had a wife and that didn't make any difference. Nothing seemed to stop these people from using slaves to serve their needs.

She couldn't help the little shiver than ran over her as she remembered the nephew's eyes on her. Even sitting down she could see that he was bigger than William and she knew that it would take little effort for him to overpower her if he so desired. From the little she had seen of him, he didn't seem cruel, like William was or perhaps he was yet to show his true colors. She could only hope that he and his cousin were not cut from the same cloth.

Chapter Seven

Richard was up early, as was his custom, but he felt well rested after the night in William's comfortable bed. He knocked on the door of his uncle's office and was invited to come in.

"Good morning, uncle."

His uncle was seated behind a huge oak desk which was covered with various papers. To one side was another desk which his aunt had told him was a typical planters' desk and had numerous small drawers with brass knobs. There was also a bookshelf lined with leather bound volumes which he assumed his uncle had brought with him from England.

"Richard, you're up early. I expected you to sleep late today."

"Habit. I'm accustomed to getting up early so I find it hard to sleep past the cocks' crowing."

"Same here," agreed his uncle. "Have you had breakfast yet?"

"No. But one of the girls offered to bring it in here for me if that's okay."

"By all means. I'll tell you a little about the plantation while you wait. I have 500 acres of which about 300 are planted with cane. The rest has crops for our own use and we grow a little cotton as well. I have about 150 slaves in the fields and seven in the house and yard."

"How long have you been using slaves?"

"Over forty years from when my father first bought the plantation. I had to sell a lot when I took over, to settle debts but I was able to keep a handful and a few indentured servants and as soon as the plantation began to prosper again, I started to replenish my stock of slaves."

"As I wrote in my letter when my fiancée and I marry I will be running her father's plantation and I plan to buy some when I introduce rice. I believe that rice will be to Carolina what sugar has been to Barbados." His uncle nodded, pleased with Richard's vision and insight. "I've heard that slaves from the West Coast of Africa know how to cultivate rice. That's mainly why I came to Barbados. To learn as much as I can from you about what to look for when I'm buying slaves, what is a good price to pay, how best to maintain them and that kind of thing."

"Well I can certainly help you there. I'll take you with me to the slave market next time I go so that you can see for yourself how to select and you can learn everything else here on the plantation."

"Are you able to use them for jobs other than field work and the house? Some people say that they are not very intelligent."

"That has not been my finding. Jethro is an excellent carpenter and I've got a boiler who works in my boiler room that is so good I wouldn't even sell him for £300 and I've been offered that much for him."

Richard was impressed and his respect for his uncle went up another notch. His uncle was obviously wealthier than he thought if he could refuse £300 for a slave.

"I've also got some intelligent girls in the house. Deborah, for one, can read and write. Her mother, Sarah, was the girls' nanny and they all came up together so when we had tutors for them, I think Deborah learned at the same time. However we don't encourage that as a rule."

"It's against the law to teach slaves to read and write in Carolina and Virginia."

"The more they're able to communicate with each other, the greater the threat of a revolt. We live in constant fear of that in Barbados. We've had several attempts over the years but they were discovered before they could be carried out and the leaders were executed. The last one was just four years ago and it was very well organized but two of the leaders were overheard talking about it and were arrested and convinced to give the names of others who were involved. After that we've had to severely restrict the movement of our slaves, for our own safety."

"I guess that is the risk of using slaves; they will eventually outnumber us. We've not got to that point yet in Carolina but I can foresee that happening as more of us get into rice and need their labor."

"What's life like in Carolina?" asked his uncle.

"It's pretty good. Probably not as grand as it is here though, at least not yet. In terms of our business, we've had some challenges with pirates but we're still doing well. A few planters have started cultivating rice and it's doing better than they expected, I believe, and we've just introduced the latest slave code which has been adopted from the Barbados code since the number of slaves being imported has grown tremendously."

"Yes I heard that," his uncle confirmed. "We've had our share of challenges here as well. The price of sugar has dropped significantly since the 50's but fortunately as the retail price has decreased in England, the demand has increased and people are using five times as much sugar as they were using before. The introduction of coffee and tea has helped sales as well since they need sugar to make them palatable. So what we've lost in price, we've been able to make up in volume."

"I've told my father that we need to diversify so that we're not at the mercy of any one line of business."

"Yes, which is why I've started distilling rum, and I've got an interest in a ship. I definitely agree that diversification is the key."

"That is why I want to get into rice cultivation which will not only be another source of revenue but will also be of benefit to our shipping business since we already have contacts in the islands and in England."

"In spite of all the negative things that are said about us, you'll find the planters here in Barbados very hospitable and willing to share information. I'll introduce you to some of them while you're here. Perhaps you can arrange to supply them with rice when you start production."

"I'd appreciate that."

"You should read Richard Ligon's book on Barbados which is somewhere in there," he gestured towards his library. "It will give you a lot of good information on the island. In fact you may borrow any of the books in my modest library. We will certainly do everything possible to make sure you enjoy your stay. In that regard I want you to know that while you're here you can make use of any of the house slaves," his uncle invited.

Richard wanted to be very sure that he understood what his uncle meant, so for clarity he repeated, "Make use?"

"Yes. For your physical needs. You're a young, virile man. I don't expect you to suffer while you're here," laughed his uncle.

Richard's body immediately stirred in anticipation as he remembered the olive skinned slave who served them the night before. Deborah, his aunt had called her.

"Any that is, except Sarah and Deborah," his uncle amended. "I don't share Sarah," he added with a slight smile of satisfaction. He offered no explanation about why Deborah was off limits as well and Richard did not feel it was his place to ask for one.

What a shame, he thought to himself. One of the others would have to do. Perhaps the young brown skinned one that had cleared the table last night.

Richard and his uncle toured the plantation on horseback after he had eaten the breakfast that was brought in by the same slave, who his uncle called Hattie.

He was sure that it wasn't by accident that she had brushed against his back as she leaned over to put his plate on the desk in front of him. The slaves he was familiar with from Carolina tended not to touch white people so he assumed that it must have been deliberate. He also knew women well enough to discern that it was a subtle invitation, one which he intended to take up soon. After all he had been on the boat for three weeks.

"We're about to start harvesting some of our canes so you've come at a good time."

"How long does that take?" Richard asked him.

"Oh, about three to four months. Harvesting canes is hard work and producing sugar is not easy. We've learned the best time to cut the canes so that we can get the most sugar from them but the earlier planters learned by trial and error. Henry Drax's instruction on how to run a sugar plantation has been of great help to many of us."

"Do the slaves work well? I've heard that they have more endurance than indentured servants."

"Generally, but from time to time they need a bit of coercion. That's why the drivers carry whips."

"Do any try to escape?"

"One or two, but they don't get far. There's nowhere to really hide on the island for any length of time. We make an example of those as a deterrent for the others and I quickly sell them off. I don't keep runners."

They rode in silence for a while observing some slaves weeding in the cane fields nearest to them. Richard watched dispassionately as one of the drivers snapped a whip on the back of a slave to hasten his pace. As the slave arched his back in response to the leather whip he idly observed that not even his horse was subjected to that kind of harsh treatment.

"You'll find that compared to other plantations, The Acreage is pretty fair. We don't overdo the whip and our slaves know that they have it a lot better here than on other plantations. On some plantations the mistress will order even the house slaves to be whipped for seemingly insignificant things but your aunt is not of that nature. Anyway she knows that I wouldn't want the house girls scarred, especially Sarah and Deborah; it decreases their value."

"How much does a house slave cost?"

"Around £25 to £30. However I paid £50 for Sarah nearly twenty years ago."

Richard whistled at the sum his uncle had parted with.

"Now you understand why I don't want her damaged, for more than one reason," his uncle added with a smile.

Richard couldn't help himself, he asked, "How much would you sell Deborah for?"

His uncle looked at him sharply and said, "She's not for sale. Or for bedding," he reminded him. Richard nodded his assent.

He needed to put the girl from his mind. The last thing he wanted was to incur his uncle's displeasure while he was staying there.

Sarah bent over the wash tub and rubbed the bar of soap against the collar of the white shirt. The pile of clothes she had washed already was growing and her back was aching from bending over the tub while her hands were raw from the soap.

It was a relief to dip the clothes in tubs of cold, clean water before wringing them out and dropping them into another tub to take them to the drying yard.

She knew that the mistress assigned this task to her because it was one of the hardest jobs that a house slave had to do but at least it allowed her to work outside and enjoy the beautiful day. She would treat her hands afterwards with lanolin to soothe them and soften the skin.

She called the stable boy to carry the tub to the drying yard where some lines were strung up to dry the clothes. Fortunately at that time of the year, the breeze was brisk and the clothes would dry quickly.

After hanging up the wet clothes she went to the bath house to collect the towels that needed to be washed for that week. Emptying out the water from the last washing she poured fresh water in the tub and submerged the towels. Looking up she was relieved to see Sally coming out to help her after finishing her own chores in the house.

"I'm glad to see you Sally. My back is hurting real bad." With that she straightened up and arched her back to ease the pain.

"I know that this work does break your back," she sympathized. "They don't care how hard it is when they change their clothes every day and we have to wash them."

"Washing day is the hardest day of the week!" agreed Sarah. "I can't wait to see my bed tonight. I going to pick up the sheets I washed this morning to make room for these towels."

Sarah was walking from the drying yard to the house with her arms full of sheets when Richard and his uncle rode into the yard heading towards the stable.

"Sarah," his uncle called. "Come to my room tonight."

"Yes, master Thomas," she said lowering her head demurely as she saw that he was with the nephew. She groaned silently to herself. The last thing she wanted was to go to the master tonight. She was so tired and her back was hurting badly, but could she tell the master that? After all he owned her and she was there for his use, no matter how she felt.

So this was Sarah, Richard observed. He could see where Deborah got her beauty from, although his uncle had contributed as well. Her skin was the color of milky coffee and though he couldn't see her figure behind the sheets she carried he had no doubt that she would be well formed. His uncle certainly has good taste in slave women.

He wondered how his aunt felt about her husband blatantly sharing his bed with his mistress under the same roof as her.

"So is that how you do it, uncle? Just tell them to come to your room?"

"Well yes, my boy."

"What if they're not willing?"

"Not willing? They're slaves, they don't have any choice. But any man worth his salt can encourage them to be willing once they get there," he added with a knowing laugh as they handed the reins of the horses over to the stable boy.

Richard was amazed at all he had seen so far. If his uncle's life was any indication, the large plantation owners in Barbados lived like lords; no expense was spared to make life on the island easy and no desire was left unsatisfied.

He recognized how easy it would be to adopt the life of the Barbadian planter. Would he want to leave when it was time to go back to Carolina?

Dinner was a more elaborate affair that night. Richard was once again disappointed to see that Deborah was absent and he wondered if it was by her own choice or whether his aunt had deliberately arranged it.

It was probably just as well, he thought, as he cut into his succulent baked pork which was accompanied by chicken, cassava cakes, fried plantain, sweet potato and a large assortment of vegetables. His uncle had opened a bottle of fine French brandy and poured him a generous glass.

"What did you think of the plantation, Richard?" asked his aunt.

"It's beautiful and I can see that it's extremely well run."

"Yes it is. It's one of the best in the island," she boasted. "We'll have to throw a party to introduce you to some of our friends from other plantations."

"We'll help you plan it," his cousins said excitedly. They didn't say much in his presence and he assumed that they were still a bit shy around him.

"The women will use any excuse to throw a party," his uncle complained good-naturedly, "but it will be good for you to meet some of the other planters and settlers on the island."

"We can have another one to celebrate the end of the crop," his aunt continued.

"Yes but we still have the harvesting and boiling to get through," his uncle reminded her. "We may need to borrow a couple of girls from the house to help this year and Jethro too. We need all hands to help out during harvest," he told Richard.

"Well I'll certainly do my part. Just tell me what you want me to do," offered Richard.

"Thank you, son. I'll definitely take you up on that." Thomas already liked Richard a great deal. He wished that William was more like him.

The combination of the sumptuous meal and the brandy made him wonderfully content and having had that hunger satisfied, he began to wonder how he could discreetly arrange to have the other dealt with. He couldn't just invite Hattie to his room with his aunt there. How was he to do it?

"Richard, join me in my office so that we can plan tomorrow. Ladies excuse us." His uncle rose and Richard did the same, asking the ladies to excuse him as well.

"Tomorrow I'll take you to the far side of the plantation and into Jamestown where I have some business," said his uncle opening the door to his office.

"Fine. I stopped in Jamestown on the way up. It has an interesting history."

"Yes, indeed. It's where the first settlers landed. Have another drink." His uncle poured him another large brandy. The retreat to the office was obviously more intended to drink brandy than to talk about the next day.

Richard had heard that drinking was another pastime on the island that was greatly indulged. While he did not have a problem with having a drink he did not like the feeling of losing control which accompanied imbibing vast quantities of spirits, so he tended to be moderate in his drinking.

"By the way, uncle, I was trying to think how best to discreetly tell Hattie to come to my room."

His uncle laughed. "Just tell her."

"But I cannot do so in front of the ladies," protested Richard.

"They are well aware of what the girls are used for, you know. But if you're shy about it, I will take care of it for you," assured his uncle.

Richard was happy to allow his uncle to deal with that particular issue.

Chapter Eight

Deborah settled down under one of the trees in her favorite spot with a sigh of contentment. It was Sunday, the day that all the slaves looked forward to, as it was their only day of rest. The house slaves alternated their days off since someone always had to be available to look after the family's needs. There was breakfast to be prepared before they left for church and as they were to have lunch out today, only a light snack would need to be prepared for later in the evening when they returned.

Deborah was relieved that she was not on duty today and could wash her hair. Sunday was the only day that she had the opportunity to do it and she always came out to her spot, as she thought of it, to dry it. She pulled her brush through the damp tresses, working out the tangles before she spread it over the front of her blouse for the warm sun and the brisk breeze to dry. The scrap of towel that she had draped over her shoulders did little to protect her blouse from the damp that seeped through it.

Task finished, she leaned back against the smooth trunk of the tree and enjoyed the view and the solitude that the spot afforded her. The sound of the wind gently disturbing the leaves was a welcome relief from the constant chatter and gossiping of the house slaves.

Hattie was the worst. Thursday morning she had come into the kitchen late, blaming the fact that she had overslept on the nephew who had called for her the night before. Yawning and stretching contentedly she told them, with a satisfied smile, that it was very late when she left his room and that he had given her a shilling. Deborah wasn't sure who she was more disgusted with; the nephew who was betrothed and still bedding Hattie or Hattie for thinking it a privilege to be bedded by him for a shilling.

Picking up the book she had borrowed from the master's office she found where she had left off before and then flipped back a few pages to refresh her memory before reading on.

Although slaves were not encouraged to read and write, the master knew that she had learned along with the girls and he had never objected. He had even consented when she had courageously broached the subject of borrowing books from his office, provided, he had said, that she was discreet.

She soon became lost in the pages of Shakespeare's First Folio and the final scenes of Romeo and Juliet. Before long Juliet had thrust a dagger into her breast when she discovered that her husband Romeo was dead.

Deborah was not moved by the tragedy; in fact she was annoyed that Juliet would chose to take her life rather than live without Romeo. What sense was that? She had the one thing that Deborah desired – freedom, and she chose to end her life because of love? Did such love exist outside of plays? She had never seen it and she would probably never experience it, even if it did exist.

Richard had declined his aunt's offer to accompany them to church the night before. This was one day that he could laze in bed for a change and besides he had wanted to explore the grounds of the house at his leisure. Walking around to the eastern side where he had not been before, he saw in the distance a small grove of trees that appeared to be on the edge of a cliff and he was interested to see the view from there.

He was almost upon the grove when he noticed a woman sitting under a tree reading. His heart gave a jolt of anticipation as he drew nearer and realized that it was Deborah, with her wavy brown hair released from the confines of the ever present handkerchief and falling over her shoulders to just graze the top of her breasts.

He strolled towards her quietly and unhurriedly, not wanting to alert her to his presence before he got closer to her. He had almost succeeded when he caused a pair of wood doves to suddenly take to flight as he passed by them.

Startled eyes swung in his direction and he noticed that she surreptitiously tried to hide the book she was reading under her skirt. She seemed undecided whether to stand up as he approached or remain seated where she could hide the book. He solved her dilemma by saying: "Don't get up on my account."

Deborah did not answer. Her heart had increased its pace as soon as she saw who had invaded her private spot. As a slave she knew that she should get up but she didn't want him to see the book and she was relieved when he took the decision away from her. What was he doing in her spot, anyway?

He was dressed simply in a pair of well fitted breeches and a cotton shirt opened at the neck. His longish dark hair was secured at his neck with a ribbon but a few strands had come loose and swung by his ear. He really was too good looking for his own good. He looked down at her from his great height making her wish now that she had stood up. She briefly glanced at his face and found his eyes on her hair.

His gaze made her feel suddenly vulnerable and the seclusion of the grove that was restful only minutes before now seemed threatening. Her hands began to shake and she hid them in the folds of her skirt, furious with herself for the fear that was beginning to rise in her.

There would be no-one to hear her if he chose to take advantage of her out here. She hoped that Hattie was enough to satisfy his needs. She wondered if she had been to his room again last night.

"What are you reading?" he asked.

"Reading?" she repeated stalling.

"Yes. I saw you with a book." Deborah couldn't deny it so she reluctantly pulled the book from under her skirt.

"Shakespeare's First Folio," she disclosed. "Master Thomas allows me to borrow books from his office," she added defensively.

"I didn't think you'd stolen it. Besides he told me you could read."

They had discussed her? Deborah wondered what they had said. She hoped Master Thomas had warned him to stay away from her.

"So which of the plays were you reading?"

"I just finished Romeo and Juliet," she grudgingly admitted.

"Ah, yes, the romantic tragedy. I saw it once in England. Were you able to understand it?" he asked.

She immediately bristled. Just because she was a slave did he think she was lacking in understanding? How she hated his air of superiority. How superior was he when he was betrothed and yet would still bed another, even if she was a slave. His morals certainly were not superior.

"Yes, thank you," she answered sarcastically and immediately froze at her insolence, wondering what punishment it would bring.

To her surprise he laughed. Richard knew that she had overstepped the bounds with her sarcasm but he admired her spirit. Just to provoke her he added, "Yes, thank you, Master Richard."

He was surprised to see her face blanch but he did not know that his words, so close to those that William had used before dragging her to his bed, had the power to shake Deborah and remind her of her vulnerable position.

"Yes thank you, Master Richard," she forced a demure tone and he was disappointed that she had backed down so easily.

"So what did you think of Mr. Shakespeare's play?"

He really wanted to discuss the play with her? Deborah was immediately suspicious. Slave women and free white men did not converse, far less discuss plays. Any interaction they had was purely physical. Why was he asking her thoughts about the play? She hesitated, remembering that this was the mistress' nephew. Would he tell the mistress that he had caught her reading the master's books?

Richard's eyes roved over her face, seeing the suspicion and hesitation before she schooled her features so that her face was like a blank page. He was surprised how much he disliked that blank look which hid all her emotions.

His eyes continued to travel the length of her hair, following it to the contours of her breasts and he had the sudden desire to run his fingers through the wild tresses and pull her close so that he could taste her temptingly full lips.

His mouth watered as he wondered if hers would be as sweet to the taste as they looked. Desire darkened his eyes to almost black and he looked away towards the horizon as he struggled to marshal his wayward thoughts, lest he forget his promise to his uncle.

Deborah saw him looking at her hair again and had the sudden urge to plait it and hide it under her towel. If she gave in to the urge he would know that he disturbed her and she didn't want to give him that satisfaction. Besides she didn't want to draw any further attention to herself.

"I think that Juliet was a stupid girl," she answered his question almost harshly, seeking to break the tension that was thick in the air. "She was foolish to take her own life when she was young, wealthy and free."

"She obviously preferred to be dead rather than live without her husband. You fault her for that?"

"I fault her for taking her life for such a reason. Many people go on living after they lose loved ones." She thought of the slaves whose daughter had been taken from them weeks ago and who was as good as dead to them. "But I do believe there are some things we should be willing to die for," she added.

"Like what?" he couldn't help asking.

"Freedom." The word slipped out before she had time to think about the implications of answering so honestly.

"You yearn for freedom?"

"There is no slave that does not yearn for freedom." She immediately realized the dangerous nature of their conversion and closed her lips, determined not to say anything else. How did this man manage to make her reveal her thoughts?

"But what would you do if you were free?" he persisted. "Where would you go? Here you have food, clothing and shelter provided for you. You have everything you need," he reasoned.

"Everything but freedom," she amended, even as his questions made her search for her own answers.

She was glad when he walked towards the edge of the cliff and gestured to the landscape asking, "Where is that?" effectively changing the subject to a safer topic.

"It's the East Coast of the island. Just below this cliff, the parish of St. Andrew starts and goes all the way down to the sea."

"Have you ever been there?" Deborah looked at him in surprise. Had he forgotten that she was a slave? What call would she have to go to the East Coast?

"The only places I have been recently are St. Michael's Town and Jamestown. When I was a child the girls would ask for me to be allowed to go with them when the family visited friends on other plantations but I have never been to the East Coast."

"You were born on the plantation?"

Deborah became cautious again.

"Yes."

Richard wanted to ask her more but he sensed that this was not a topic that she wanted to discuss. Many topics were off limits to them.

"How old are you?"

"Nearly eighteen."

"You seem a lot older," he remarked.

"Being a slave ages you," Deborah was quick to return.

"It's not that you look old, you act older." Deborah wondered how old he was but didn't have the freedom to ask.

"I'm seven years older than you, if you were wondering," he teased.

"I wasn't," she lied.

"I am feeling famished," he confessed, changing the subject again. "Could you prepare something for me to eat?"

'It's my day off. Get it yourself,' Deborah thought and wished she could utter the words out loud.

"Some of the girls are working today. I'm sure any of them would get you something to eat." That was as close as she could come to saying what she really wanted to.

"I prefer you to get it for me."

Deborah could not believe how selfish he was being but then she shouldn't be surprised at anything these people did. Why did she expect him to be different? She took a deep breath to control her anger and resentment, raised herself from the ground and said formally, "Right away, Master Richard," before walking with great dignity towards the house.

Inside she was seething. How could she let his conversation make her forget that in his eyes she was nothing more than a slave? It didn't matter to him if it was her day off. It didn't matter if the only day she got to read and lose herself in stories was on Sunday. Whatever Master Richard wanted, he got. How she hated him for giving her the feeling of freedom and then snatching it away again. When would she ever be able to get what she wanted? Even if it was just time to read a book in peace.

As Richard watched her walk purposefully towards the house, something akin to guilt pricked his conscience before he deliberately pushed it aside and focused instead on the tempting sway of her hips. As his gaze travelled up to the long wavy hair bouncing against her back, he was keenly aware that her beauty and spirit stirred him like no other woman and he knew that the promise he had made to his uncle was already in jeopardy.

Chapter Nine

S arah had just finished sweeping out their hut and was collecting dirty clothes to wash when Deborah stormed into the hut.

"Sorry I'm so late back to help you clean. I was drying my hair out by the cliff when Master Richard saw me and asked me to fix a meal for him. I don't know why he couldn't get it himself, or find Hattie and ask her. She would have been glad to help him!"

"You know they don't know how to do anything for themselves," Sarah consoled her. "How he find you out there though? Out there is lonely Deborah. Anything could happen and nobody would hear you. He ain' trouble you, nuh?"

Deborah remembered how his eyes had travelled over her body and shivered a little but she couldn't honestly say that he had troubled her, apart from the fact that she found his presence somewhat unnerving.

"No, ma. Don't forget that it is Hattie he is interested in. I don't know how he could be planning to marry a woman in Carolina and still bed Hattie."

"Girl, those men don't see us as their own kind, so they don't think they're doing anything wrong. To them we just like a favorite chair; something to sink into and give them pleasure at the end of the day."

"Even Master Thomas?"

"He is a good man but he ain' much different from the rest of them when it comes to that. You think I could ever tell him that I don' feel like coming when he tell me to come to his room?"

"Have you ever tried?" Deborah challenged her.

"Girl you want me to get the skin whipped off my back?"

"I don't think the Master would ever have you whipped, ma. I'm not too sure about the mistress though."

"I know. Ever since Master William get send to England she been looking for to something to flog me and you for but she can't find anything."

They filled up a tub with water and began to wash their laundry with a bar of soap. Being a lot less than what Sarah had to deal with on laundry day, the two pairs of hands made quick work of the load.

"Ma. You ever think about being free?" Deborah asked as they spread out their clothes on nearby bushes to dry.

Sarah looked around cautiously before answering.

"Yes, child. But I think more about you being free than me. I know that you could do a lot with the learning you have. You could run a boarding house or keep a shop in Town. I hear that sometimes when a master free a slave he gives them money or property to make a start after they free."

"Have you ever asked the master if we could buy our freedom from him? We don't have much money saved up but maybe he would sell us cheap since he doesn't need the money," she laughed. Sarah joined her.

"I was going to ask him for your freedom after William troubled you but since he sent him away I didn't bother."

"I don't want to be here when William comes back. Even if the master were to put in his will that we are to be freed after he dies I don't trust William to do it. You need to talk to him about that soon."

"Next time he calls for me I will ask him. That will be the best time." She smiled the secret smile of a woman who knew the power she had over a man.

Deborah felt a sliver of hope penetrate the wall that guarded her heart. Maybe her mother could persuade the master to set them free.

The family returned from their day out at church, followed by lunch at friends who lived on a large plantation in St. Peter called St. Nicholas Abbey, late in the evening. Thomas went to sleep right away and the girls retired to their rooms leaving Elizabeth in her favorite spot on the patio to enjoy the sunset which transformed the sky into a palette of pinks and oranges.

"How did you spend your day, Richard?" asked his aunt as he joined her on the patio.

"Oh I had a wonderfully lazy day. I explored the eastern part of the plantation and spent some time enjoying the view." A picture of Deborah with her hair draped over her shoulders flashed into his mind. "It's very peaceful out there." Or would be if it was not occupied by a disturbing slave girl, he thought.

"Yes, the view is lovely. I don't go out there very often; I prefer to sit on the patio here in my favorite chair. I hope the girls fed you."

"I got Deborah to prepare something for me. I think she was less than pleased though since it was her day off."

"If she was insolent I'll deal with her!" His aunt said sharply. Too late, he realized that he may have gotten Deborah in trouble with his comment.

"Not at all. She fixed me a very nice meal."

"That girl is constantly rude. She does not know her place. Of course it's Thomas' fault. He lets her do as she pleases. She and her mother. You must let me know if she is rude to you."

Richard realized that Sarah and Deborah were a source of shame and jealousy to his aunt and she would look for any excuse to punish them. He couldn't really blame her.

"I don't know what William saw in her but he was obsessed with her. That's what got him sent away." It was as if his aunt had kept this inside her since William left and was glad to have someone to unburden to.

"Imagine that Thomas sided with those slaves against his own son!" she continued.

Richard waited for her to explain further but having vented her frustration, she now seemed reluctant to say more and he did not want to appear overly interested, although he was now curious to know what had transpired, so he said nothing.

"So tell me about your fiancée," said his aunt changing the subject. "Have you written to her to let her know that you arrived safely?"

"I must admit that I have not. Letter writing is something that I avoid like the plague. It took me months before I wrote Uncle Thomas to let him know that I was coming."

"You don't sound as if you're smitten with this young lady, if you will forgive my boldness. Otherwise you would have written her as soon as you landed."

"I've known her for a long time but I must admit that it was our fathers who pointed out the benefits that such a marriage would bring."

His aunt nodded understandingly.

"My marriage was one such as that, but I loved Thomas passionately so I was eager to come with him to Barbados even though I knew the early days would be hard. I never imagined it would turn out like this."

Richard didn't know if she was referring to their marriage, life on the plantation or both. It dawned on him that Ann would be in exactly the same position as his aunt, except for the hardship.

Would it be fair to subject her to such a marriage? He even had his own version of Sarah in Anise although she, at least, was not under the same roof. Funny, he realized that he had hardly thought about her since the first night when he compared Deborah to her and Ann had crossed his mind even less.

He knew his aunt was right though. He really should send letters to his parents and Ann to let them know he had reached Barbados safely although Bostick would assure them of that on his return. He was just about to excuse himself to go and start the arduous task when he a sudden pain gripped his abdomen.

He rubbed it surreptitiously and waited for it to pass. Instead the pain intensified and spread. He wondered if it was something he ate and them he remembered that Deborah had unwillingly prepared his meal. Did she put something in his food?

"Aunt Elizabeth, I must ask you to excuse me but I have an excruciating pain in my abdomen. I think I had better lie down."

"Oh, my dear boy! I wonder if the water has affected you. Sometimes the water makes visitors to the island ill since they are not accustomed to it. I will get Deborah to fix you one of her potions. That's the only thing the girl is good for," she could not resist saying.

I hope that it wasn't one of her potions that has me in this condition, he thought to himself.

He gingerly rose from the rocking chair and was ashamed when his aunt came to his assistance as another cramp almost doubled him over. He was amazed at how quickly the illness came on. By the time they reached his room he was covered in sweat.

"I'll get Jethro to come and help you undress and use the chamber pot if you have to and I'll get Deborah to bring you some tea to make you feel better."

She helped him into his bed and hurried out, calling one of the girls to go to Deborah's hut and tell her to find Jethro and come to the house quickly.

Richard was too weak to do anything except pray that Deborah would hurry up with the tea and that it would work fast, provided that she hadn't poisoned him in the first place. While the thought of having Jethro help him use the chamber pot was beyond humiliating, he hoped that he would appear before he had an embarrassing accident.

As another series of cramps ravaged his body, he could not bite back the moan that escaped his lips. He had never felt so ill in his life. Did he come to Barbados only to die?

"Deborah, Deborah!" Rachel called outside her hut. Deborah took just a second to appear in the doorway as it was such a rare occurrence for the girls to come to her hut.

"Mother told you to find Jethro and come to the house quickly," she continued breathlessly. "Cousin Richard is sick."

Deborah's heart skipped a beat. She paused only to turn back to her mother who was on her heels to ask her to find Jethro while she rushed to the house. She had plaited her hair but did not even stop to pile it under a handkerchief.

"Do you know what kind of sickness he has?"

"I think it's his stomach. Mother said something about the water affecting him or it may have been something he ate."

Deborah began to feel a little anxious. She thought of the food that she had prepared for him earlier that day. It was lamb stew that had been left back from the night before and bread.

Did she heat it up enough? Was she responsible for his illness or was it the water?

She reached the kitchen and lit the fire in the hearth. Quickly filling up the kettle from the bucket of water on the counter, she suspended the handle over the crane and swung it into the hearth.

Looking through her herbs in their clay jars she took out two small cloth bags containing chamomile and peppermint leaves. She poured some of each into a tea pot and paced the floor waiting for the kettle to boil.

Her mother always said that a watched pot took longer to boil and she felt sure that this was true. She could hear the mistress heading to the kitchen, probably to find out what was taking so long.

"Deborah, how much longer will you be? Poor Richard is in agony. Jethro is with him now but I know your tea will soothe his stomach and replace much needed fluids. I don't know what has brought this on, but I feel terrible!"

"I'm coming now mistress. I'm waiting for the kettle to boil." Deborah felt terrible too. Terribly guilty.

"I'm going up to my room to change out of these clothes. I will check on him in a few minutes.

"Yes, ma'am."

Richard felt marginally better after using the chamber pot. He was now fully convinced that pain and discomfort were the perfect antidotes for pride and he was just grateful that he had Jethro there to help him and take away the contents before returning the pot in pristine condition and ready for the next use. He had also helped him to undress and change into a robe.

Deborah balanced the tray in one hand and knocked at the door. Memories of knocking on this door almost two years ago and the painful events that followed made her hands shake. She steeled herself to enter the room that she had not seen since that night.

The door was opened by Jethro who stepped aside to allow her to come in.

"How is he now?"

"A little better after using the chamber pot but the worse ain' pass yet. He real weak already." Deborah nodded and made her way to the bed where she put the tray on the bedside table.

Richard was lying under a sheet and looking extremely pale. His dark hair was almost black with sweat and his eyes were closed.

"Master Richard," she said softly. "I brought you some tea to settle your stomach."

His eyes flickered open and it took him a moment to focus.

"Were you so upset that I interrupted your day that you decided to poison me?" he asked weakly but with a straight face.

"Master Richard! I ..I..." Guilt stole the words of denial from her mouth because she still wasn't sure if she was responsible for his illness.

"I jest. I'm sure that if you wanted to poison me I would be dead already. Although I do feel as if I'm halfway to Hades."

"You should not jest, sir! Slaves have been put to death just for the suspicion that they tried to poison their master or mistress."

"I wouldn't want you to be put to death. Not before..." Richard didn't even get to finish his sentence before another cramp seized him.

Deborah was quite glad that he hadn't finished what he was going to say; she had a feeling it would not be something she would want to hear.

Watching him dispassionately, she poured him a cup of tea that had been sweetened with sugar then got Jethro to help him to sit up so that he could sip it so that she didn't come into intimate contact with him.

"I've never felt this ill in my life," confessed Richard. "I'm shocked at how fast it came on. I was just thinking how pain is the perfect cure for pride. Having to be helped on and off a chamber pot has robbed me of all pride, you'll be pleased to hear."

Deborah bit back a smile and said, "Yes I am. Unfortunately I know it will come back as your strength returns." He managed a weak smile.

"Thank you for the tea Deborah."

"You don't have to thank me. I am here to serve you," she added sullenly.

Richard couldn't even muster the strength to tell her how he would like her to serve him and where and how often. It was just as well; he'd probably teased her enough for one day.

Chapter Ten

The Acreage, Barbados
March 27, 1696

Dear Father and Mother

I am finally writing to let you know that I arrived safely although I'm sure that Bostick has already informed you of that.

I am currently recovering from a very bad stomach ailment which may have either been caused by something I ate or the water which, Aunt Elizabeth says, often affects visitors to the island until they become accustomed to it.

As soon as Uncle Thomas heard about my illness, he sent for the doctor as he and Aunt Elizabeth were very worried. There was not much the doctor could do except advise me that the illness would run its course and to continue to drink lots of fluids and to only drink water which had been boiled first in case it was the water that was affecting me.

Aunt Elizabeth had one of their house slaves sleep on a pallet in my room so that he would be available to help me to and from the chamber pot during the night. I lost count of the times he had to empty it. Can you imagine me being helped to and from a chamber pot? What I have learned from this is that illness cures pride.

I have to confess that I felt so ill I thought I would die, so I was grateful for his assistance. Thankfully one of the other house slaves, who is quite knowledgeable in the use of herbs, kept me regularly supplied with some kind of herbal tea which helped me greatly.

You would be shocked at the weight I have lost just in the two days but I have no doubt I will put it back on in short time as my aunt spreads a very good table. I plan to accompany Uncle Thomas on his duties tomorrow, for two days in my room are more than enough to drive me to distraction, as you can imagine.

Apart from my illness, I have thoroughly enjoyed Barbados so far. The island is beautiful, as is the plantation and I have been made to feel very much at home. Uncle Thomas and Aunt Elizabeth send their regards. They have gone out of their way to ensure that all of my needs have been met.

Please give my best regards to Ann and let her know that I will write to her soon. I must confess that this sickness has left me weak and it has been a challenge to even write this letter. Also give my regards to Charles and Charlotte.

Yours respectfully
Richard

Richard folded the letter with a thankful sigh. Although he was not fully recovered, he felt considerably better than in the last two days and had therefore made the effort to write the tardy letter.

If it was not for Jethro who hardly left his side and Deborah with her teas which helped to settle his stomach, he would have surely been a lot worse off.

She had come quietly, three times a day with a pot of tea and left Jethro to help him sit up and drink it. He was surprised at how much he looked forward to seeing her come in with the tray of tea even though she didn't stay. Her hair was always bound in a handkerchief but he could not forget how glorious it looked bouncing against her back as she walked to the house.

Hattie came in both days to wipe him down and get the stale smell of sweat off him, something he was sure that Jethro could do. While he appreciated the bed baths, he found himself irritated with her constant chatter and had to beg her to stop. Moreover he was surprised that he was not the least bit aroused by her ministrations. He put it down to the illness and hoped that it would pass quickly.

A knock on the door interrupted his thoughts. Since Jethro had returned to his duties in the house and yard he called, "Come in."

Deborah tentatively poked her head around the door. Noticing that Jethro was absent she hesitated on the threshold.

"Come in," he invited again.

"The mistress got the cook to make some broth to help you build back up your strength and she asked me to bring it up."

"Thank you. I am grateful for all you did for me when I was ill."

He knew that he did not have to pay her but he had put aside two shillings to gift her with.

"These are for you." He offered her the coins.

Deborah's pride made her want to refuse his money but the conversation she and her mother had had a few days ago about buying their freedom made her hold her tongue. Which was more important, pride or freedom?

"Thank you," she managed, putting down the tray with the broth and taking the coins. She dropped them in her pocket and was heading for the door when he stopped her. "Read to me for a while. I'm dying of boredom."

She hesitated, glanced at the door she'd left open and back at him.

"Slaves are not supposed to read."

"Just for a few minutes," he said with a charming smile. "You can read while I eat. You had better close the door then so that no-one sees you."

This was said so differently from the way William had ordered her to close the door that she obeyed with no feeling of trepidation.

"Ok," she agreed looking around for somewhere to sit. Did she really have any choice?

"I'll sit on the bed and you can have this chair."

With that he crossed to the bed and propped up the pillows so that he could sit up. Deborah handed him the bowl of broth and took the book that was on the bedside table.

Turning the chair towards the bed, she sat down and the warmth that had been left by his body in the chair cocooned her, giving her an unwanted feeling of intimacy with him.

She read the title on the cover of the book: "The True and Exact History of the Island of Barbadoes 1657 by Richard Ligon."

"I've been increasing my knowledge of Barbados," he said. "This book is very insightful; although I'm sure the island has changed a lot since Mr. Ligon wrote his true and exact history. I've marked my place."

Richard waited for her to find the place he had marked and was not disappointed when he saw streaks of red appear on her cheekbones and her nostrils flared slightly in anger. She refused to look up at him.

"'Observations upon the shape of Negroes,'" she read stiffly.

Deborah was mortified to read aloud the account about the female form of negroes written by Mr. Ligon, as if he were a student of science and was simply making observations of some life form that was not human. Why did he not write a similar piece on the form of white women? She was sure that the nephew was doing this on purpose! She set her face and continued tonelessly.

"'The young maids have ordinarily very large breasts, which stand out so hard and firm, as no leaning, jumping, or stirring, will cause them to shake anymore than the brawn of their arms. But when they come to be old, and have had five or six children, their breasts hang down below their navels, so that when they stoop at their common work of weeding...'"

"What is going on here?" The mistress demanded throwing open the door. From her outraged tone, one would think that she had found them indulging in more inappropriate behavior than reading. Deborah was almost relieved to see her although she knew it would mean trouble.

"I asked Deborah to read for me while I ate my broth," Richard explained calmly.

"Slaves are not allowed to read!" His aunt replied, "If you want someone to read to you, one of your cousins will do it. I'm sure that Deborah has work to do in the kitchen. Take yourself off, girl! I will deal with you later," she added dismissing her with a shooing motion of her hand.

Deborah gritted her teeth to hold back a remark that would be guaranteed to earn her the flogging that she was sure the mistress was itching to give her. Seething with the humiliation of being dismissed like a dog, she dropped the book on the chair and left the room without another word, head held high.

"You're going to give that girl ideas. She already acts ..."

The mistress' voice became inaudible as Deborah walked down the hallway, anger infusing her body and making her back straight.

The nephew knew that slaves were not encouraged to read or write so he should never have asked her to read to him. She had no choice but to obey him and in doing so she had stirred up the wrath of his aunt. She wished that he had never come to Barbados. She had a feeling that his visit would mean nothing but trouble for her.

"She already acts as if she's not a slave! Have you ever seen her with her eyes cast down?" his aunt continued. Richard wisely kept silent.

"I don't know what it is like in Carolina, but in Barbados we do not encourage our slaves to read and write. It will only help them to plan rebellions." This was said more calmly. "We've had several uprisings in the past, the last was but a few years ago and I for one am mortally afraid of it happening again, and successfully this time. We heard that the slaves were planning to kill the masters and take as wives only the mistresses who were comely." She shivered in distaste. "Thankfully it was discovered before it came to pass."

"I'm sorry, aunt. We have similar laws in Carolina for that same reason. It's easy to forget that Deborah is a slave, especially since she's so well spoken." And beautiful, he added silently.

"Exactly my point! She certainly does not act like one and that is the fault of Thomas. As I said before, he lets her do as she likes. However I will deal with her and remind her that she's nothing but a slave in this house."

"Please don't punish her for this," Richard protested. "I asked her to read and she could hardly disobey me, so it's not really her fault." His aunt nodded reluctantly, unable to argue with that.

"As you say." She smiled briefly to allow him to think she would let the matter rest there. "I hope to see you downstairs later now that you're feeling better."

Elizabeth shut the door behind her carefully although she really wanted to slam it in frustration.

What was it about that girl? Had she used witchcraft on the men in the family? Thomas favored her, William was obsessed with her and now it seemed as if she was working her spell on Richard. She couldn't believe that he had her reading to him. And he actually said that he forgot she was a slave! The girl must have put something in his tea to bewitch him.

What next? Would he be inviting her to dine with them instead of serving them at dinner? The girl had caused enough disruption in her family.

Chapter Eleven

As soon as Richard was better, Elizabeth began to plan his party. Once they had set the date she and the girls spent a whole day writing letters of invitation, which they got Jethro to deliver on horseback. In addition to their closest friends, they had invited the governor, members of the House of Assembly and other high officials in the island.

No expense was to be spared on the party to introduce Richard to the Barbadian settlers; or at least those that mattered. The menu they selected boasted, along with local fare, imported foods such as pickled oysters, caviar, olives and anchovies as well as a variety of desserts.

Once the invitations had gone out Elizabeth called together all the house slaves and announced that she was having a party to introduce her nephew to their friends and acquaintances in two weeks and were expecting about 100 people.

"We will use the sitting room for the party so the furniture will have to be removed. Jethro your job will be to act as butler and direct the guests to the sitting room. Deborah, Cassie and Hattie you will serve. We will have light food rather than a big meal. I will borrow one or two of the skilled workers to serve the drinks."

"Sally you will need to wash all the glasses and small plates we have before the party. Get the girls to help you. I have some material that I bought in Town recently and Sarah you are to make an outfit for Jethro and dresses for the girls to serve in so that I won't be disgraced by their appearance. I will draw a sketch for you to follow. OK, you can get back to work now."

"This is so exciting, mother!" exclaimed Mary. "We've not had a party in ages."

"You can wear your new dresses that we bought in Town last month so that you look your best when the eligible young men come. There are so few of them here in Barbados, we might be forced to send you to England to wed."

They tittered excitedly.

"I'm sure our friends will faint dead away when they see how handsome cousin Richard is," Rachel boasted.

"I'm just glad that he's put back on a bit of weight," admitted Elizabeth. "He had looked so drawn after his illness. I felt simply terrible!"

"He's fine now mother."

Richard had felt well enough to venture out with Thomas by the Wednesday and Elizabeth was glad that he no longer had any cause to interact with Deborah. She made sure that Hattie and Cassie served dinner and she knew that Hattie went to his room some nights. There was little that happened in the house that she did not know.

She had no problem with him bedding Hattie; after all that's what men did. Hattie was harmless. Deborah, on the other hand, was not and she intended to make sure that Richard didn't lose his head over her, like William did. The less he saw of her the better.

The mistress gave Sarah a sketch of a dress and several yards of coarse blue linen with a smaller amount of blue and white striped material to make the dresses and aprons for the girls. When she had finished making them, Deborah tried on hers, took one look at the bold neckline which would no doubt draw the attention of the male attendees of the party and declared that she would not wear it.

"Child, you don't have any choice; the mistress told me how to make the dresses."

"I don't want all of those men eyeing me and thinking that I am available. I'm not wearing it!"

"So what you going to wear then?"

Deborah thought for a moment and then remembered the beautiful green satin dress that her mother had given her on her sixteenth birthday.

"I'll wear the dress that you gave me when I turned sixteen. I haven't had anywhere to wear it before."

"That would look real nice but the mistress will be vexed if you don't wear the dress that I made. Girl, you looking to upset the mistress? What I goin' tell her when she sees that you not dressed like Cassie and Hattie? I would have to ask the master if you could wear it since he is the one that gave me the material to make the dress for you. He don't really get involved in things to do with the house though so I don't know what he will say."

"Yes, talk to the master because I am not wearing that dress."

Although Sarah planned to get the Master's permission, she had a bad feeling about it since she knew that the mistress had not been happy with Deborah since she had found her reading to the nephew and this would only make things worse. She wished that Deborah was not so stubborn; it would only lead to trouble.

Deborah opened the trunk where she had carefully packed the dress nearly two years ago. Although she had put some sachets of dried flowers in its folds, it was slightly musty so she shook it out and took it outside to drape it over a nearby bush to air. She would get her mother to iron it when she was doing the other two.

It was truly beautiful and showed her mother's fine talent with a needle. More important the neckline was respectable and would not attract lustful eyes. Her mother's talent was truly wasted as a slave, doing the laundry, ironing and sewing for the family when she could be making a living as a seamstress if she was free.

Deborah sighed as heaviness settled over her like a mantle. Would they ever be free? She knew that wearing the dress would rouse the mistress' anger but she was prepared to face the consequences to experience the freedom to choose what she wanted to do just once. At least her dress would make her feel free, if only for one night.

Deborah plaited her hair and coiled it around her head in a coronet. The style emphasized her slender neck and sculptured cheekbones and made her look more exotic than usual.

Picking up the freshly pressed dress she stepped into it and Sarah came to help her button it up. As she turned around, tears sprang unexpectedly to Sarah's eyes.

"You look like a beautiful free woman tonight. None of those women will be able to hold a candle to you but I hope you ready to deal with the mistress. Although the master said that he didn't see why it should matter what dress you wear, when the mistress she see you she ain' going to be too happy."

"Tonight, I don't care. I feel like a free woman." The feeling was addictive and she wanted more already.

She and Sarah headed to the kitchen which was already a hive of activity. Their entrance brought a sudden hush as the house slaves noticed Deborah.

"Girl, you look like the mistress of the house," said Cassie in awe.

"How come you ain' dress like us?" Hattie asked. The dress fitted her well and the daringly low neckline emphasized her ample bosom.

"I have no desire to make anyone think I'm offering anything other than the food." Deborah retorted.

"That dress look real nice, Deborah. Where you get that from?" Sally asked her.

"My mother made it for my sixteenth birthday."

"Girl, you goin' turn some heads tonight. Hattie, the nephew may call for Deborah tonight instead of you," Cassie teased. Hattie glared at her and said nothing. Deborah fervently hoped not.

She couldn't help the shiver that went down her back at the thought. For a moment she wondered if she had made a mistake by dressing as she had. She hadn't wanted to bring attention to herself with the revealing dress but was she doing it anyway by setting herself apart?

Jethro appeared in the doorway. "The mistress said that you can start serving the food. A good set of people here already."

That started a flurry of activity as the cook began to hand out trays of food for the girls to take out. Deborah hung back as long as she could but eventually took her tray from the cook and headed for the dining room.

Richard tried to remember the people he had been introduced to as he stood with the family to greet their guests. The Bayleys, the Newtons, the Watermans, the Littletons, the Pierces, the Sharps. His head was swirling with all the names and he knew that he would remember few.

They were dressed as finely as the gentry in England and in fact many of them were from among that class who had relocated to Barbados to capitalize on the wealth to be had on the island. He knew that they must be deathly hot in the imported fashions which were terribly unsuited to the climate. He certainly felt warm in his jacket and waistcoat over a fine linen shirt and breeches. The cool breeze blowing through the doors that opened onto the balcony was a welcome relief.

"Christopher, it has been a long time." His uncle greeted a man who was several years older than himself. He was richly attired and his waistcoat strained to contain the paunch which betrayed his love for food.

"I haven't been out much since my wife passed away."

"Yes, of course. This is Elizabeth's nephew Richard Fairfax from Carolina. Richard this is Christopher Coverley, one of the richest men in Barbados." Coverley laughed but Richard noticed that he didn't deny it.

"Good to meet you. What brings you to Barbados?" he asked extending his hand.

"Business."

"What business are you in?"

"My family is in shipping but I'm looking to get into rice production when I go back."

"Rice. Sounds good. We need to talk later and see how we can do business together."

"I look forward to that," said Richard shaking his hand again.

"I think we can stop the formal greetings now and mingle with our guests. Anyone who comes later can meet Richard as we circulate." Thomas said.

He was anxious to talk to some of the other planters about Jamaica and the growing sugar industry there which could be a threat to theirs. Maybe he should invest in Jamaica.

"Yes," agreed Elizabeth. "I think most of our guests are here anyway and I'm getting weary of stand..." She bit off her words abruptly as a vision of beauty proffering a tray came into sight. It was Deborah in a beautiful satin gown that looked as well made as some that were worn by the guests. The family turned to see what had caught her attention.

Richard's breath caught at the sight of Deborah's striking profile as she smiled politely at a group of planters. They seemed to him to be taking their time selecting whatever she was offering and the way they were devouring her with their eyes, he could just imagine what they wished she was offering.

He had never seen her in anything other than the plainest garb which she seemed to wear like armor, so the sight of her in satin, as well dressed as any of the guests, hit him squarely in the chest. A lot lower the truth be told. He was surprised at the possessiveness he felt on seeing the men's reaction to her. It was not as if she was his but he certainly wanted her to be.

He glanced at his aunt to see her tighten her lips before she made excuses and ushered the girls to greet some friends, leaving Richard and Thomas alone.

"Deborah seems to have caught the eye of every male here," Richard observed. Mine included he thought silently.

"Yes. She certainly looks beautiful tonight," Thomas agreed nodding.

"You may have some offers for her after this," Richard said, feeling him out.

"It's well known that she's not for sale."

"At any price?"

"I'm in no desperate need of money. Why the interest?"

Richard sighed deeply, his eyes seeking out Deborah across the room. "She stirs me like no other," he confessed quietly.

Thomas eyed him thoughtfully and clapped him on the shoulder. "I understand completely. If you can convince her to come to your bed, I'll not intervene."

"You said that I only have to tell them to come," Richard reminded him.

"Not Deborah. She has been through enough. I'll not have her subjected to more. Come, let us talk with our guests," his uncle said, gesturing him towards a group of planters.

Richard would have liked to ask more, but had to be contented with the fact that his uncle had at least given him permission to pursue Deborah. He smiled even as his body tingled with anticipation.

Richard and his uncle joined a group of planters who were drinking glasses of Thomas's fine French brandy and discussing the challenges that Antigua was facing with getting their sugar to England.

"I've heard that late last year they could not get their sugar shipped to England because of the war and they had to wait months before England was able to send any help."

"Yes. That was good news for us since we were able to get our sugar to market first," another planter added.

"Now I see why you invested in a ship, Thomas," praised a man whose flushed face suggested that he had already had a lot to drink. "No one will be able to stop you from getting your sugar to the motherland."

"I don't intend to be held to ransom by anyone," Thomas agreed.

"So what brings you to Barbados?" One of the planters asked Richard, changing the topic.

"I'm here to observe how you manage your African slaves as I plan to buy some when I go back and use them to cultivate rice."

"Barbados wouldn't be so successful without their labor. However they now outnumber us badly. We had a close call in '92 when they planned a rebellion."

"So I heard," Richard said.

"We've had to curtail a lot of their movement and we don't allow them to meet together anymore. Because of their numbers, we have to keep them in line through fear and punishment. Thankfully our slave code gives us legal right to do so without reprisal."

"The slave code has made us like gods; we have the power of life and death in our hands." Another planter declared.

"They've just adopted a new one in Carolina based on yours."

"Good move that. Helps to keep them under control."

"Speaking of under control, when is William coming back?" This was from John Bowyer, the father of William's friend Henry. "Henry's been like a fish out of water without him here. Not that it's been a bad thing because I've actually been able to get some work out of him." Thomas laughed.

"That's what I'm hoping for when William gets back. It probably won't be before late in the year or next year though. I trust that England will make him into a better man."

"I spent two years there myself and I think it made a better man out of me. And if not better then certainly stronger. When you're born in the colonies, you're often looked down upon so you have to be strong enough to overcome that and get on with whatever you're there for." Richard told them.

"You certainly turned out well, my boy," Thomas praised him. If William turned out half as well, he would be happy.

"Thank you uncle."

"Speaking of turning out well, Thomas, that girl of yours has turned out very well. I have not seen her since William left," John remarked, his eyes boldly roving over Deborah as she made her way towards them with a tray.

"Pickled oysters." She announced, proffering the tray.

"I may need them, especially if you're offering yourself to go with them," John joked. Deborah was revolted and would have liked nothing more than to throw the oysters in his sun-wrinkled face. The man was as old as Master Thomas and just as disgusting as his son.

"You randy old goat," another planter said. "Don't you have enough girls to keep you busy on your own plantation?" He helped himself to an oyster.

"None as lovely as this one," he replied taking one himself with his eyes still on Deborah. "Have you changed your mind about selling yet, Thomas?"

Richard was silently disgusted with the old lecher but he could fully understand his interest in the ravishing slave girl. He looked at Deborah who wore a blank expression on her face as the men talked about her as if she was not there, but the now-familiar flaring of her nostrils and the color on her cheeks betrayed her anger.

"I've already expressed my interest," Richard interjected, watching her closely, "but my uncle couldn't be persuaded." The men laughed in sympathy.

Deborah's eyes flew up and collided with his and he was pleased to see hers widen in shock at his bold confession. The look was quickly replaced by one of intense dislike. Rather than put him off though, it served to challenge him. He allowed his gaze to roam the length of her and his eyes became more intense. She gave him a cold glare before she lowered her eyes.

"OK, Deborah," said Thomas indicating that she could leave.

Deborah was relieved to move away from the group of lecherous men. What did the nephew mean by that? Had he really offered to buy her from the master? He was just as bad as the rest of them. After discussing Shakespeare with her and asking her to read to him, he still thought her nothing more than a chattel that he could buy for his use? Why had she believed he was any different?

She had not thought he was like William, but she now couldn't be certain. One thing she was certain about was that she didn't like what she had seen in his

eyes when he had looked at her. It had been uncon-
cealed desire.

"Elizabeth, what a lovely party. And how handsome
your nephew is!" exclaimed her friend Dora Pierce. "It
must be nice having him here now that William is away,"
she added.

"Yes indeed."

"You should really find him a nice girl to marry and
keep him in Barbados. I wouldn't mind him for my own
Mary-Ann," admitted her friend, Hazel Newton.

"I know what you mean. We really need more of our
kind on the island especially since hardly any indentured servants are coming here now," agreed Dora.

"That thought did cross my mind, but unfortunately
he's already betrothed to a girl in Carolina." They all sighed
with disappointment and then laughed at themselves.

"He's been such a help to Thomas and he says he's
looking forward to helping out during the harvest."

"There speaks someone who knows nothing of the
horrors of harvesting cane. I practically lose all my
house girls to the work," complained Hazel.

"Speaking of house girls, I must say that you dress
yours very well Elizabeth. The one in the green, in particular, looks as well turned out as many of the ladies
here tonight."

"Thank you Dora." Elizabeth pasted a polite smile
on her face which ably covered up the anger seething
inside her as she looked at Deborah again.

Not only had Deborah deliberately disobeyed her by wearing something of her own choosing, but she drew the eyes of every man in the room, Richard's included! She wondered where she had got the dress from. No doubt Thomas! It wasn't surprising that she thought herself above the others. Well it was high time she reminded the girl that she was nothing more than a slave in her house and under her control. She now had a good reason and she would do it at the earliest opportunity!

Chapter Twelve

T he Barbadian planters, Richard noticed, indulged in drink like no other people he had encountered and each group he joined insisted that he have a drink with them. He didn't resist, hoping that the alcohol would dull the desire that rose in him each time his eyes fell on Deborah as she served. The fact that she appeared oblivious to his presence, while he could not keep his eyes off her, was a blow to his pride and he was determined to get a response from her one way or the other.

The opportunity arose when he saw her crossing the room with an empty tray to go to the kitchen. Quickly begging the excuse of a group of young ladies that his cousins had insisted he meet, he exited through the nearest doorway and reached the hallway ahead of her and was able to block her path.

She came to an abrupt halt when she saw him, her startled eyes meeting his. She made to move around him and he moved as well, cutting off her exit.

"You look beautiful tonight, Deborah," he praised quietly.

"Thank you," she murmured lowering her gaze, even while she kept the tray between them.

He leaned closer and said, "Come to my room after the party." The smell of brandy was strong on his breath. Before she could move back he bent his head and branded her with a kiss on the side of her neck.

A shiver tickled her back and she pulled away shocked; not sure if it was because of his bold action or her response to it. "I'm afraid that's not possible." Her voice was unsteady.

"What do you mean, that's not possible? You will do as I say." His pride was stung and he forgot what his uncle had warned him only hours before.

In a panic Deborah scrambled for a response and finally said, "I am indisposed, Master Richard."

The alcohol he had drunk made him slow to process the information and it seemed to take an age before he understood her meaning. His mouth twisted in displeasure at the news and he uttered a curse before turning away to stride down the hall.

Deborah resumed her way to the kitchen, with a slight smile of victory on her face. She couldn't use that excuse forever so she would have to get her mother to speak to the master soon. He obviously had not told the nephew that she was not for bedding.

Dawn was painting the sky in pale pinks when the last carriage departed from The Acreage. While the family wearily climbed the stairs to their rooms, the slaves were faced with the task of restoring the house to order before the family woke up later in the day. Thankfully it was Sunday so after they had cleaned up they could take their own rest.

If the success of the party was to be judged by the amount of alcohol consumed, then the slaves who worked serving the drinks could attest that it was a very success-ful party. They packed about a hundred empty wine and brandy bottles into crates before helping Jethro to put the furniture back in place in the sitting room. Deborah and the other women walked about picking up glasses and plates to take into the yard just outside the kitchen, where several tubs had been set up to wash and rinse them.

The sun was half way up the sky when they finally headed to their huts for much coveted sleep. Deborah was so exhausted that she barely managed to take off her dress before falling onto her pallet to sleep.

She awoke several hours later, disoriented to find herself in bed in broad daylight. Wincing as she sat up, she heard her mother bustling about in the front room.

"Ma, what time is it?" she called to Sarah.

"It looks to be around four or so," Sarah replied pok-ing her head through the door. "You hungry? I made some pone."

"Yes, but I want to wash my hair before it gets any later. I'll eat something when I come back."

Deborah washed inside the hut then carried a bucket outside and filled it with water so that she could wash her long hair. The soap that she had made, scented with lemon balm, gave her hair a fresh lemony scent. Drying it as much as she could with a small towel she headed out to her favorite spot leaving it loose for the wind to finish the job.

She had not had the opportunity to get a new book from the master's office as they had been busy preparing for the party so she had nothing to read but she would just enjoy the view and relax for a few minutes. As she made her way around the back of the house towards her oasis, an unaccustomed feeling of well being came over her.

Richard saw Deborah heading for her favorite spot from his bedroom window. He had woken up an hour or so earlier with a headache induced by the vast quantities of brandy he had consumed the night before; another reason why he avoided drinking too much spirits.

He recalled his encounter with Deborah in the hallway and now cringed at his crassness. He couldn't believe he had ordered her to come to his room. It was just as well that she had been indisposed, or so she claimed. He wouldn't put it past her to lie about that. He had never needed to force a woman into his bed and he was not about to start now. She might be a slave, but he had enough pride to want her to be willing to come to him and he vowed that when she came to him, she would indeed be willing.

The desire to follow her was strong and he battled with himself for a few minutes before he gave up the fight and slipped out of his room, hoping that he would meet none of the family. From the amount of spirits his uncle had consumed, he was sure that he would be asleep until nightfall and he hoped that the ladies were still spent. Luck was with him and he made his way out of the house unseen and down to the grove of trees where he knew he would find Deborah.

Deborah saw him coming from the distance and her heart gave a little lurch. She preferred to call it fear but if she was truly honest with herself, she knew it was really anticipation. She was assured that her lie at the party would give her safety from any inappropriate advances, at least for now, so she wasn't really afraid of him in that way.

This time she stood up as he came closer so that he would not tower over her as he did before, although she still had to look a way up to see his face. He stopped fairly close to her and as her eyes stared at the top button of his shirt, she couldn't help but notice the breadth of his shoulders under the shirt he wore this evening.

"You needn't have stood."

"I'm supposed to," she replied.

"Do you always do what you're supposed to?" She kept quiet knowing that wearing the dress to the party provided her answer to the question.

"I came to apologize for my behavior last night which I attribute to the vast quantities of alcohol I consumed," he offered rather than pursuing the answer to his question.

"Since when does a master apologize to a slave?" asked Deborah rhetorically.

"I am not your master," he replied quietly, "but I would like to be," he added in a husky voice.

"I am not for sale!" she declared.

"Don't be too sure about that," he retorted confidently. Deborah hesitated, now unsure of her bold statement. Would the master really sell her to the nephew? Had they come to some sort of agreement that she had not been told about yet? How she hated the fact that she could be bought and sold.

"Would it be so bad to be owned by me, Deborah? I would be good to you," he promised in a low voice, closing the distance between them to run the back of his fingers down her neck. Her skin felt like silk to his touch and an image of him kissing her neck came back to him. Had he done that last night or had he imagined it? He slid his fingers into her hair to see if it felt as silky and pulled her gently towards him.

Deborah jerked her head back as his fingers on her neck and in her hair stirred unfamiliar feelings in her body.

"You don't want to be owned by me, but I think you already own me," he continued musingly as she said nothing. Her eyes met his questioningly. "I saw you pass my window and said that I would not follow you, yet here I am. Do you not own me?"

Deborah dismissed his confession. "That is hardly the same thing. Anyway, it is not me that owns you. It is your lust. But I'm sure that Hattie will be only too willing to take care of that."

"And you're not." It was a statement.

"No. I am not."

"One day you will change your mind."

"Never!" Deborah assured him.

"Never say never," he said arrogantly, walking away. He would remind her about those words when she came to his bed.

Deborah seethed at his retreating back. She would never desire the infuriating, arrogant nephew and she couldn't wait until he left Barbados.

Monday morning dawned clear and bright. It was a beautiful day in the island. The kitchen was abuzz with talk about the party and how much food and drink had been consumed. Cassie had served breakfast to the men and reported that the master was going to Jamestown later in the morning to do some business but had asked Master Richard to check on the slaves working near the house since the overseers would be involved with harvesting the first set of canes.

"He does more than Master William ever did 'bout here. The master goin' be sorry when he gone back to Carolina," Sarah said.

I will not, thought Deborah, remembering his boast to her as he walked away from her the day before.

"Me too," piped up Hattie. "He is a real good man. I never had any like him before," she confessed with a satisfied smile.

Deborah remembered the tingle that ran through her body when he sank his fingers in her hair and for a brief moment wondered what it would be like to find out what Hattie was talking about. Her face burned as she caught her wayward thoughts and told herself that

Hattie was welcome to him because she certainly wasn't interested and she didn't care how good he was.

"I'm going to pick some herbs from the back garden. I haven't picked any for a long time and most of the bags are almost empty," Deborah announced, hurriedly picking up a basket. She really didn't want to hear any more of Hattie's stories at the moment. The girl had no shame and was willing to share all sorts of intimacies that Deborah could do without hearing about.

As she went out the back door she heard Cassie saying, "Sarah, the mistress ain' ask you nothing about why Deborah didn't wear the same dress as us?"

"To tell the truth, I ain' see the mistress since the party and I hoping that she forget."

"I don't know 'bout that. You shoulda see her face when Deborah come in wearing that dress. In fact you shoulda see the nephew face too. I peep at him and I nearly burst out laughing to see how he was looking at your girl child. Hattie you better enjoy it while it last because he soon goin' to be calling for Deborah instead of you."

"Don't say so, Cassie," Sarah begged her. "I don' want no more trouble for Deborah."

"He ain' like Master William, you could see that," comforted Cassie.

Just then the kitchen door burst open and Jethro ran in, sweating and agitated.

"Where Deborah? The mistress want to see her."

"Why she send you? What she want?" asked Sarah standing up.

"I don' know what Deborah do but the mistress tell me to bring a whip and find Deborah. She want me to flog Deborah. Losee, I don't know what to do. The master never ask me to do anything like that. How I supposed to flog Deborah? But I can' tell the mistress no. I don't know what to do." He paced up and down.

"Flog Deborah? For what?" Sarah's voice rose in fear as she asked the question but she already knew the answer. Dread pooled in her belly as she realized that the mistress had at last found something that she could use to punish Deborah.

"Oh loss, she wait 'til Master Thomas turn his back to plan this. What to do?"

"Jethro, have you found that insolent girl yet?" The mistress' voice penetrated the door before she pushed it open.

"Where is Deborah?" She looked around the room.

"She out picking herbs," Hattie volunteered, earning her glares from all the slaves.

"What she do, mistress?" asked Sarah fearfully.

"As if you don't know. I should flog you as well! I expect either the dress or the rest of my material to be returned to me immediately and burn that dress that Deborah wore to the party. Jethro, find her and bring her to the whipping post in the yard. It's time to teach that girl a lesson."

"It is my fault mistress. Flog me instead of Deborah. She didn' mean nothing by it. She didn't like how the dress was fitting and the master said..."

"Jethro, you heard me," Elizabeth interrupted, ignoring Sarah's plea. "If that girl is not stripped and tied to the post in ten minutes, you will get the flogging instead." With that she left the kitchen and went to sit in her favorite chair on the patio.

139

Pandemonium broke out in the kitchen. Sarah started to cry and Jethro looked torn as if he would cry too. He didn't know what to do. He jumped when Deborah appeared at the back door with her basket full of herbs. Seeing her mother in tears, she dropped the basket and rushed to her.

"What is the matter?"

In short time she discovered what her fate was to be for rebelliously refusing to wear the same dress as the other slaves. She realized, too late, that she had played right into the mistress' hands. She suddenly didn't feel so brave when she saw the leather whip in Jethro's hand and the regret in his eyes.

Panic flooded her as she recalled seeing one of the runaway slaves tied to the whipping post and whipped until his back was a crisscross of bleeding welts and his voice was too hoarse to cry with the sting of each blow after a while. She began to shake and back away from him.

"Sorry Deborah, but she say that if I don' do it, she goin' whip me. I sorry girl, but I got to obey the mistress. I gine try not to hit you too hard but I don' know how you does stop a leather whip from stinging." With that he pulled Deborah through the house to the patio where the mistress was calmly rocking in her chair.

"This has been long in coming," the mistress said looking up. "You've crossed me once too many times. Tie her to the post Jethro and gave her ten lashes."

Deborah refused to give the mistress the satisfaction of seeing her fear but her legs felt as if they couldn't hold her up as Jethro reluctantly pulled her into the yard.

"What's going on, mother?" asked Rachel as she and Mary appeared on the patio.

"Nothing that concerns you. Go back to your rooms until I tell you to come out," she instructed in a hard tone. Being unaccustomed to their mother speaking so harshly to them, they rushed to obey, lest they risked her wrath.

In the kitchen, Sarah was being restrained by Cassie as she fought to go to help Deborah.

"I can't let her scar up my child. Oh why the master not here today? He would never let her do this. What to do Cassie? What to do?"

"Go and get Master Richard. He out by the plantain patch. Go quick!" Cassie released her and Sarah ran, knowing that she was racing against time.

Deborah was pulled over to the whipping post by a reluctant Jethro and on the mistress' instructions the back of her dress was ripped open, exposing her back and falling away at the front to reveal her naked breasts. Jethro loosely tied her hands to the post, averting his eyes, all the while saying he was sorry that he had to do it or else the mistress would do the same to him.

There were very few slaves around, apart from the house slaves, to see her shame and for this she was glad. Images of whippings she had witnessed tormented her mind. Could she stand the pain without crying out? She did not want to give the mistress the satisfaction. Even as that thought entered her mind it was quickly replaced by fear that made her body tremble against the warmth of the wooden post as Jethro stepped back and raised the whip.

Richard reined in his horse and pulled up under a tree to watch the young slaves pulling weeds from among the plantain trees. Further down he saw some other children weeding the vegetable gardens, laughing as they competed to see who had the biggest pile of weeds. The morning was beginning to heat up and it was looking to be another beautiful, but hot, day in Barbados. He realized with a start that he didn't even miss Carolina.

A sudden commotion caused his horse to rear up slightly and he looked up to see Sarah rushing towards him like a mad woman with fear in her eyes. His heart missed a beat and he swung down from his horse to meet her, knowing that something terrible must have happened to Deborah.

"Master Richard, Master Richard, come quick, come quick!" she panted. "The mistress making Jethro flog Deborah," she pulled at his hand in agitation, not realizing what she was doing.

"What? Where is she?"

"The whipping post in front the house."

Richard jumped on his horse and flew back in the direction that Sarah had come, not waiting to see if she followed. His breath came in quick bursts as he urged the horse to move faster, envisioning Deborah tied to the post. He remembered seeing the drivers urging the slaves to work harder with a lash of the whip and his mind protested at the thought of Deborah being subjected to that pain.

The sound of the leather whistling through the air was the last thing Deborah heard before pain exploded across her back and she couldn't help the cry that escaped her lips as she felt the searing burn of the whip.

As Richard approached the house, the sight of Deborah, stripped to the waist, with her hands tied to the post and a welt already marring her back, sent a physical pain through him. He caught sight of Jethro's distraught face as he raised the whip and brought it down again.

Richard cringed as Deborah arched her back and another thick red welt appeared.

Tears involuntarily ran from her eyes and Deborah knew that she could not survive eight more of those strokes without humiliating herself. How she wished she had never worn her own dress. The few hours of pleasure at making her own choice could in no way compensate for the fiery pain in her back. Too late she recognized that her rebellion was wrong and it had done nothing but lead her right into the hands of the mistress.

Where are you God? I confess I was wrong. Will you stand by while I am whipped? She agonized silently. Do you not care about me? The pain of rejection in her heart was almost as intense as the pain in her back.

"Stop!" She heard a shout. "Stop Jethro!" The sound of Richard's voice penetrated the haze of her pain and she wept in relief. Had her prayer been answered? Was God real? Dare she believe that he cared about her after all?

As Richard jumped from the horse and grabbed Jethro's hand in mid-air he glimpsed the patent relief on the slave's face.

Pushing Jethro out of the way he quickly untied the rope that had loosely bound her hands and gently turned Deborah who collapsed into his arms with tears streaming down her face. He cursed himself for his weakness but couldn't help but look at her firm breasts before he pulled up her torn dress to preserve her modesty. Shudders shook her body as she buried her face in his shirt sobbing.

"What do you mean by interfering here, Richard?" his aunt demanded rushing from the patio.

"Uncle Thomas would never condone this, aunt," he said angrily over Deborah's head. He couldn't believe how angry he was with her for punishing Deborah this way. "He told me himself that the house slaves were never to be whipped because they're too valuable to be scarred."

"The girl is insolent and deserves to be taught a lesson!"

"I will let you take that up with Uncle Thomas when he comes home but for now I ask that you leave her alone."

His aunt stalked off without another word and he handed Deborah over to Sarah who had finally made it into the yard, breathing as if her heart would explode.

He strode angrily over to the horse, climbed in the saddle and rode out without a backward glance. He knew that he had probably made an enemy of his aunt and he was angry with her, angry with himself and angry with Deborah for putting him in that position in the first place. He should have known from the time he set eyes on her that the girl would cause him nothing but trouble.

Chapter Thirteen

On reaching their hut, Sarah put Deborah to lie down and picked a piece of aloe which she crushed and smeared gently over the welts on her back.

"Do you believe in God, ma?" Deborah asked thoughtfully as Sarah performed her ministrations.

"You mean that Jethro was telling us about?"

"Yes," Deborah confirmed.

"I know the children's tutor used to teach them about this God but my mother used to tell me about Olódùmarè which is the creator that her people believed in and the Orishas which are gods or spirits that are different forms of Olódùmarè. Maybe they are the same. I don't know. Why you ask me that?"

"I've been thinking about him recently so when Jethro was whipping me, I prayed to him and the same time Master Richard came and saved me. I wonder if it was by chance or if he is real and he heard me."

"I don't know child. If he real, why he didn't help you when Master William called you to his room?" Deborah had no response to that but she suddenly remembered William dragging her across the bed and pulling back his hand to deliver a blow to her face which for some reason never came. Did the same God stop him from harming her more? Was he there with her even as William took her innocence? She didn't know what to think; what to believe. Exhaustion overtook her and she succumbed to sleep without even knowing when it happened.

Sarah was glad when Deborah fell asleep, overcome by the morning's trauma and tiredness from the party but she knew that when she woke up her back would probably pain her terribly.

She was grateful that Jethro had not put his full strength behind the whip, or it would have been much worse and that Master Richard had not gone to Jamestown with the master and had been near to the yard. Maybe that was God's doings.

The way that he had jumped on his horse and taken off to stop Jethro from whipping Deborah, made her think that Cassie was right. He seemed to be interested in Deborah, even though he still called for Hattie to come to his room at night. Perhaps the master had told him he couldn't have Deborah; she hoped so.

She wondered how things would be in the house with the mistress now that Master Richard had stopped Jethro from carrying out her orders. What would the master do? Would he take the mistress' side? Would he be vexed with her for causing this trouble although he had said that Deborah could wear the dress? She was surprised that the mistress had not ordered her to be whipped too; after all it was she who had disobeyed her in not making Deborah wear the dress.

In spite of everything she couldn't bring herself to burn the green dress; she had put too much time and love into making it and it was the best dress she had ever made. She would hide it in Deborah's trunk until she had the opportunity to wear it again someday, hopefully as a free woman.

Someone knocking on the door of the hut roused her from her thoughts and she opened it to find Master Thomas and Master Richard outside.

"Sarah, I just got back to the plantation and Richard told me that he had to stop Deborah from being whipped by Jethro. What happened?" Sarah stepped outside and closed the door behind her.

"It was my fault, Master Thomas. It was about the dress that I asked you if she could wear to the party. The mistress was vexed because Deborah disobeyed her and didn't wear the one I had made for all the girls so she told Jethro to flog her or he would get flogged himself."

"Thankfully Sarah found me quickly and I was able to stop him after just two strokes."

"A good thing Jethro was trying not to hit her too hard so the skin didn't break but her back has two big welts and it is real sore," Sarah told them.

Thomas closed his eyes, at the upheaval in his family yet again. It always seemed to involve Deborah in some way. Maybe he should sell her for the sake of peace in his house.

"Can I see her?" Richard asked, looking towards his uncle for permission. He nodded and Sarah stepped aside to let him in.

"She's in the back room sleeping."

Richard bent his head to get through the door and glanced around the dim room which was sparsely furnished but well kept and clean. The floor was packed dirt and the walls of the hut were made of wattle and daub with plantain leaves for the roof.

He went through to the back room and saw Deborah lying on a pallet on the floor. Her back was bare and a thin sheet covered her from the waist down. The smooth skin of her back was flawed by two long red welts which were smeared with some sort of slimy substance.

The room's one small window provided enough light for him to see a similar pallet on the floor next to Deborah's, a trunk and an old chest of drawers with a basin and a jug on it. There were few personal items in sight; just a comb and a brush on the trunk.

This was where Deborah and Sarah lived? He was shocked at the primitive accommodations that his uncle's favorite slaves lived in. Had his uncle ever been in here? He thought of William's soft bed that he slept in every night and the ornate furnishings in the house and he felt a tug of conscience at how he took them for granted while Deborah lived like... a slave. That was what she was. Why did he seem to have trouble remembering that?

Looking down at her he could make out the swell of her breast as she slept on her stomach with her head cushioned on her arms and he was surprised to find that it was not only desire that stirred in him but an overwhelming feeling of compassion. He sent up a brief prayer of thanks that he had been able to save her from a worse beating and bent to stroke her hair gently before turning to leave the room.

"How is she?" His uncle asked as he rejoined him.

"She's still sleeping but I'm sure her back is going to be very sore and stiff when she wakes up."

"OK Sarah, you can go," Thomas dismissed her.

Richard hesitated, not sure how to broach the subject of the living conditions of the two women as they walked towards the house.

"I'm surprised the house slaves don't sleep in the house. What is there to prevent Sarah or Deborah from being violated in their hut by one of the overseers or the other slaves?"

"Only the threat of a flogging for the offender, I suppose. But you're right. They should probably be in the house for protection and that way they would be close by in case they're needed during the night or something. Sarah and Deborah used to live in the house when she looked after the children. I don't even recall when they moved out. I will talk to Elizabeth about finding somewhere for them, although after today that may not be a very popular decision."

"Speaking about lack of popularity, I'm sure that I won't be popular with my aunt for intervening today. I told her that you didn't want the house slaves scarred since it would diminish their value."

"Don't worry, I'll deal with her."

Thinking it best to avoid his aunt for the time being, Richard headed for the kitchen, to the accompaniment of his growling stomach to ask the cook to pack something to take with him to eat while his uncle went in search of his aunt. He was warmly greeted by the cook who was more than happy to pack a good sized lunch for the man who had rescued Deborah.

Meanwhile Thomas, not being one to put off unpleasant tasks, headed for his wife's room where she was resting after lunch. He knocked on the door and was invited to come in.

Elizabeth was propped up in bed reading a book. Thomas noted the lavish four poster bed with several fluffy pillows at her back and a beautiful white quilt lying across the foot of the bed. A mahogany chest of drawers stood to one side with gilded brushes and combs, jewelry boxes and all kinds of bottles and jars. A lady's writing desk, with a carved chair was strategically located in front of a window to catch the light.

Thomas realized with a start that he had not been to Elizabeth's room in ages. In fact he found it impossible to remember when they had last been intimate. Not for many years, to be sure. An unfamiliar feeling that felt almost like shame came upon him but he told himself that she was probably glad not to have to fulfill her marital duties.

A look of surprise crossed her face as she saw that it was him but she quickly schooled her face and presented him with a slightly inquiring stare.

"Good day, Elizabeth," Thomas began. "I hope you do not blame Richard for interfering today. He and I had a discussion not too long ago and I told him that the house slaves were never to be whipped because any scars on them would diminish their value. That is why he stopped Jethro from carrying out your orders."

"I have invested a lot of money to ensure that you have all the help you need in the house and I'm sure you can appreciate that in the event that I were to sell any of them, I don't want to lose any money on my investment. In fact the house slaves should be living in the house so I need you to find somewhere to put them. And that includes Deborah and Sarah. I recall that they used to live in the house when Sarah looked after the children. When did they move out?"

"I moved them out when we no longer needed a nanny. They certainly didn't need to be in the house anymore. They have been nothing but trouble to me and now you want them to live in the house again? Because of that slave, you no longer visit me as a husband. Because of her daughter I have not seen my son in nearly two years and now my nephew seems to be bewitched by her as well. I have had enough Thomas! I want them sold!"

Thomas felt the beginning of a headache. It was not as if he did not have enough to deal with concerning the plantation but now he had Elizabeth's relentless nagging. His only solace was in bringing Sarah to his bed some nights and Elizabeth was insisting that he get rid of her? Was the woman trying to totally destroy his peace?

"You will do as I say and find somewhere to accommodate them. I will give some thought to your concerns. In the mean time, let there be no more incidents of whipping." She gave a brief nod; satisfied that he had at least not refused to consider her request.

"Deborah will be indisposed for a day or two while her back heals." He searched her face for any sign of remorse and was not really surprised to see none. "I will see you at dinner." With that he left the room.

Deborah woke up as the evening sun forced its way into the hut through the small window and streamed across her face. She tried to turn onto her side and the sudden pain and stiffness in her back arrested her movement. For a moment she was confused at the discomfort and then the memories of the day came back to her.

The whipping, as much as the abuse she had suffered at William's hands, cruelly reminded her that she was a chattel with no control over her body or her life and that her fate was in the hands of the master and mistress who could do whatever they wanted to her. Heaviness settled over her like a thick blanket, wrapping her in a cocoon of depression that left her sapped of energy.

Reluctantly rousing herself, she wondered how she would be able to put on a dress and go in to help prepare dinner. Unsure of how to get up without causing further pain to her back she lay on her side for a few minutes and remembered the relief she had felt when she heard Richard's voice shouting at Jethro.

The gentleness with which he had untied the ropes that bound her and held her to his chest while she wept softened a part of her heart, even as she blushed in shame that he had seen her nakedness and her humiliation.

She should have thanked him for saving her from the beating but she was too overcome at the time and besides he had seemed angry when he rode off, as if she had done something to upset him. It was probably because of the friction she had caused between him and his aunt.

She heard her mother in the front room and was glad that she would be able to help her get up.

"Deborah, you awake yet?" she called.

"Yes, but I don't know how to get up." Sarah came into the back room.

"The master just told me that you're to have a day or two to recover so you don't have to help with dinner."

Tears of gratitude sprang into Deborah's eyes. "I don't know why I'm crying all the time but you don't know how glad I am to hear that. I was just trying to figure out how I would put on a dress to go and help."

"When the master calls me again I am going to ask him about freeing us, especially after what happened today."

"I should thank Master Richard for stopping Jethro."

"Yes. He came to see how you were earlier when you were sleeping."

"You let him in?" Deborah exclaimed. "With me half naked?"

"It wasn't anything he didn't see today already," Sarah reminded her. "And anyhow, the master said yes, so what was I to do? Anyway he looked worried about you. Cassie like she was right when she said that he interested in you."

"He's not interested in me; he's only interested in my body. He stopped me in the hallway at the party and told me to come to his room afterwards," she admitted in disgust. She didn't tell her mother that he had kissed her neck or that his kiss had made her shiver.

"Oh loss! What you told him?"

"That I was indisposed. He wasn't too happy about that." She laughed as she remembered his reaction.

"This is nothing to laugh at, girl. You can't use that excuse forever. I goin' have to try and talk to the master about him."

Deborah didn't reply. For some reason, she didn't feel afraid of Richard's interest in her anymore.

Chapter Fourteen

Dinner was a somewhat strained affair. Although his aunt greeted him civilly and even apologized for the misunderstanding of the day, she was still rather cool towards him.

The slaves were also particularly careful, as if they were afraid of drawing his aunt's attention and finding themselves at the end of a whip. Nevertheless, he felt sure that the meal was more salty than usual and the Beveridge that he normally enjoyed was more watery than he was accustomed to. His aunt said nothing but he noticed that her face tightened when she tasted the food and drink. It was the slaves' silent protest of the events of the day.

"We're going to have a few changes in the household," announced Thomas. "I've decided to move the house slaves, with the exception of Jethro, into the house. That will make them more accessible if they are needed during the night and if we have bad weather. Room will have to be found for them downstairs."

"That's a good idea father," said Rachel. "When Richard was ill I had to run all the way to Deborah's hut to find her and Jethro."

"Yes, well Jethro will have to remain in his quarters."

"I think this is a good move as well, uncle. Living indoors will probably also ensure better health for them since they won't be living in damp conditions which I'm sure they must be in the rainy season." His uncle nodded.

Richard was pleased with his uncle's willingness to listen to his suggestion and act on it. He only wished that his father was as open, then they wouldn't be butting heads in the business all the time.

"Richard, are you up to joining in the harvesting tomorrow?" His uncle asked.

"Certainly," he answered.

"You obviously don't know what you're getting yourself into," warned his aunt and he was glad that she seemed warmer towards him, otherwise his visit would be very strained. "Make sure you wear long sleeves and a pair of long pants. I'll order a bath for you afterwards. You're going to need it."

"Thank you Aunt Elizabeth, I certainly appreciate that."

Richard slept badly that night. His dreams were filled with scenes of Deborah, tied to the whipping post with Jethro wielding the whip again and again and he couldn't get to her. Images of her back streaming with blood and her voice calling his name tormented him and caused him to jump up with a start.

When he had ridden into the yard that evening, she had been waiting for him near the stables, wearing a loose shirt over a dull brown skirt which revealed her bare feet. Her long hair was plaited and hung over one shoulder giving her a youthful look in spite of her ordeal and making Richard feel ancient in comparison.

As he dismounted and handed the reins to the stable boy, he noted that Deborah was avoiding eye contact with him.

"I just wanted to thank you for rescuing me today," she had said humbly keeping her eyes lowered. With sudden insight he realized that she was ashamed that he had seen her in her weakness and humiliation. It was so unlike Deborah that for a moment he could not think how to respond.

Then it came to him and he had told her with all the seriousness that he could muster, that she was now indebted to him and he would be calling on her to collect his payment soon. When she drew in an angry breath and stalked off, muttering that she should have known better, he smiled at her retreating back.

Just to make sure that she was truly herself again, he shouted to let him know when she was no longer indisposed and would be available to come to his room. She had turned around to glare at him and say: "You may have rescued me, but you do not own me," before storming off in the direction of her hut.

He smiled as the image filled his mind again. She would make the rest of his stay in Barbados very interesting. He couldn't believe that a month had gone already. That only gave him two months before he had to go back to Carolina. He wondered why he lacked excitement at the thought.

Throwing off the sheet he got out of the warm, comfortable bed which made him remember the thin pallet that Deborah slept on. He was glad that his uncle was dealing with her accommodations and then wondered why it mattered to him. Maybe he selfishly wanted to have her close at hand; not that she would willingly come to his room. Yet.

He washed quickly with the warm water then had been left while he was still asleep and dressed in a long-sleeved cotton shirt and loose pants that would keep him cool while protecting him from the cane leaves. Pulling on boots and picking up his hat he headed out the door to join his uncle for breakfast before they went out to the fields that were being harvested. He had planned to try his hand at cutting canes today and his uncle had said that he would show him how the cane was processed afterwards.

He had read about the processing in Richard Ligon's book and it seemed very complicated to him. He was looking forward to seeing how it all worked and how the slaves were used to carry out different functions, especially the boilers who were so valuable because of the work they did. If they could be trained to carry out functions that were highly critical to the successful processing of the sugar, then surely the ones he bought would be highly efficient in the farming of rice.

The thought of Ann flitted in and out of his mind and he found that as he strained to recall her features, all he could think of was olive skin, green eyes and long wavy brown hair. The woman had indeed bewitched him and there was only one way he knew to get a woman out of your system. He would work on that soon.

Richard was no stranger to hard work but he soon realized that cutting canes was in a category by itself. One of the overseers gave him a broad curved machete and told him to cut the cane stalk as close as possible to the root since most of the sugar was concentrated in that part of the cane and they also needed a good length to feed through the mill.

Although cane was part of the grass family, Richard could find nothing soft about it as he wielded his machete. The pith which contained the juice was encased in a thick woody rind that was resistant to the machete and required a good deal of strength to cut through it. He soon learned that it was easier to cut the stem at a joint than directly through the rind. Since the leaves were not allowed to go through the rollers he then had to strip them off the stem with strokes of his machete while holding the cane in one hand.

By the time he had a fairly substantial pile of canes to show for his efforts, his hands were raw, and his arms and back were stiff. He was pitifully glad when the overseer instructed one of the slaves to load his pile onto the cart, leaving him free to join his uncle, because he didn't think he had the strength to load them himself.

"How was it Richard?" His uncle asked knowingly.

"This is the most back breaking work I've ever done and I often work alongside the crew on our ships."

"Harvesting canes is not easy and processing is even harder. We'll go and see the grinding and boiling after lunch. You better ask Deborah for something to put on your hands when you go in for lunch."

"I'm sure she would offer pepper instead of a balm," laughed Richard tiredly.

"What have you done to upset her?" His uncle asked expectantly.

"I told her that she owed me for rescuing her and that I would collect soon. I couldn't resist teasing her," he admitted, drawing a laugh from Thomas.

"I'm sure that riled her up."

"It did what it was supposed to do, give her back some spirit. I was afraid that the whipping had broken her."

"Slaves are supposed to be broken, Richard, but I know what you mean. Deborah has spirit." He sighed. "Your aunt wants me to sell her and Sarah."

"And will you?"

"I will not let Elizabeth dictate to me what to do although I'm sure there would be more peace in my house if I sold them. But I'm not ready to give up Sarah yet."

"If you decide to sell Deborah you know that I want to buy her."

"You would take her back to Carolina with you? I don't think your fiancée would be too happy with that."

"You're right. I must confess that I have almost forgotten that I am betrothed."

"Beautiful slave girls will do that to your memory," his uncle laughed as they went to clean up for lunch.

Richard watched as the canes were removed from carts and loaded into troughs where the dirt was washed off them.

From there his uncle led him to the mill house where the canes were fed through vertical rollers, made of wood but covered with metal, to extract the juice. He had seen the windmill that was used to generate the power to turn the rollers on his first tour of the plantation and had heard that this was the best season for harvesting because of the high winds and low rainfall which were characteristic of this time of year.

"Why is that slave standing around with a machete doing nothing?" Richard inquired.

"His job is to cut off the limb of anyone who gets caught in the machine." Richard searched his uncle's face for signs of joking but found none and realized that he was deadly serious.

He observed the greenish liquid that was extracted from the canes as they were ground in the mill which was then run in cisterns under the ground to the nearby boiling house for the next part of the process.

The heat that met them at the door of the boiling house almost made him stagger back. The place must be as close to hell as you could get on earth, Richard decided after a minute. About five huge copper kettles of decreasing size were being heated over a common furnace which accounted for the stifling heat. Richard did not know how the slaves could stay in here for hours keeping the furnace burning since it could not be allowed to go out or the sugar would be ruined.

The juice discharged into the largest kettle where a boiler stood by with a long ladle to skim impurities off the top before transferring the liquid to the next kettle. As each kettle got smaller, the heat in it intensified making the liquid thicken and turn dark brown. It was the job of the boilers to know when it was time to transfer the liquid into the next kettle. Richard could now understand why they were so valuable.

"What is that they're putting into the mixture?" Richard asked, wiping the sweat from his forehead with a handkerchief.

"It's quicklime. It helps the liquid to form grains. After that the mixture, which is sugar and molasses, is put into a cooling cistern. We then have to drain off the molasses to get the sugar so it's put into clay pots in the cooling room and drained for about three weeks. The sugar has to be spread out in the sun to dry before it is packed into bags and sent to Town. I use the molasses to make rum in the distillery."

"This is quite an investment in machinery," Richard noted looking around.

His uncle nodded. "That's why only the biggest plantations can do the processing. It is definitely a significant investment. Seen enough?"

Richard nodded and they were almost at the door when a slave came running from the mill house.

"Master Thomas, Master Thomas come quick! Jacko hand get catch in the rollers and Sambo had to cut it off."

"Oh, God!" Thomas took off running. "Send one of the stable boys for the doctor in Jamestown."

Richard followed him, unsure of what he would find. There was chaos in the room, with all the slaves recounting to his uncle what had happened at once. Fortunately Jacko had passed out from the shock and someone had wrapped his hand, or the stump, in a dirty looking sack. It appeared that his hand had only been cut off at the wrist, thanks to the quick action of Sambo. Blood was all over the floor and more seeped through the sack.

"Get him to his hut and clean up this blood," instructed Thomas. "Throw out that batch of juice. What a waste of good cane juice."

"Does this happen often?" Richard asked shaken, as they walked into the yard, taking several deep breaths.

"Not very, thankfully. But that's why we have Sambo standing by. At least he only lost the hand and not the whole arm but what's the use of a slave with one hand? I'll have to decide what to do with him when he recovers."

"I had no idea that cultivating sugar was this hard."

"Make no mistake, it is a very rewarding business but it is one of the hardest ways to make money. There are a lot of problems to deal with: pests, weeds, diseases, fires and now we have, added to those, competition from Jamaica. Because of its size it can produce sugar in volumes that we can't and the soil there is virgin whereas our soil is wearing out and we have to constantly manure it to put back in the nutrients."

Business was a constant challenge, especially starting something new like rice cultivation. Richard knew that not only would he have to invest significantly to drain the land so that rice could be planted and to buy slaves to cultivate it but there was no guarantee that it would pay off. Anything could happen to the slaves, like the accident today or they could succumb to diseases and die. Then again business was always a risk, so he had to be certain that this was in fact the course he wanted to take. After all he was giving up his own freedom to pursue it.

Chapter Fifteen

When the house slaves heard that they were to move out of their huts and into the house there was much rejoicing, never mind that the rooms that were to be given to them were by no means large and would have to be cleaned out. Just to be under a roof that was not made of plantain leaves and to have a floor under their feet that was not dirt was pure luxury for them.

Sarah and Deborah were to share a room at the end of the hallway that was being used as a store room, while the others were to share a larger room near to the door that led to the kitchen. When Sarah had lived inside the house, she had a room just off the nursery, before the mistress ordered her to move into a hut in the yard when she was no longer needed as a nanny. She had never complained to the master and he didn't seem to realize that she was no longer in the house. The only time he saw her was in his room anyway.

The room they were to occupy was not as big or as nice as the one upstairs but it was an improvement on the hut they lived in and it had a sizeable window which overlooked the drying yard and was breezy.

"Isn't it strange that we are to move back into the house after all these years?" Deborah remarked to her mother. "I wonder if it has anything to do with Master Richard's visit to our hut?" she mused.

"You think he said something to shame the master about how we were living?"

"If he said anything, I don't think he would have said it in a way to shame the master, but he may have pointed out the benefits of having us under the same roof."

"All I know is that I am glad to be living in the big house again so that we won't have to run through the rain to do our work and I won't have to leave you in the hut alone at night when the master calls for me."

Deborah didn't even realize that her mother had worried about that since she had never felt unsafe in the hut. Nevertheless she much preferred to be living in the house, even if it put her in closer proximity to Master Richard.

Jethro was given orders to make simple cots for them and Sarah was to make mattresses to fit them which she would stuff with cotton that was not good enough to sell. Although far from luxurious, the beds would be a welcome change from the pallets that they slept on.

Deborah reflected on how Richard's presence was changing their lives, and she had to admit for the better. She had no idea how much more hers was about to change because of him.

Richard's conversation with his uncle about buying Deborah dug in like a stubborn mule and refused to leave his head. Questions kept him awake at night. Should he buy Deborah? Would she resent him if he did? She had told him more than once that she did not want to be owned by anyone, especially him. Did he really need to buy her to get her into his bed? Would it be worth it? She might turn out to be as cold as she acted sometimes. Although in spite of her coldness he sensed that she was not as immune to him as she pretended.

He remembered the last time he had found her by the grove and buried his fingers in her hair. She had pulled back with a look of panic on her face but he had sensed that it wasn't fear of him as such, so perhaps it was more fear of the feelings he had stirred in her. He hoped so.

If he was staying longer in Barbados he could take his time and break down her resistance but he barely had two months left and he wanted her badly. He wasn't even interested in calling Hattie to his room anymore, he only wanted Deborah.

He had to get this girl out of his system. Thoughts of Carolina, his fiancée and Anise were far from his mind. All he could think of was Deborah. Every time he closed his eyes before he went to sleep, the picture of long wavy brown hair and green eyes seemed to be stamped on the inside of his eyelids and the image of her as he untied her from the whipping post was implanted firmly in his mind.

So if his uncle was willing to sell her to him, and he seemed on the verge of doing so, then she would be his. But that did not mean she would come to him willingly and he wanted her to be willing. What would be an incentive to her? What did she want more than anything? Her freedom. He knew that he couldn't take her back to Carolina with him so he would agree to free her when he left. That would probably be the worse business decision he had ever made.

The girl must have totally bewitched him for him to even consider that. His uncle would probably think he was crazy and if his father found out he would surely be convinced that he was right not to let him have the full run of the business or to buy a plantation. Richard smiled. He didn't care. Right now he couldn't think of anything he could buy that would give him as much pleasure as owning Deborah.

Thomas lay back against pillows replete as he watched Sarah put back on her plain skirt and blouse that were by no means attractive. He wondered at that. His wife wore the latest fashions from England but he was unmoved by her. Sarah wore cheap, drab clothes and she stirred his blood. How was he to let her go? Who could he sell her to and be assured that they would treat her well? He didn't see how he could ever sell Sarah. And did it make sense to sell Deborah to Richard when he was going back soon? Not only that but it wouldn't really appease Elizabeth.

As if she read his thoughts Sarah said: "Master, I'm afraid for Deborah. After what happened this week I don't know what else the mistress will try to do."

"Don't worry about Deborah. She will be fine. I have spoken to the mistress."

"What about Master Richard? He seem to have his eyes on her. I don't want anything happening to her again like what happened with Master William."

"Richard is not like William, Sarah." Sarah knew that but she also knew that lust could sometimes drive men to do things that they would not normally do.

Sarah took a breath to give herself courage. It was now or never. She went and sat on the bed resting her thigh against his. "Master Thomas, would you ever think about freeing Deborah and me?"

"I have thought about freeing you in my will and leaving you a little money to buy some property." Even as he said it, he knew that he should amend his will to make sure that happened even if he sold Deborah to Richard.

"Thank you, Master but suppose Master William don't carry out your wishes?"

"Sarah, you worry too much," he dismissed her fears but Thomas knew that she had real cause to worry about William.

Should he consider freeing them before he died? He could count the number of slaves who had been freed in wills on one hand, far less while their masters were still alive. That was just not done. That didn't mean it could not be done. He would have to give it some more thought.

Maybe if he freed Sarah, he could set her up in Town and see her whenever he went to town. That way he would still have her and not have to put up with Elizabeth's nagging. He would not see her as often, but if he needed relief in between his visits he could always call Cassie or Hattie.

"I will think on it, Sarah."

"Thank you Master Thomas." Impulsively she grabbed his hand and rested it against her cheek.

"Good night, Sarah." He smiled at the gesture.

"Good night, Master Thomas." Sarah let herself out of the room quietly with a hopeful smile on her face. At least he had not said no.

Elizabeth heard the door of Thomas' room closing and gritted her teeth. The slave woman was leaving her husband's bed which she had not been invited to share in years. The pain of rejection surprised her for surely it should have diminished by now.

She wondered what she could do to hurt him as he hurt her. Although he had never struck her, as some husbands were known to do, that didn't make her pain any less real. Even though she knew that the slaves he had bedded over the years were just for physical relief and to show that he was lord of all he owned, she still resented it, especially his relationship with Sarah. Was it more than physical? Could he possibly love the slave?

She hated the fact that Thomas had the freedom to do whatever he wanted while she had no control over her own life. She was just as much a chattel as the slaves that he owned. First William had been sent away and she had no say in the matter. Then Richard had stopped Jethro from whipping Deborah when she had ordered him to do so. He even had Richard as his ally rather than hers, even though he was her nephew.

The two of them were growing very close, spending hours shut away in Thomas' study, discussing who knew what, and she could see that Thomas had become very fond of Richard. Would he take William's place in Thomas' affections? Would Thomas try to persuade him to stay in Barbados and help run the plantation? What would that mean for William?

Now Thomas was bringing the slaves into the house after all these years and she felt certain that it might be due to Richard's influence. Her title as mistress was a farce, for even the house slaves defied her and did what they wanted. Well Sarah and Deborah anyway. That was why she had to get rid of them.

Thomas had said he would give some thought to it but she wondered if he was to be believed or if he was just pacifying her. Well she would make his life unbearable if he didn't get rid of them soon. For when they were gone, she would regain control of her household and maybe even win her husband's affections once again.

Sarah hurried out to her hut, thankful that she would not have to leave the house in the darkness for much longer. She hoped that Deborah was still awake because she was eager to tell her what the master has said.

He had not actually promised to free them right away but at least he had said he would think about it and he had already planned to free them in his will. She didn't trust William though so she could not afford to rely on that.

She pushed open the door excitedly and latched it behind her before she rushed into the back room. The moonlight was streaming through the small window and she could see that Deborah was lying awake waiting for her.

"Deborah, girl, I have good news. The master said that he plans to put in his will that we are to be freed when he dies, but I told him that we don't know if William will do that, so it would be better to free us now."

"What did he say to that?" Deborah asked sitting up.

"He said that he would think about it."

Deborah did not want to get her hopes up. She would have to see it before she would believe it. She could see no benefit to the master if he freed them, especially when he could sell them, make some money and keep the mistress quiet at the same time. Could he really be trusted to free them or was he just telling her mother what she wanted to hear?

Chapter Sixteen

Richard and his uncle retired to the office after dinner as they had become accustomed to doing. His uncle poured brandies for them which they enjoyed in contemplative silence.

They had come to enjoy this time together when they talked about the workings of the plantation, the issues facing the colonies and plans for the future or sometimes just sat in silence as they did now. For Richard it was what he would have liked to have with his father while Thomas felt the same with respect to William so without the two even being conscious of it, they were becoming as close as father and son.

The sound of crickets in the yard hardly penetrated their consciousness until it stopped, probably at the passing of the stable boy or one of the house slaves.

"You become so accustomed to the crickets that you don't notice them unless you really listen carefully or unless they fall silent for some reason," Richard commented breaking the silence. His uncle nodded.

"It's almost like a wife," joked Thomas. "Their constant harping can become like background noise until you're forced to really listen to them. That whipping Deborah had has forced me to listen to Elizabeth. She is adamant that I sell Deborah and Sarah and to tell the truth her constant nagging is beginning to wear me down."

"As I said, I would be happy to buy Deborah if you decide to sell her, although I'm sure that is not what Aunt Elizabeth has in mind." His uncle agreed.

"What would you do with her when you go back to Carolina? Take her with you?"

Richard thought for a moment. He couldn't take her back to Carolina with him; that would cause too much of a furor from his mother, not to mention his fiancée.

"No. As you can imagine that would cause all kinds of trouble. Once I satisfy this hunger that I have for her and get her out of my system, I would set her free before I go back Carolina."

"I wouldn't put money on getting her out of your system," warned his uncle. "I still haven't got Sarah out of mine after nearly eighteen years and I'm having a hard time contemplating selling her. I don't know what it is about these slave women but they just seem to get into your blood. I will go ahead and get my lawyer to prepare the papers to sell Deborah to you for, shall we say, £20?"

"That is very generous of you, since I know that you could get three times as much for her if you wanted to."

"Not at all my boy. Besides she can continue to work in the house while you're here so we'll have the benefit of her services but she will be under your protection and looking after your needs will be her first priority."

"I like the sound of that," Richard smiled in antici-pation. "Shall I tell her?"

"I will do it. After all she is my property as well as my blood. Be good to her," warned Thomas.

This was the first time Richard heard Thomas acknowledge that Deborah was his blood and it was totally unexpected. Such things were never mentioned or acknowledged, although they were commonly known.

"On my oath, sir," Richard replied solemnly. Thomas nodded satisfied.

A few days later Cassie came to the kitchen to report that the master's lawyer was meeting with him in his office and she had heard them through the door talking about selling a house slave but she didn't hear who it was.

Her words struck fear into everyone as they knew that in spite of the mistress' verbal abuse from time to time, The Acreage was one of the best plantations to work at and no-one wanted to be sold into a situation that was worse.

"I hope you heard wrong, Cassie 'cause 'better the devil you know than the devil you don't'," said Sarah. She loved all the house slaves, even Hattie was growing on her, and she wouldn't want any of them to be sold. She knew it wouldn't be her or Deborah. After all, the master was thinking about freeing them.

"That's not always true," Cassie corrected her. "Don't forget what I came from. I was so happy when I come here. You wouldn't understand because you have it good here."

"Well a devil is still a devil," Deborah contended. She had a bad feeling about this. She wondered if the mistress had finally convinced Master Thomas to sell her. Fear started in her belly and became full blown panic when a message came a little later that the master wanted to see her in his office. Immediately she started to shake. Sarah hurriedly got up and came to hold her.

"Don't worry; you know that the master would never sell you." Deborah wasn't convinced but she nodded as calmly as she could.

Shaking legs took her to the master's office where she stood outside the door for a minute before she gathered her courage and knocked.

"Come in," he invited. It was the last thing she wanted to do.

Pushing open the door she said, "You wanted to see me, Master Thomas?"

It appeared that the lawyer had left because he was alone, sitting behind his desk with papers in a neat pile in front of him. His hair looked as if he had been running his hands through it and his unaccustomed disheveled appearance caused her further panic. He was going to sell her. She knew it as certainly as if he had said it already. The mistress had finally got her wish.

"Yes Deborah. After your whipping, which Richard thankfully stopped, I realize that I need to do something to keep the peace in the house so I have decided that the best option is to sell you." At the stricken look on her face, he hurriedly held up his hand.

"Don't worry. It is not as bad as it sounds. I'm selling you to Richard and you will continue to live here and look after his needs while he is in Barbados so you won't be separated from your mother."

Deborah hardly heard what he was saying. A myriad of emotions began to chase around her mind. Disbelief that the master was selling her, hurt that she was nothing more to him than property, anger that Richard had gotten what he wanted, fear of what it would mean for her and then contradictorily, relief that it was Richard and not one of the lecherous old planters.

"You're selling me to Master Richard? How will that help to keep the peace? Will he take me with him when he goes back to Carolina?"

"He will let you know about that. I've had the papers drawn up and it's only for him to sign now. He wants to talk to you before he signs them though so I'll leave him to do that." She was in a daze, numb at the thought that the master would sell her.

"I wouldn't do this if I didn't think he would be good to you. I would trust him with my life and I trust him with yours."

Deborah was shocked at the betrayal that she felt in spite of his words. She never thought the master would sell her; after all she was his flesh and blood. She had fooled herself into thinking that it meant something to him. She almost laughed at herself; she had thought she was special. Now she knew that she was just another slave even though his blood ran in her veins. Tears sprang to her eyes and she quickly turned away lest he saw them. So much for his promise to think about freeing them; she should have known better.

"You might not think so now, but this is the best thing for you," he consoled. Deborah didn't see how so she said nothing.

"OK, you may go now. Richard will talk to you later." She blindly turned away and practically ran to her grove, not caring that it was the middle of the day and she had chores to do. What more could they do to her now? She was just exchanging one master for another. She remembered Richard's words when she told him that he would never own her. He had said "Don't be too sure about that!" And he was right. He owned her, or he would soon enough. Freedom was as far away as it ever was. She buried her face in her hands and wept.

Richard found her there half an hour later, still distraught. The sight of her misery unexpectedly touched his heart and made him want to hold her in his arms as he had done that day by the whipping post, but he knew that she would reject his comfort this time. He dropped down next to her, leaned back against the tree and looked out at the view. Immediately she shifted until there was distance between them and dried her eyes, adopting a stoic expression.

"You know there are many women who would be happy to be owned by me?" Richard provoked. He was glad to see fire flash in her eyes and she snapped, "I'm not one of them! I don't want to be owned by anyone!"

"Well unfortunately for you, you will be owned by me so you'd better adopt a respectful tone before I beat you."

Her head swung around to him in shock. "You wouldn't!" She didn't seem as certain as she sounded.

"No I wouldn't, Deborah. Listen, I have a proposition for you. I have promised to pay my uncle £20 for you, a real bargain I might add, but I have told him I will free you when I leave Barbados."

Once again shocked eyes met his, this time with a glimmer of hope in them.

"I don't believe you!" she accused. "Why would you do that?"

"I can't take you back to Carolina with me, for obvious reasons."

"What is your proposition?"

"While I am in Barbados you will come to my bed willingly whenever I call for you provided, of course, you are not indisposed." At this Deborah blushed furiously giving away her lie.

"You lied!" Richard accused her now as he saw the guilt on her face. He had to laugh at her quick thinking and he knew, without a doubt that he would not be bored for the remainder of his time in Barbados.

"You expect me to prostitute myself for my freedom?"

"Well it's a lot better than dying for your freedom, do you not agree?"

"That is a matter of opinion," she said so softly that he could barely hear her.

"Why is sleeping with me so appalling to you? Surely you are not innocent of the intimacy between men and women?"

She was silent for so long that he thought she would not answer him. When she finally spoke, her voice was hard.

"No. Your cousin brutally introduced me to it when I was sixteen. He had been eyeing me for months and enjoyed taunting me like a cat with a mouse and then when he got tired of his game, he pretended to be ill one night and asked for me to bring some tea to his room and then he took what he wanted. He always got what he wanted. And he wanted me."

Richard was shocked at the surge of anger that erupted in him at the thought of William violating her. If his cousin was in front of him now he would be hard pressed not to beat him senseless. Although he was already clearly without sense. Snatches of conversations dropped into his mind and the pieces began to fall into place.

"Is that why he was sent away?"

"Partly, but I think he was in trouble with some merchants in town as well."

"Deborah, I would never hurt you in that way. You can trust me."

She was torn. Could she offer herself willingly to Richard in exchange for her freedom? It was so tempting. She now mocked herself for judging the women who sold themselves for the money to buy their freedom. Would she be any different? Could she give up her self respect and the rights to her body for her freedom? Was she willing to pay the price? Then again she didn't have any rights to her body now anyway. He could buy her and just use her at his will if he wanted to. He didn't even have to buy her; he could have her for free as long as the master gave his permission. So why was he buying her?

Freedom beckoned to her. It was what she'd always longed for, what she'd always dreamed of and now it was within her reach. All she had to do was give herself to him willingly. That was all. That was all.

It's wrong. A voice in her head chided her. Jethro's voice saying, that if they sinned they would be slaves to sin, echoed in her head adding to the other voice. She ignored both. She could be free in two months!

Richard waited in anticipation. He really didn't need her agreement. Once he signed those papers she would be his and he could do whatever he wanted with her. However the thought of being with her against her will did not sit well with him, especially in light of what she had just revealed to him.

With great deliberation she turned to him and said, "I will do it. I will come to you willingly while you are here in exchange for my freedom. How can I be sure that you will free me when you leave?"

"You will have to trust me. And I need you to keep that to yourself for now because my aunt does not know."

At Thomas' request, his lawyer had prepared manumission papers at the same time as the sale documents but he would not tell her that. For some reason he wanted her to trust him. He reminded himself yet again that she was just a slave; she had no right to question his integrity. She really didn't even have to agree to come to him willingly, but what pleasure would there be in forcing her? He wanted her to come to him of her own free will although, he acknowledged with a twinge of conscience, the lure of freedom was almost unfair bait. Still, he had given her a choice and she had taken it.

Deborah looked into his eyes and saw the sincerity in them and for the first time in her life she felt hope and a song was birthed in her soul. It was a song of freedom.

Deborah returned to the house in high spirits to find the slaves in the kitchen speaking in hushed tones which fell into silence at her appearance. Nobody seemed to know what to say.

Sarah rushed over to her asking worriedly, "Where you went girl? What the master tell you?"

"Cassie was right. It is me he is selling, but only to Master Richard."

"What? He going back in two months. What he want to buy you for? He going take you back to Carolina with him?" Sarah's voice rose in panic.

Deborah hesitated, not sure how to answer but she was saved by Hattie butting in. "Master Richard buying you? For what? He never even called you to his room!" she added jealously.

"So you still going to work in the house? What you going to do?" This was from Cassie.

"I don't know. They have not signed any papers yet so I don't know what will happen. I was so scared when the master told me that he was selling me and although I don't want anything to do with Master Richard, I am glad that it is to him and not anybody else. At least I will still be here. For now anyway."

"That mean, he ain' going be calling for me any-more?" Hattie asked glaring at Deborah.

"Girl, what you think?" asked Cassie rhetorically.

"That real unfair. She always getting the best of everything. You think that you better than us," she said turning to Deborah, "but you just a slave too." With that she ran out of the kitchen.

Hattie was right. She was just a slave. She had simply exchanged one master for another and she had agreed to give her body to her new master in exchange for her freedom. Who was she to judge Hattie or any-one else? She was no better than they were. In truth she was worse because they saw nothing wrong with what they did. She, however, believed that it was wrong and she was still going to do it anyway.

Chapter Seventeen

T he cart driven by Jethro bounced over the rough roads and Richard was glad that he had chosen to ride his horse as his uncle sat beside Jethro enduring the bumpy ride. They were heading to a plantation in St. Peter, which had run into financial trouble and was selling off slaves today, to find one to replace Jacko. His uncle had said that he would also take a look at the house girls since he would be without Deborah and possibly Sarah in a couple of months.

Richard could not believe how his visit to Barbados was turning out. When he left Carolina he never imagined that he would end up owning a slave, far less one as beautiful as Deborah. He had signed the ownership papers only yesterday and now was £20 poorer but he felt richer for his possession. He owned Deborah. The thought gave him a feeling of power and excitement.

It was Thursday but he would make himself wait until Saturday night before he called for her. He wanted to take his time and he didn't want to have to get up and go out on the plantation the following day. Besides anticipation was half the pleasure.

His aunt was patently displeased about the sale of Deborah to him. She had wanted her sold and Richard could imagine that she had hoped for a cruel master to buy her. He had not even told her that he had planned to free Deborah when he left. She would no doubt feel that Deborah had once again triumphed over her. He had asked her not to mention the purchase if she wrote to his mother; he would prefer if they never knew of his madness.

Yesterday his uncle had summoned Deborah to his office after they had signed the papers to tell her that she was now owned by him. Richard recalled the panic in her eyes as they met his briefly before it was replaced by the blank look that she was so skilled at adopting. He wondered if she regretted their agreement.

Even in her usual drab clothing with her hair hidden in a handkerchief she was beautiful and he felt the pride of possession. She was now his. He couldn't prevent the quick smile that flitted across his face as he eyed her from head to toe and thought with a great deal of satisfaction, 'Mine'.

The cart turning up a driveway shifted his attention and dragged him back into the present. In the distance he could see a plantation house that looked as if it hadn't had a coat of paint in several years with a few of the shutters hanging drunkenly against the windows. It was obvious that the owner had no extra money to spend on maintaining the house.

There were already several horses and carts in the yard but Jethro found a place to park under a shady tree. Richard swung down from his horse and tied it to the cart as his uncle alighted with an agility that belied his age. He greeted several of the planters that hung around chatting while they waited for the sale to begin. Richard recognized most of them from the party and reacquainted himself with them.

"You looking for more slaves Thomas?" asked John Bowyer as a way of greeting them.

"One of my boys lost his hand in the mill last week and I need to find one to replace him. I may also take a look at the house slaves because I just sold Deborah to Richard."

John spluttered into the jug of water he was drinking. "I thought she wasn't for sale! I would have paid you handsomely for her."

"Well Richard was persistent and the wife was beginning to nag about getting rid of her and Sarah."

"You selling Sarah?" he asked unbelievingly.

"Not yet, but no harm in looking."

The owner of the plantation, an unkempt looking man who had the bloated look of a heavy drinker, invited the planters to draw nearer as the overseer brought out the slaves. The men were dressed in ragged pants and no shirts while most of the women wore skirts only, their breasts bare for all to see.

Richard looked around at the planters and noticed that no-one seemed to think this state of undress to be unusual. Perhaps his uncle clothed his slaves better than most.

The slaves were led forward one at a time with their attributes listed for the buyers. Richard's uncle appraised him of what to look for in a quiet voice.

"Look for strong arms and shoulders. Check for whip marks on their backs because that can tell if the slave is either lazy or rebellious. You don't want those. Check the eyes to see if they are yellow or white which will tell you if they are healthy or not."

Richard nodded and watched as his uncle approached a tall strapping looking fellow and examined him. The man's expressionless face reminded him of Deborah's and a fleeting thought of what the man was thinking about this physical examination passed through his mind.

His uncle made an offer for him when his turn came to be auctioned and acquired him for £30. He was not interested in buying any more women for the fields so he waited until the house slaves were brought out.

There were only three women and one young girl who could be about thirteen who clung to one of the women to whom she bore a strong resemblance. They were not bad looking women but none could compare to the house slaves at The Acreage. Richard now realized that his uncle's reputation for having the most beautiful house slaves was not exaggerated.

"I don't see any that I fancy to replace Deborah," confided his uncle. As if Deborah could be replaced, thought Richard.

"I need a young girl to help my wife," one of the planters announced. "I'll pay £15 for that one there," he offered pointing at the terrified slave girl. Since no-one else was interested in such a young slave the owner nodded his acceptance and indicated that he could come and get her.

The girl didn't seem to understand that she had been sold and continued to cling to her mother. The planter sent his boy to get her and take her to their cart while he paid his money and did the paperwork to transfer ownership.

Richard stood transfixed at the trauma that unfolded before his eyes. Mother and daughter clung to each other, and began to scream at the master. The slave who was sent to collect her pulled at her waist while the mother tried to beat him off with one hand while holding her daughter with the other. The overseer rushed forward with his whip raised and threatened to use it if they did not stop the ruckus.

Remembering the welts on Deborah's back Richard hoped that the fear of the whip would restrain them, but the pain of being torn apart was obviously greater than the fear of the whip. When they still refused to part he brought down the whip across the mother's back and she arched her back and instinctively loosened her hold on the girl, giving the slave the opportunity to grab her and run with her under his arm like a sack of flour.

The girl's screaming and crying were haunting but the pure anguish in the eyes of the mother, not knowing if she would ever see her child again, or what fate awaited her at the hands of this new master, pierced the indifference that had been built around his heart and he knew beyond all doubt, that the belief held by many of the planters that these slaves were creatures with no intellect or emotions was a lie.

The journey back was silent and Richard wondered if the others were also in shock over what had transpired.

He soon realized by surreptitiously looking at their calm and unaffected faces, that it was only him who had been shaken by the traumatic parting. This was nothing unusual for his uncle or even for Jethro; it was part of life on the plantation. Slaves were bought and sold with as little emotion as buying a horse, probably even less.

Is that how Deborah felt when he bought her? As if she was little more than a farm animal? He had thought she was overreacting but now he saw firsthand what it truly meant to be a slave and he felt sick inside that he may have made Deborah feel that way. Did he feel bad enough to free her now, rather than when he was leaving? A battle waged between his conscience and his flesh and his conscience surrendered after a half-hearted fight. He just did not have the strength to release her before he had his fill of her. He cursed his weakness but found that he had no real desire to be strong.

On reaching the plantation, Richard handed the reins of the horse to the stable boy and headed straight for the grove overlooking the East Coast. He needed the calmness of the scenery to penetrate his disturbed thoughts and be a balm for the guilt that was pricking at his conscience.

He shed his jacket and leaned back against the smoothness of the tree trunk, opening the first few buttons of his shirt to allow the breeze access to his chest.

The beauty of the evening soothed his soul and settled his thoughts until he was able to justify his decision not to free Deborah right away.

He reasoned that they had reached an agreement, which she had made of her own free will, so he was not deceiving her in any way or forcing her to do anything against her will. He would free her at the end of the two months when he went back to Carolina and he would have had what he wanted and she would have the freedom which she desired.

With that decision made he got up and headed towards Deborah's hut. His uncle had told him that the girls would be ready to move into the house on Saturday and he was glad that Deborah would not have to leave her hut in the yard to come to him at night.

He knocked at the door and it was opened by Deborah who stepped outside to greet him. He was pleased to see that her hair was not concealed under the handkerchief but she was in her usual skirt and blouse. He would have to see about getting her some more attractive clothing for the duration of his visit.

"Hello Deborah. Did my uncle tell you that we signed the papers today?"

"Yes. That's why I'm not helping with dinner tonight. I understand that you will have to give permission if you want me to help in the house since I now belong to you." The latter was said almost bitterly.

"Well, you should be glad that I'm a generous master because I am giving you the next two days off to rest and prepare yourself."

"You are indeed a generous master," she said sarcastically. "I am not any more tired than usual so why do I need to rest? And what am I to prepare myself for?"

He leaned closer and said: "For me. I want you to come to my room on Saturday night after dinner. Wear the green dress that you wore to the party." Richard saw dread fill her eyes as she realized that he truly owned her now and what that meant.

"Very well, Master Richard," her voice shook slightly.

"I like this new obedience, Deborah. While you're being so accommodating, how about a kiss to seal our bargain?" he teased.

She stepped back, expecting him to kiss her mouth but instead he took one of her hands and planted a moist, warm kiss in the palm, lingering for a few moments as he searched her eyes.

Deborah snatched her hand away as tingles ran up her arm but the heat remained, as if he had branded her for the entire world to know that she now belonged to Richard Fairfax.

Chapter Eighteen

S aturday dawned with a clear sky that promised a
truly beautiful day. The beauty and peacefulness
of the morning contrasted sharply with the nervous
churning of Deborah's stomach as she contemplated the
night and what it would bring.

It took them little time to pack their meager posses-
sions, much of which was cast offs from the household.
Soon that will change, she told herself, if the nephew
could be trusted to keep his word. She remembered
the look in his eyes as he asked her to trust him and felt
assured that she could. But what would she do when
she was free? She had a little money saved but it wasn't
enough to buy a property or start a business. Would he
give her some money to start out? She hadn't considered
that in her agreement.

After Jethro and the stable boy came to take their
things over to their new room, she washed her hair
before heading out to the grove to dry it and spend
some time alone. Her life was about to undergo a major
change; in fact the change had already started. It felt
strange to think that the master no longer owned her,
but Richard did instead.

Never would she have imagined that happening when she had heard the master reading the letter from him a few months ago. Had he only been here for a month? Why did it seem so much longer? It was as if he had come to the plantation and just fit in as if he belonged and had always been here. Now she would belong to him, not just by means of a legal document but by his possession of her body. Her stomach churned again.

She couldn't help but remember the night that William had lured her to his room and the pain and shame that she had endured. She was not afraid that Richard would be like William for he had had opportunities where he could have taken her against her will and he had not, but that didn't stop the dread she felt as the day grew older.

She had accepted his proposition and it was too late to back out now. Her body for her freedom. She acknowledged that it was more than just her body she was giving up; she was giving up her pride, her beliefs and her self-respect. She knew that it was wrong. He was not her husband and he was betrothed to another. But it was worth it for her freedom, wasn't it? She could do this for two months; go to him willingly when he called for her. No real harm would be done.

Would she be required to pretend that she enjoyed his attentions? Was that part of their agreement? Just two months, sixty days. How many times could he call for her in that time? Surely not that many. And then she would be free.

Deborah took a leisurely bath in the bathhouse on Richard's instructions, a luxury that had not been available to her before and her mother helped her into the green dress. She put up her hair as she had worn it at the party and took a deep breath to steady her beating heart. She was being prepared like a bride for a wedding but this was far from the joining of two lives, this was simply the joining of two bodies. Shame swept through her that she had agreed to this until she ruthlessly pushed it aside and reminded herself that it was for her freedom. She was prepared to pay any price for that.

"You look real pretty," Sarah complimented her. "Don't worry, you know that Master Richard isn't like William and anyway Hattie only had good things to say about him." That was supposed to make her feel better?

She felt awkward. She didn't know what to do. Should she go up to his room and wait for him or should she wait until he called for her. Who would he send? What time was it now? Had they finished eating dinner? She could eat nothing because of the knots in her stomach.

A knock at the door made her jump nervously. It was Cassie telling her that Master Richard had asked her to come up to his room in a few minutes. She squeezed Deborah's hand comfortingly and said, "He's a good man, don't worry."

It was all very well and good for them to say but that didn't stop the trembling that had started in the pit of her stomach.

Cassie stayed a few minutes to chat with them, telling Deborah that Hattie was not too happy with her for taking her place with Master Richard and that the mistress didn't look too pleased when Master Richard sent her with the message but the master had smiled and slapped him on the shoulder.

"Girl a few minutes gone. You better get upstairs." She said getting off the bed to head for the kitchen to finish her chores.

Deborah looked at her mother, took a deep breath and walked out the door.

The walk to Richard's room seemed to take a lot less time than she remembered. Before she was ready, Deborah found herself standing outside the thick mahogany door and she raised her hand to knock. She heard a chair push back and before she could gather herself, the door opened and Richard stepped back to let her in.

She stood awkwardly, unsure of what to do. Should she greet him? Should she wait for him to say something? Why did she suddenly feel so shy when she had spoken boldly to him on many occasions?

"You look even more beautiful tonight." He took both of her hands in his and drew her further into the room. Two lanterns were turned down to give the room intimate lighting which made her feel more comfortable than the stark brightness of William's room that night.

"Would you like a drink?" He indicated a bottle of wine and two glasses which were on the desk.

"Yes, thank you." She was glad for any excuse to delay the inevitable.

She couldn't help but admire his grace as he crossed the room and how well he filled out his black jacket and breeches.

He poured a small glass of wine for her and a larger one for him. She had tasted wine only once before and she couldn't really say that she had liked it but now she was glad for the fortifying drink which she sipped.

Richard knew that he wasn't doing justice to the fine wine as he drank it in a few gulps and quickly drained the glass. He couldn't believe Deborah was finally here in his room and he was eager to be with her. After all, he'd done nothing but imagine this for the last two nights; in fact longer than that. Taking the glass from her hand, although she had barely tasted the wine, he put it on the desk and drew her closer. He could feel her shaking.

Gentle fingers unwound her long plait and freed her hair from its confines until it streamed down her back.

"Beautiful," he said as he buried his fingers in her hair. "And mine."

William's words came back to haunt her but were quickly banished as Richard bent his head and kissed the side of her neck and nibbled his way across to the pulse that was beating frantically at the base of her throat.

Raising his head, his eyes focused on her lips which were stained with the wine, making her instinctively lick them. Taking this as an invitation, Richard sipped at each corner of her mouth and then slowly stroked her sealed lips with the tip of his tongue, tasting the wine he had barely allowed her to drink. Deborah shivered in response and parted her lips obediently.

His hand at the back of her head urged her even closer and he slanted his head to one side as he tasted each delicious crevice that he discovered. Deborah was drowning in sensations that she had never felt before and her hands crept up to his shoulders for support lest her knees give way.

Of their own volition her hands reached up to tangle in his hair. This was the first time she had voluntarily touched him, any man for that matter, and she found that the sensation of her fingers in his hair was pleasurable. He obviously felt the same way as he shuddered, giving her a feeling of power that she didn't know she had.

His kisses became more demanding and Deborah found herself giving all that he silently asked for. When he drew back they were both breathing as if they had run a race. Deborah lowered her head to his chest in shame. She couldn't believe she had kissed Richard like that and enjoyed it.

"Your mouth is as delicious as I imagined it would be," he whispered huskily. Deborah cringed in embarrassment. She wished he wouldn't say these things to her.

He lifted her chin and she found herself staring into eyes that were no longer navy blue but black with desire. She would have looked away but he held her chin and said: "You have nothing to be ashamed about. Desire is natural and beautiful when it is pure."

Distracting her with intoxicating kisses, he sought the buttons at the back of her dress and with an expertise she could only imagine how he came by, he soon pushed the dress from her shoulders. Before she had time to be embarrassed at standing before him in her undergarments he kissed her again, bringing her hands to his chest and encouraged her to unbutton his shirt. He quickly shrugged off his jacket and shirt and stood before her clad only in his breeches.

When she innocently explored the hardness of his chest and his muscled back, he sucked in his breath and pulled her into his arms, burying his face in her fragrant hair. She marveled at how right their embrace felt.

"Beautiful," he said again hoarsely and she gloried in the fact that he was so affected by her.

He picked her up in his arms and gently deposited her on the bed which was as soft as she remembered from the last time. This time however she didn't try to escape; she moved over to make room for him as he peeled off his breeches and joined her, pulling her on top of him so that she felt powerful and in control.

She bent her head and boldly initiated a kiss which he soon became the master of. Rolling her over he pinned her under his heavy body but she didn't feel any panic, instead she welcomed his weight and tangled her legs with his.

Richard drew back and took a breath to steady himself and slow down the pace. He did not want to rush this but Deborah was making it very difficult. It took all his strength to control his desire to lose himself in her but even more than the physical release he craved, he wanted to erase the horror of her experience with William. His greater desire for their first time together was to create a memory so beautiful that it would stay with her long after he had left.

Richard held Deborah in his arms until her shudders subsided. He languidly smiled in satisfaction against her hair. Deborah was amazed that being intimate with him could be so totally different from what she had experienced with William. The memory of that violation was now firmly banished from her mind by Richard's gentle touch and patience.

Now that the ecstasy had faded she began to feel ashamed at her response and that she was in his bed. This wasn't the consummation of a marriage, she was his slave and she was in his bed in exchange for her freedom. Funny how easily she had forgotten that with the caresses of his hands and mouth on her body. The truth was as shocking as a bucket of cold water in her face. She struggled out of his embrace and turned her back to him in an attempt to hide the tears that now trickled from her eyes.

Richard immediately leaned over her in concern and asked: "What's the matter? Did I hurt you?" She shook her head. "Then what's wrong?"

"This is wrong! I'm with you in exchange for my freedom and you only bought me because you desired my body. Oh..," she gasped in horror as she suddenly remembered something, "I even forgot that you have a fiancée in Carolina." To tell the truth Richard had forgotten as well.

"What of it? It felt right and we both enjoyed it." Deborah could not deny that it felt right but feeling right didn't make it right. And she would never have been in his bed if he had not promised her freedom. Then again, after tonight, maybe that was no longer true. She now understood what Hattie meant. He had been so patient and gentle with her that the ice around her heart that had begun to melt the day he rescued her was now just about gone and that scared her more than a whipping. He was leaving in two months.

"You think too much," he complained pulling her back against him. The warmth of his embrace and the languor of her body made her begin to feel sleepy in spite of her restless thoughts and her eyes began to close.

"Shouldn't I go back to my room?" she murmured sleepily.

"No. Stay where you are. I will enjoy sleeping with you in my arms." His last thought before he fell asleep was that she felt entirely too right in his arms.

Chapter Nineteen

The sun in her face woke Deborah or she would probably have slept until noon. Stretching contentedly she wondered why she was on a soft mattress and why her body felt so relaxed. Images of Hattie coming into the kitchen weeks ago stretching contentedly came back to her and she suddenly remembered the source of that contentment. Richard! Shame shocked her into wakefulness. She was no better than Hattie.

"Good morning," greeted Richard. Deborah's head swung around to find him lying on his side watching her.

In the light of day Deborah was mortified and pulled the sheet up to cover herself as she remembered their time together.

"Too late for modesty now," teased Richard earning him a glare.

"I shouldn't be here. Why didn't you wake me up?"

"Have you got something to do? Somewhere to go? You forget that your job is to serve me now."

"How could I forget?" she asked sarcastically. "I hope I served you well."

"Oh, you definitely did. You're worth every pound I paid for you," provoked Richard. Deborah raised her hand to slap his face but he caught it before it found its mark.

"Now I promised that I wouldn't hit you but I should have made you promise the same, you little minx. Does this mean that the honeymoon is over?" he teased.

"This isn't funny Richard. This is not a honeymoon. I have sold my body for freedom. This is something I always said I would never do," she agonized.

"Well if that is the case, I paid £20 for your services, something I always said I would never do, and do you see me agonizing about it?" As if to prove his point he bent to kiss a ticklish spot on her neck. "And it's Master Richard to you." He couldn't help adding.

"You are so infuriating!" she scolded shoving him off and escaping from the bed.

"Well if you're getting up, go and get me some breakfast and bring it back to bed. I am famished woman, and I need to regain my strength."

Deborah picked up a pillow that had somehow gotten pushed off the bed during the night and threw it at him. He caught it easily and put it behind his head while he sat up to watch her get dressed with a satisfied smile. He was right; he could not have bought anything with the £20 that would have given his as much pleasure as Deborah.

Since it was Sunday only some of the girls were working in the house. For that Deborah was grateful since she didn't feel up to facing their knowing looks. She returned to her room, had a quick wash with a bowl of water she found there and changed into her everyday clothes before heading to the kitchen.

The family had already left for church and Cassie, her mother and the cook were sitting down to eat some porridge. She was relieved that Hattie was not there.

"Good morning," Deborah greeted hesitantly.

"Morning? It's nearly noon girl," teased Cassie. Sarah smiled and continued eating her porridge without commenting.

Deborah blushed and told the cook, "Master Richard would like his breakfast now. I'm to take it to him."

"All right, just now I goin' fry some bacon and eggs for him. Sit down and eat some porridge."

"Thank you. I am starving!"

"Master Richard didn' feed you last night?" Cassie asked just to get a reaction from Deborah. "It's a good thing Hattie not working today because she ain' too happy with you."

That was too bad for Hattie. She'd had the pleasure of Richard's attention for a month and Deborah could even understand her anger, but her freedom was at stake so Hattie would have to get over it.

As the smell of frying bacon and eggs filled the kitchen, Deborah got up to fix Richard some tea to go with it. Her mouth watered at the scent of the cooking meat and wondered if he would offer to share it with her. The cook had been more than generous with her portions.

Holding the tray with his breakfast in both hands she headed up the stairs and to his room at the end of the corridor. She balanced the tray in one hand while she knocked and waited for him to invite her in.

Richard opened the door again, this time clad only in a pair of tight breeches which left little to the imagination. He took the tray from her and walked over to the desk and put it down. Deborah's eyes trailed after him in secret admiration.

"Something smells good," he remarked lifting the cover off the plate. "Surely the cook doesn't expect me to eat all this. Come and have some." Deborah hesitated and then checked herself. The slave mentality was so engraved in her that she felt she should not eat with him. It was funny how slaves could share their master's bed but not their table.

Richard pulled her to sit on him and fed her pieces of bacon. The smoked salty meat was delicious. She couldn't remember the last time she tasted bacon; probably when she used to practically live with the girls or on the rare occasions that the cook would let them have the tiny burnt bits that were left over after she made the family's breakfast.

How she had risen in status, she scoffed at herself; having the luxury of two days off, sleeping past dawn and now eating bacon and eggs with her master. She could easily get used to this life. What had happened to the days when she scorned status and said she preferred freedom? She reminded herself that the privileges were only for two months, and that was assuming that Richard did not tire of her before then; after all Hattie had not lasted more than a month.

Harvest was well on the way so every hand was put to work. Richard had another hard day of working in the fields but, unlike the slaves, he could stop cutting when he got tired and move on to another task like loading the canes which was a lot easier.

He groaned as he stretched his back after picking up another load and putting it on the cart. The only thing he would do tonight when he got into his bed was sleep. At this rate he wouldn't have the energy to call for Deborah very much in the next two months. He knew that he didn't really have to work so hard but he wanted to earn his keep since his uncle had refused to take any money from him, except of course the £20 for Deborah.

He was glad that the end of the day was drawing to a close and that he could soon head back to the house.

As the family sat down to dinner a few hours later, his aunt handed him a letter that had been delivered that day.

"It must be from your fiancée," she said with a pleased look. He almost thought she seemed happy to remind him that he was betrothed, especially since she so heartily disapproved of his liaison with Deborah.

The last thing he wanted was a letter from Ann to remind him of his responsibilities in Carolina and he almost groaned when he saw it but he put the letter next to his plate and said, "Thank you, Aunt Elizabeth. I will read it later."

Deborah and Cassie brought in their meal and he couldn't help his eyes following her as she crossed the room and put out the food. Vivid images of her in his arms flashed before him making him distinctly uncomfortable in his chair and the letter beside his plate added to his discomfort in other ways. He looked away from her and caught his uncle's amused look.

"The harvest is progressing nicely and we should be finishing about the time you're ready to leave, Richard. At least there have been no more incidents of anyone getting caught in the grinder and the new boy seems to have settled in well."

"Good. I know you need all hands on deck but was wondering if I could go into Town tomorrow," Richard asked.

"Of course, my boy. You don't need my permission, but you may have to drive yourself there because I can't spare anyone. Do you think you can find your way?"

"I will take Deborah with me. I'm sure she can make sure that I don't get lost."

"Do you have business in Town?" His aunt asked curiously.

Richard hesitated, not really wanting to tell her that he was taking Deborah to buy some clothes to replace the drab skirts and blouses that she wore. He couldn't even explain it to himself but he wanted to give her something that would please her.

"Yes. I need to meet with our agent here and I really should send some letters home." Yes, it was long past the time he should have written to Ann.

Richard was too tired to even share a drink with his uncle in his office. Instead he made his excuses and headed to his room where he stripped off his clothes, put on a comfortable robe and sat up in bed to read the letter. He broke the seal with reluctance, for some reason not wanting news of what was happening in Carolina or in Ann's life.

April 5, 1696

Carlisle Hall,
James Island, Carolina

Dearest Richard
I can't believe that you have been gone for only five weeks because it has felt like five months. The days drag by and my thoughts are constantly with you, wondering how you are doing and if you are enjoying Barbados.

I'm certainly enjoying Barbados very much, Richard thought as an image of Deborah came to his mind. But I'm sure that's not what you mean.

My only relief from missing you is to attend an occasional party but even then I miss your presence and I am reminded of that time on the terrace at the Berkeley's party which does not help. Charles has been kind enough to escort me if my parents are not attending. I have been spending quite a lot of time with your mother and Charlotte and I was very worried when I heard that you had been ill. I hope you have fully recovered your strength.

My father is eager for you to come back with all the things you have learned so that you can begin to make the changes you and he have spoken about. You know that business is not of interest to me but I'm sure that you will be successful at whatever you are planning to do.

I hope you have not met and fallen in love with any beautiful Barbadian women who will try to convince you to stay because I miss you terribly and can't wait for you to come back so that we can start our life together.

All my love
Ann

PS Looking forward to receiving a letter from you soon although I know how you hate to write. A brief note will suffice.

Richard sighed. He would write to Ann early in the morning and mail it when he went into town, although to be truthful his mind was not to it. As for her concerns about him falling in love with a Barbadian woman, she had no worries there, although he had to admit that a certain beautiful slave girl was occupying his every thought. However one did not fall in love with slaves. As soon as he had his fill of her, he was sure that she would not possess his thoughts as she did now.

The thought flitted through his mind that he could call for her but the truth was that while his mind was willing his body was weak. He was just too exhausted.

He put the letter on his bedside table and turned down the wick of the lantern until it went out. The smell of Deborah on the pillow beside him stirred him in spite of his tiredness and while he struggled to find the energy to call for her, sleep decided the matter for him.

Deborah lay in her cot and listened to her mother's even breathing. She was excited that she and Richard would be going to Town tomorrow for she didn't know the last time she had been into Town.

She had thought that he would call for her tonight. She was glad that he hadn't, so that she didn't have to battle with herself as she did every time she gave in to him, but she missed the warmth of his body next to hers and the strength of his arms around her. She missed his intoxicating kisses and his addicting caresses.

Stop it! She scolded herself. She did not want to be thinking of him in that way. She wondered if he had already tired of her. Had she lasted even less time than Hattie? Was it because she did not please him? No, he had said that she was worth every pound he paid for her. As if that was a compliment!

So she would keep her part of the bargain and it would be strictly business. He was betrothed and he was going back to Carolina in two months. She was a slave and he was free. The only thing she wanted from him was her freedom.

The next day was somewhat overcast which perfectly matched Deborah's mood. She wasn't sure why she was feeling so low in spirits; it certainly wasn't because Richard did not call for her last night. She put on the best dress she had apart from the green one and met him in the driveway where the stable boy had brought the carriage.

Richard was already seated with the reins in his hands looking impatient. He gave her a hand up and she took the seat next to him, making sure that she was as far as possible from him.

"Ready?" he asked and she nodded but did not reply.

After travelling for quite a while in silence he asked if everything was all right.

She said yes briefly but did not elaborate.

Richard was acquainted with enough women to know that she was lying. He therefore knew that when she could not contain herself any longer he would find out. He almost smiled when a mile or so down the road, Deborah asked, "Are you regretting our arrangement?"

"What do you mean?"

Did he mean for her to spell it out? "You did not call for me last night so I wondered if you called Hattie to come to you instead."

She couldn't seriously believe that! "Deborah the only reason I did not call for you was because I was incapable of doing anything other than sleeping after working in the fields all day."

"Oh," she replied mollified.

"Were you worried that I had tired of you already?" he teased.

"I was hoping that you had," she lied, "but then you might try to get out of your promise to free me. That's all I want."

"I can't imagine ever getting tired of you," he assured her and raised one of her hands to his lips.

Deborah was not sure why the day seemed so much brighter than it had before they left, especially since the sky was still covered with grey clouds.

Chapter Twenty

At breakfast on Wednesday Thomas brought Richard up to date on what had been done the day before. He was pleased with the progress of the harvest but said that they needed to start harvesting the more mature canes that were on the outskirts of the plantation otherwise they would begin to lose their sugar content.

Nobody looked forward to harvesting them because the stems were harder to cut and their distance from the mill meant that they had to wait long periods for the carts to come back from taking the canes to the mill, which often resulted in a backup of canes to load.

His uncle told him that it was easier to burn those canes, but the fire had to be managed carefully so that it did not get out of control. Then the canes had to be processed the same day otherwise they would spoil and the juice would be no good. That usually meant running the mill and boiling house through the night.

"Do you have water out there?" Richard asked.

"There's a well near the field and we always have buckets on hand in case we need them. Don't worry, we do this all the time."

Richard finished eating and returned to his room to collect his hat as well as a large handkerchief in case he needed to protect himself from inhaling the smoke. Deborah was tidying the bed which had become disheveled during the night. Would he ever get enough of this woman? Rather than getting her out of his system she seemed to be getting further under his skin.

Deborah's heart sped up when Richard entered the room.

"We're burning canes today so I need a kerchief to cover my nose."

She paused in straightening the bed just to feast her eyes on him as he dug through a drawer looking for a large handkerchief.

Richard turned around to catch Deborah looking at him with blatant desire on her face which evoked an immediate response in him. She held a pillow in front of her as if in defense but he crossed the room and took it from her, tossing it on the bed as he pulled her close.

"You have no idea what you're doing to me with that look in your eyes," he warned her.

"What look?" She asked innocently.

"The look that says ..." he whispered the rest in her ear and Deborah blushed. He kissed her thoroughly before reluctantly pulling away and saying huskily, "I've got to go."

For no apparent reason Deborah began to feel a sense of foreboding and didn't want him to go, but she could hardly say so.

"Be careful," she said instead.

"You sound like a wife," he teased. "I'll be careful," he promised. "I wouldn't want to miss tonight," and was gone.

As she fluffed the pillows a letter that was on the bedside table floated to the floor. She had noticed it the night before and she was sure that it was the one from his fiancée. It had seemed to accuse her as she shared his bed that night.

Picking it up she began to wonder what she had written. Had she told him she was missing him? Shared intimate secrets? What was she like? She was very tempted to read it but she put it back without giving in to the temptation.

She quickly finished tidying the bed and gathered up his dirty clothes. She would wash them along with the dress, skirts and blouses he had bought her in town yesterday. She still could not believe that Richard had bought her clothes because he hated seeing her in the same drab slaves' clothing. She did not know what she had done to deserve such treatment but she would enjoy it while it lasted.

Sarah was doing the laundry when Deborah joined her to wash Richard's clothes and hers. The day was already hot but there was a strong wind that dispelled the heat and would dry the clothes quickly.

"Master Richard treating you real good," Sarah said smiling as she gestured at the new clothes. "I'm glad. You happy with him?"

Deborah smiled a little secret smile and admitted, "Yes, ma. More than I expected to be. And he promised to free me when he goes back to Carolina," she confided. "But the mistress doesn't know so don't tell the others."

"I'm real glad, Deborah! I knew he was a good man." She hugged Deborah in delight. "Maybe the master will

219

free me too." Deborah fervently hoped so. Maybe the master would give her a little money to help them. She still didn't know what she would do once she was free.

Turning back to the clothes, she finished washing them in a few minutes and took them to the drying yard in a bucket. Without consciously thinking about it she hung Richard's on the line and spread hers on some nearby bushes. Slaves did not hang their washing with their master's.

She had spread the last shirt on the bush, a green and white flowered one of the softest cotton, when she turned to find Hattie behind her. She jumped in fright as she had not heard her walk up and was about to scold her for startling her when Hattie said, "I don't know what you gave Master Richard but you got him bewitched. He buy them new clothes for you?" she asked jealously.

Deborah nodded, feeling guilty and ashamed since she had scorned Hattie for accepting a shilling after sleeping with Richard and here she was accepting clothes. In a strange way, she felt sorry for Hattie that Richard had moved on from her and she wondered how she would feel when he went back to his fiancée.

Richard listened as his uncle and the overseers went over the plans to burn the mature canes. The area was about ten acres and was next to a field of young canes which would not be ready for harvesting until the following year.

The plan was to widen the track between the older and younger canes to create a fire break to protect the young canes and provide an access to load the burnt canes onto carts once the field cooled down and the canes could be cut. There was already a rough cart road between them but it had become overgrown in the rainy season.

Once the bush edging the field of young canes was cleared they would start what his uncle called a perimeter fire which was the quickest way to burn the canes. He had said that this type of fire had to be handled carefully since it was hotter and moved faster than any of the other methods of burning.

Richard and a crew of about twenty slaves began to cut back the overgrown bush from the far end of the field and worked their way down. He was happy that it was not as back breaking as cutting sugar cane and this allowed them to make rapid progress. A cart followed them so that they could pile the cuttings into it.

The overseers signaled with the agreed gun shot that they were ready to start the fire. It was progressing well and burning away from where Richard and the gang were cutting, when the wind shifted suddenly and several sustained gusts from the south created a new head and flames, aided by the wind, reached towards them like hellish hands. The intense heat caused them to shrink back.

"What's happening?" Richard shouted to a slave over the crackle of the flames

"The wind shifted," he answered. "Best get out quick," he warned even as he ran.

"Run," Richard urged the other slaves even as he ran back to help the driver of the cart to control the panicking horse. The horse reared up and its hoof clipped him on the temple before it bolted down the track as Richard collapsed to the ground, stunned by the blow. The handkerchief, which he had been holding over his nose, blew from his hand as he lost consciousness.

Thomas had ridden down towards the track in time to see the slaves run out.

"Where is Richard?' he asked one of them who gestured towards the track, coughing. Thomas jumped from his horse and ran towards the track where he found Richard lying on the ground with blood trickling from a cut on his head. He picked him up under the arms and began to drag him out and was relieved to see one of the slaves appear to help carry him.

Loading him onto the cart, Thomas anxiously checked to see if he was still breathing and was relieved to see his chest move. Once they moved away from the smoke, Richard began to cough violently before slipping back into unconsciousness.

Thomas didn't know how much smoke he had inhaled and how bad the cut on his head was but he didn't look good. He swore to God that if he spared Richard's life, he would give up something that was important to him in exchange: Sarah.

Deborah saw the smoke in the distance and once again a nervous feeling came over her. She tried to tell herself that the master was accustomed to doing controlled burning but the feeling would not go away.

A high gust of wind made her look frantically in the direction of the fire and she was frustrated that she could not see anything apart from thick smoke that rose in the air, thankfully downwind from the house.

She paced up and down in the yard, unable to sit still and unwilling to examine why she was so worried about Richard.

It was almost a relief when half hour later she saw a cart racing into the yard. She started running towards it, knowing already what her premonition had told her. As the cart came to a halt she rushed to it to find Richard lying unmoving in the back, with blood all down his face and on his shirt.

Her heart froze as she gazed in disbelief at his still form and everything seemed to slow down around her. She couldn't believe this was happening. Surely Richard could not be dead, not when she was just beginning to have feelings for him.

Thomas rode into the yard, shouting for Jethro to help get Richard into the house, even as he jumped from his horse. Chaos erupted in the next few minutes as Elizabeth and the girls rushed out to see what was happening and the house slaves appeared in the doorways.

"Deborah, get some water and cloths to clean the wound," the master instructed. "I've already sent for the doctor. Quick!" he snapped when she still seemed dazed.

She snapped out of it and ran to the kitchen to boil water and find clean cloths, sobbing in relief that Richard was still alive.

Chapter Twenty-One

B y the time the doctor arrived just over an hour later, Deborah had cleaned the wound on Richard's head and sat in the chair next to his bed watching him closely. She was worried that he had not regained consciousness, even when Jethro helped her to take off his filthy shirt which reeked of smoke so that she could wipe him down as best as she could.

Thomas led the doctor in and waited while he performed his examination and pronounced that Richard had a concussion and that he was to keep quiet for the next few days. He advised that he would probably have a headache and may experience nausea or vomiting. He gave them warning signs to watch for and said to call him right away if they saw any of them, otherwise he would return in two days.

When he left, Deborah went down to the kitchen to make some chamomile tea with skullcap to ease the pain in his head when he woke up. She wished that she could do more and felt helpless that all she could do was wait.

The sun was beginning to go down when Richard opened his eyes and found Deborah restlessly folding the clothes in his drawers. He would have smiled if his head was not throbbing so much. He searched his memory for the cause and remembered trying to calm the horse in the fire and getting hit on the head by its rearing hoof. He couldn't recall how he had got out of the track or back to the house.

"Why the sudden desire to fold all my clothes?" he asked in a rough voice.

Deborah dropped the shirt she was folding and sped around, relieved that Richard had woken up.

"You're awake! We were all so worried about you," she added as she crossed to the bed. She was concerned with his pallor and was about to ask how he felt when he murmured, "Chamber pot," just seconds before she pulled it from under the bed and he emptied his stomach into it.

She gave him a cup of water to rinse out his mouth and put the lid on the pot and left it by the door to empty later.

"Thank you. I feel like I've been kicked in the head by a horse," he joked weakly.

Deborah was relieved that he could still joke even though he looked so ill. She gently stroked the hair back from his forehead which was wrapped in a bandage.

"I made you some tea for your headache. I'll just go and warm it up. The doctor said that your head would be aching when you woke up and that you might feel nauseous. Do you feel dizzy?"

"No but my throat is raw and my head hurts like the devil."

"I'll be right back," promised Deborah heading for the door. She picked up the chamber pot to empty outside and hoped that he didn't need to use it before she came back.

She ran into Rachel in the hallway and informed her that Richard had woken up. It was so strange to be speaking to her as if she was a stranger, when they had played together as children and did so many things together. Soon she would be free to speak to them as an equal and not as a slave. She smiled to herself as she pictured how horrified the mistress would be.

Richard closed his eyes against the pain and marveled at the fact that he was still alive since he knew that a well placed kick from a horse could kill a man. Maybe there was something that he still had to do with his life, so he silently thanked God for sparing it.

Richard was restless. Once again he was confined to his room in Barbados. The pain in his head had lessened to a dull throbbing and he had not vomited since the first night. The doctor had come a little while ago and although he seemed pleased with his progress he instructed him to rest for a few more days and not to move around too much.

He wondered where Deborah was. He enjoyed having her around fussing over him and when he remembered how annoying he'd found Hattie's attention, he wondered why he didn't feel the same with Deborah.

His thoughts seemed to bring her into the room and she quietly knocked and opened the door. He brightened on seeing her in one of the brightly colored skirts and blouses that he had bought for her that day in Town. He was surprised at how much he had enjoyed treating her to new clothes, especially since Ann's interest in clothes had often annoyed him.

"I was just wondering where you were," he told her.

"Why, were you missing me?" she flirted with him. Deborah did not normally talk to Richard so boldly but she was happy that he was recovering well and that the doctor was pleased with his progress.

"Come over here and I'll show you how much," he promised huskily.

"Now behave yourself. The doctor said that you're not to move around too much so you need to keep quiet."

"I promise not to move too much. You can do everything."

"Richard! You are wicked!" He loved the fact that he could easily shock her and he took every opportunity to do so. She had called him Richard so maybe she no longer saw him as her master but as her lover. He smiled at the thought.

"OK. Read to me instead. At least for now," he conceded.

"You know what happened the last time I read to you. Your aunt was not at all pleased."

"Well you belong to me now so she can't do anything about it." Deborah sobered up. She kept forgetting that she belonged to Richard and she feared that he not only owned her but, worse yet, he was beginning to own her heart.

"I'll go down to Master Thomas' library and see what I can find. As long as it isn't Richard Ligon's

'Observations upon the shape of Negroes'. You made me read that on purpose, didn't you?" She accused him.

"I could not resist. You should have seen your face when you saw what I'd asked you to read. And I have to admit that his observations were very accurate," he said lowering his gaze to the subject matter.

"I would throw something at you but you have not recovered fully as yet. I'm going to find a book. Maybe Macbeth or something equally sinister."

Richard smiled as she left the room. He couldn't imagine ever getting bored with her. She was constantly changing and the fact that she was a slave in no way demeaned her, no matter what she thought. If she was like this as a slave, what would she be like when she was free? Unfortunately he would not be around to see it. He planned to leave at the end of June which would give him two clear months in Barbados and he intended to make the most of that time.

Thomas managed to take some time from the harvest to stop by Richard's room to see how he was doing. He was glad that he seemed well on the way to recovery. He still felt guilty that Richard had been injured on the plantation and he was thankful that his life had been spared.

That reminded him of his promise to God that he would give up Sarah if he spared Richard's life. He would call his lawyer as soon as he had a break from the harvest and start putting things in place to have the manumission papers prepared. He would set her free but that didn't mean he couldn't continue to visit her. He would buy her a property in Town where she could live and have a shop of some kind.

His conscience pricked slightly that he was not in fact giving up Sarah, he was just moving her to a different location and he would not own her anymore. God knew that he couldn't live without her altogether; she had become a very important part of his life. To give her up altogether would be like losing a limb.

"I'm certainly glad to see you looking so much better," Thomas greeted Richard.

"I have the best nurse," Richard said. "Deborah has been at my beck and call and she hasn't complained once. I'm only sorry that she's taking the doctor's orders of no movement very seriously. What's the point of having her this close to me if I can't do anything about it?" He complained.

Thomas laughed at his disgusted expression. "Does that mean you haven't got her out of your system yet?"

"I haven't had enough opportunities to do so to tell the truth, but I can't see it happening," he admitted. "I decided today that I will go back to Carolina at the end of June so hopefully I'll be cured by then."

"I will be very sorry to see you go. When you were unconscious in the cart, you looked so close to death that I made a pact with God that if he spared your life I would give up Sarah."

Richard didn't know what to say because he knew how much Sarah meant to his uncle.

"He did his part, I will do mine, so I'll get my lawyer to work on manumission papers soon and I will set her free when you free Deborah. I'll buy a property in town for her and give her enough money for the two of them to start a business of some sort."

"Thank you for your petition on my behalf. I'm glad to hear that you'll be freeing Sarah because I was worried about what Deborah would do without her, but to tell the truth I haven't thought much beyond the next two months and how she would survive. I find it hard to think rationally with that woman around," he laughed at himself.

"So all is well?" Thomas inquired.

"Very well. She's everything I imagined she would be. She told me about William," he broached the subject carefully, "but she is over that. Well over it," he added with a satisfied smile.

"I am glad," Thomas said seriously. "That's why I was so careful to protect her from the men who wanted to buy her, but I knew that I could trust you to be good to her. I wouldn't have sold her to anyone else."

Richard was humbled and before he could even find the words to express what his uncle's words meant to him he continued: "You have become even closer to me than my own son. If you ever consider staying in Barbados I want you to know that you would have a place here. I'm not getting any younger and I could use a good manager for the plantation."

Richard was astounded at Thomas' offer and was embarrassed to feel a lump in his throat that his uncle, after only knowing him for a month would trust him to that extent when his father did not.

"I'm very honored by your offer, sir but my future is in Carolina."

"If you ever change your mind, let me know." Richard nodded, still overcome with emotion.

Deborah knocked softly on the door and opened it when Richard invited her to come in. She stopped as she saw Thomas sitting in the chair by his bed but they both gestured her to come closer. Richard patted the bed next to him but Deborah was not so bold as to sit next to him on the bed with Master Thomas present and chose to remain standing. She had to remind herself that he was no longer her master but seventeen years was hard to undo.

"Is this young man treating you well?" Thomas asked her, searching her face.

"I would like to treat her even better but the doctor has convinced her that I'm to keep quiet."

Deborah blushed, suddenly shy in front of her former master.

"And well you should. You've been kicked in the head by a horse, boy. If that didn't shake you up, I don't know what will. But you didn't let Deborah answer my question." Both of them looked expectantly at her.

"He's been very good to me," Deborah admitted, looking at Richard with an uncharacteristically shy smile. Richard smiled back at her and held out a hand to her. Deborah could not ignore the gesture and came closer to give him her hand. Richard kissed the palm, tickling it with the tip of his tongue which made her tingle and look quickly at Master Thomas to see if he had noticed. He was smiling at them with a look of approval on his face.

"I will leave you two now. I don't think I'm needed here."

Deborah made a half-hearted protest but Richard said quickly, "Thanks for the visit."

As the door closed behind his uncle he pulled Deborah closer until she was sitting next to him on the bed. Taking the handkerchief from her head, he unraveled her hair and buried his fingers in the thick locks all the while holding her eyes captive with his.

He was pleased to see her eyes darken with desire but she was still protesting half-heartedly about the doctor's orders even as his lips closed over hers. After two days of not touching her, he felt a surge of desire and his kiss quickly became demanding. Deborah kissed him back as if she too had been starving for the taste and feel of his mouth on hers.

As he began to unbutton her blouse she stilled his hands and said with great reluctance, "I don't want to do anything to hinder your recovery. I'm serious Richard; the doctor was adamant that you should not move around much for a few days."

"OK. I'll show you what to do so that we keep the doctor happy," he said resuming what he had started.

In less time than seemed decent Deborah collapsed against his heaving chest, satisfied that the doctor's orders had not been violated too badly.

Richard held her in his arms and said breathlessly, "Don't you know that you're the best medicine for me?"

Yes, but not for much longer. Deborah thought silently.

Chapter Twenty-Two

A month later

Richard looked out over the plantation and was able to see new vistas from his vantage point as many of the fields were now bare of the tall sugar cane. There was just over a month remaining of the harvest and everyone was looking forward to the end of the crop. He realized that by the time the crop was officially over he would be on a boat back to Carolina.

He hoped that his aunt had forgotten about her plans to have another party to celebrate the end of harvest because he knew that he wouldn't feel like celebrating. In fact as the end of June drew closer he began to be filled with restlessness and he didn't need to examine its source that closely to recognize that he was being torn between Barbados and Carolina. He had come to love Barbados and life on the plantation, but the opportunity to run the Carlisle's plantation and make his own way was still very strong.

His thoughts turned to Deborah as they did so many times during the day. His uncle had been right; she was no closer to being out of his system. He realized that it wasn't even just physical desire that he had for her because many nights he was too exhausted to even lift his hand but he still called for Deborah just so that he could sleep with her in his arms.

Eventually he ordered her to move into his room rather than returning to hers each night. He knew that his aunt disapproved but his uncle had given his permission. Besides it would only be for five more weeks. Five weeks, or thirty-seven days to be exact. He had already arranged with Bostick to leave with the boat on June 30.

His uncle had told him only today that Deborah's birthday was tomorrow. He wanted to give her something special; something that she would have to remember him by when he left. He didn't have time to go into Town to buy anything. What could he give her?

Her freedom. The thought floated to him on the breeze. Her freedom? Before he left? Then she would have no reason to stay with him. Would she be willing to stay if she had her freedom? He didn't want to lose her yet. He felt good when she was around. She made him laugh and challenged him at every turn and she made him feel powerful when she was shuddering in his arms. He had been right when he told her that he couldn't imagine getting tired of her.

Could he risk losing all that by giving her the freedom she longed for now? The document had been prepared over a month ago; all he had to do was write in the date and sign it. He felt that she had feelings for him, but were they strong enough to keep her with him if he freed her now?

❧

May 25, 1696

The beautiful day mocked Deborah's heavy mood. Two years after her fateful sixteenth birthday when she had rued the fact that she was a slave, nothing had changed. Granted she would have her freedom when Richard left at the end of next month and the anticipation she felt could not be explained to someone who was free, but now she found that it was somewhat diminished by the thought of him leaving. How had her emotions become so involved? She had planned to treat this as a business arrangement and she remembered swearing to him that she would never want him. What a joke! He now owned her, body and soul. When did she begin to love him? And how she would recover when he went back to Carolina?

"Why so glum?" Richard asked coming to hug her from behind while she plaited her hair.

"I've been a slave for eighteen years. That's enough reason, isn't it?" she muttered.

"Maybe this will cheer you up. Happy birthday," he said handing her a folded document.

Master Thomas must have told him. "What's this?" She opened the document and started to read.

The Acreage, St. James
Barbados

It is hereby made known that on the twenty fifth day of May in the year of our Lord sixteen hundred and ninety six, I Richard Fairfax of Charles Town, Carolina, currently residing in Barbados, have liberated, manumitted and set free my slave Deborah Edwards of the age of eighteen years old and I hereby liberate, manumit and set free the said slave and discharge her from all service or demand of service to be hereafter made by me or by persons claiming by, from or under me.

In testimony whereof I have hereunto set my hands and seal the year and date aforesaid.

Signed: Richard Fairfax
Sealed and delivered in the presence of: Thomas Edwards and Peter Hall

Deborah looked in disbelief at the document. She literally held her freedom in her hands. After all of these years, after the tears she had cried, after crying out to God, she was free. Tears sprang from her eyes and poured down her face as she stood before Richard, clutching the paper to her breast.

"I am free?" she whispered in disbelief through her tears. He nodded feeling something expand in his chest which made it hard to breathe or to speak.

She sank to her knees at his feet and bent her head saying, "Thank you, thank you, thank you."

Richard dropped to his knees before her, lifted up her chin and wiped away her tears with his handkerchief.

"You are free to go but I would like you to stay until I leave. Will you stay, Deborah?"

Richard knew that his request was not fair, after all Deborah had waited her whole life for this moment. He had given up the incentive to keep her here. Would she stay with him of her own free will?

Deborah could not fully grasp the fact that she was free. No-one could tell her what to do or where to go? No-one could demand her body? She could make her own decisions? She could tell Richard that she was leaving and he could not stop her. For the first time in her life she was free to do what she wanted. As she looked into his eyes and saw the vulnerability in them and the need for her that matched her need for him, she knew she would stay with him while he was in Barbados. She nodded.

"Yes, I'll stay."

Richard closed his eyes in relief and released a breath he did not even realize he had been holding. He hadn't known until then just how important her answer was to him.

Tonight was different. Tonight was the first time that she would be with Richard as a free woman, not because he held the promise of freedom to persuade her, but because she chose to be with him. It was a powerful and exciting feeling. She took a leisurely bath, dressed with particular care and then sent a note to the dinner table by Cassie. She smiled as she recalled what she had written.

Miss Deborah Edwards requests the pleasure of your company in your room after dinner. Don't have dessert. Dessert awaits you.

She couldn't believe that she could make a joke about being dessert after William had referred to her that way two years ago. Richard had healed her with his love and gentleness. Love? Was it love he felt for her or simply desire? After all, he had never said the words.

Richard took the note that Cassie had surreptitiously handed to him and opened it beneath the table. He couldn't contain the laugh that escaped his lips or the anticipation that surged through him at Deborah's boldness and the thought of her waiting for him upstairs.

His aunt glanced at him questioningly but he smiled and said, "Private joke. Sorry."

He passed the note to Thomas discreetly. He had told him earlier of his decision to free Deborah today and that she had decided to stay until he left.

He practically devoured his food, not even caring what he ate, wanting to get to the end of the main course as quickly as he could. Why did this woman excite him so much? All he could think about was her note and imagine her waiting in his room.

As soon as Cassie removed his plate, he pushed back his chair. His aunt looked up in surprise as he made his excuses.

"I'm afraid I'm much too full for dessert right now," he apologized. "I may just have something in my room later if I feel peckish." His uncle smothered a laugh.

"That's quite all right, my boy. Don't let us detain you. I'm sure you're anxious for your bed tonight. Don't bother to come out tomorrow. Make sure you get a good rest."

"Thank you, uncle. That's very generous of you." With that he put down his napkin and eagerly headed for his room.

Deborah stood as Richard burst into the room. His breath caught at the picture of her in one of the new dresses he had bought in town and her hair loose over her shoulders and down her back.

"Dinner finished already?" she asked teasingly, as if she knew that he had wolfed it down without noticing what he had eaten.

"You knew very well I would have no idea what I ate after I read your note. You wanton woman," he accused. She laughed delightedly, her spirit free.

"It is my birthday! It is as if I was born for the first time today and I was born free," she said with joy. Richard was pleased that he had given her that joy.

"I know that you could have waited until you were leaving to give me my freedom but you gave it to me today as a gift. You do not know how much that means to me. Thank you," she finished humbly.

"Now although it's my birthday, I want to give you a gift," she said taking off his jacket and dropping it over a chair. "Tonight I give you the gift of myself; not because I want my freedom or because you own me, but because I choose to."

Richard was both humbled and exalted by her words. He pulled her into his arms and buried his face in her hair; his heart full of an unnamed emotion that threatened to overwhelm him.

Raising his head he looked into her eyes and then bent to kiss each eyelid, her nose, the corners of her mouth, all with light butterfly kisses. He trailed kisses down her neck to the ticklish spot he had discovered, making her squirm. He gently sucked on a sensitive place on her neck, branding her with his mark.

Deborah unbuttoned his shirt and pushed it off his broad shoulders, enjoying the sensation of his smooth warm skin against her hands. She rained kisses on his chest, nipping and branding him as hers in reciprocation.

Richard suddenly pulled her head up and plundered her lips with a passion that he could not seem to restrain. Deborah gloried in the fact that she could move him with just a few caresses and met his kiss with the same intensity. They quickly divested themselves of any hindrances between them, coming together with an urgency born of the realization that their time together was short.

Later they leisurely explored each other as if trying to imprint on their minds memories that they wanted to last the rest of their lives.

Chapter Twenty-Three

June 29, 1696

T homas paced up and down as he waited for Sarah to come to his office. This was more difficult than telling Deborah that he had sold her to Richard because he at least knew that Richard would take care of her and that she was still going to be in the house. With Sarah it was different. He was going to be freeing her and it was harder than he imagined it would be.

It was not just the thought that she would no longer be owned by him or be available to him but he realized that she would be without his protection as she and Deborah would be living in Town, so far away if she needed him. He had bought her a small property there earlier in the month; a two bedroom house with a shop front where she and Deborah could run some sort of business.

He had decided to give her Jacko as a slave since he couldn't do much on the plantation with one hand and he would give her one of the women from the field to help out.

Sarah knocked at the door and he bid her to come in. She looked as if she had come in from doing the laundry as the front of her dress was wet and her hands looked wrinkled from being in water for too long.

"You wanted me Master Thomas?"

"Yes Sarah." He paused as if to collect himself. "Since Richard will be leaving tomorrow and Deborah will be free to go, I have decided to grant you your freedom now."

Sarah put a hand over her mouth as tears sprang to her eyes.

"You freeing me now, Master Thomas?" she repeated.

"Yes, Sarah. I'm freeing you now." The words were hard to say because in his heart he wanted to keep her. "I found a small house in town for you and Deborah where you can live and have a shop of some sort and I will give you Jacko as well as Mamie, one of the field girls to help you out."

"You giving me slaves? Master Thomas I don't want to own anybody."

"You and Deborah will need their help."

Sarah was overcome with all the information and had to sit down. Things were changing so fast. Master Richard was leaving tomorrow, Deborah was free and now the Master was freeing her and giving her property? She couldn't believe it.

"I'm also going to give you £100 for you to set up a shop and live on until you start to make some money from the shop."

Thomas knew that Sarah couldn't really comprehend having that sort of money so he would give it to Deborah and let her deal with the finances.

"It's not going to be easy to let you go, Sarah. From the time you came, you have made my life happier. I still want to see you. When I'm in Town I will come and spend the night or the weekend with you." This was more of a statement than a request but she nodded.

He went to his desk and picked up a document. "This is the document that says you are free. Keep it safe so that no-one can ever make you a slave again."

"Thank you, Master Thomas," she said clutching the paper. "I can't believe that this happening. Deborah and I talked about being free but I never believed it would be so quick. She is going to be so happy when she hears this, because I know that she was worried about me." Thomas nodded.

"Would you come to me tonight, Sarah? We only have a few days before you leave."

"Yes, Master Thomas." She left the room quickly and he knew that she was going to find Deborah to tell her the news. He was torn between joy for her and a deep sadness that his life would no longer be the same without her.

Richard could not believe that he would be on a ship bound for Carolina the next day. His trunks were packed and waiting, only the things he would need for tomorrow remained. Deborah had packed it in spite of his protests that she was no longer his slave. He wasn't surprised though because in the month since he'd freed her nothing had changed. She still cleaned his room, washed his clothes and looked after him. Either it was a habit that was hard to break or she just wanted to do it for him out of love. He preferred to think it was the latter.

Lying in bed now with her head on his chest, a feeling of longing sought to overwhelm him. It was as if they had already parted and he was experiencing the separation even though she was still here. He remembered leaving Ann in Carolina with hardly a pang and yet here he was torn up inside at the thought of having to part from Deborah. He certainly had not felt this way about Anise either, although he had enjoyed her attentions. He didn't know what it was about Deborah but the thought of leaving her tomorrow made him feel as if his heart was being torn out and left behind in Barbados. Maybe it was.

Thoughts began to torment him. Would she meet some free man and get married? Have children? After all she was only eighteen, even though she seemed so much older. The thought of her in another man's arms gave him a sick feeling in the pit of his stomach. He tightened his arms around her as if in protest.

"What's the matter?" she asked. She had also been deep in thought. She felt as if she was mourning the loss of Richard already and he had not yet gone. She couldn't imagine how she would feel when he got on that boat tomorrow. Her heart grieved silently.

"Nothing that I can do anything about."

"I was just remembering when I heard your uncle reading the letter you sent. I disliked you instantly." She laughed softly.

Richard looked at her in surprise. "Why? You didn't even know me."

"No. Nor did I want to. You had told him that you were coming to Barbados to see how he managed his slaves so that you would know what to do when you bought some for your plantation. You were talking about us as if we were animals to buy and sell."

"I didn't mean you."

"Until you freed me, I was a slave too. Just because I worked in the house or my skin was whiter does not make me any different. Because I had the opportunity to learn how to read and do other things does not make me more intelligent than them. They are people just like me."

Richard was silent. He still saw Deborah differently, no matter what she said. In fact he had never seen her as a slave.

"Tell me what you plan to do now that you're free and my uncle has freed your mother," he said changing the subject to a safer topic.

"I'm so glad that Master Thomas freed her too. You know that he has bought her a house?" Richard nodded. "I can't believe that we will actually own a house."

"My mother is going to make clothes to sell and I will sell herbs, soaps and things like that. That's what I know best. Master Thomas said that he would help me make some contacts with merchants from England and France and I can bring in herbs and things on his ship." She was very excited at the prospect of running her own business and being independent.

"I'm sure that you'll be very good at it. Look how well you healed me with your teas, when I had that stomach ailment and again when I had the concussion."

"About that stomach ailment; I have a confession to make," she started.

"What? You really did try to poison me?" he asked in disbelief.

"No, but I felt very guilty because I didn't know if I had heated up the food I gave you properly and if it was because of that you were sick. You see, I was very upset when you came and invaded my grove on my day off and then demanded that I get you something to eat. I was so tempted to tell you 'Get it yourself' but I could not of course."

"I could not tell by the way you walked off with such dignity. That was when I knew that I wanted you." Deborah smiled.

"I wasn't sure if you would have me flogged so I bit my lip to keep from answering you back."

Richard sobered. "I would never have flogged you. When Jethro was flogging you, it was as if I could feel the pain in my own body." He hugged her tighter.

"I truly understood pain that day and I swore that I would never again be rebellious. I was crying out to God to help me when you rode into the yard and shouted for Jethro to stop."

"You were? I didn't even know that you believed in God."

"I was not sure then, I was wondering if he was real; but now I do. I'm convinced that your coming to Barbados was part of some divine plan because so much has happened since you came, for the better. I feel as if you were sent here on a mission."

"Thank you for your kind words, Deborah, but I don't think that God would use the likes of me for any divine purpose. I'm the worst of sinners. I have a fiancée in Carolina as well as a mistress and here I am in bed with you, to say the least."

"You have a mistress in Carolina?" Deborah said in disbelief, sitting up. To her that was even worse than having a fiancée because she knew now that his marriage was an arrangement but having a mistress was by choice.

"I used to, but she may have moved on to someone else. You have successfully removed both from my mind. Let me just hold you until the dawn then I will leave without disturbing you so that we don't have to say goodbye."

They became silent, their thoughts filled with the memories of the few months they had had together and reluctantly of the days to come when those memories would grow dim and be replaced by others of which they would not be a part.

Early the next day

Richard slipped out of bed while it was still dark. Deborah stirred but thankfully did not wake up. He washed quickly with the water in the jug and dressed without lighting a lamp. He quietly picked up his trunks and deposited them outside the door for Jethro to pick up.

Returning to his room he put some money wrapped in a piece of paper on the bedside table and took one last look at Deborah as she lay on her stomach with her hair gloriously down her bare back as he liked it. That was one of the images that he would take with him to Carolina. She had changed his life in ways that she did not even know, opened his eyes to see things differently and stolen his heart, leaving him with a gaping wound where it used to be. He knew that time would heal the wound but his heart would always remain in Barbados.

Deborah woke up with a start as if a noise had penetrated her sleep. The room had an empty feeling about it and even without seeing Richard's side of the bed empty; she knew that he was gone. Something on the bedside table caught her eye as she looked over at Richard's side of the bed. She eagerly opened the folded up paper thinking that it was a note from him. Instead she found money. On counting it she discovered it was £20 and although she was disappointed that he had not left a note she knew that he was making sure she was taken care of. After all what else was there to say?

Pain seized her, causing her to curl into a foetal position clutching the pillow that he had slept on to her chest, as if it could somehow ease the pain there. His familiar smell on the pillow overwhelmed her and she buried her face in it smothering the sobs that shook her body.

She had what she had always wanted; her freedom. But now it was hard to rejoice when a part of her had been torn away and was on the way back to Carolina.

Chapter Twenty-Four

Elizabeth stood at her bedroom window and watched the laden cart crawl down the driveway under its load, with Jethro handling the reins and Jacko at his side. Sarah, Deborah and one of the field slaves sat in the back squeezed into the small space that they were sharing with their trunks.

She smiled victoriously. They were finally out of her house and out of her life. She would have preferred if they were leaving in the back of the cart of some cruel owner but at least she didn't have to put up with their hurtful presence any longer. She was now truly mistress of her own house again.

Thomas had said that he would buy two more girls for the house and this time she would make sure that she was there to pick them herself. She did not want another Sarah on her hands.

He had not said so, but she was sure that he had bought Sarah a house and given her some money to start out. She would have a look at the records in his office next time he went out. He would no doubt be going into Town a lot more frequently now. She would be fooling herself if she thought that he had truly given up Sarah.

At least she wouldn't have to endure the humiliation of knowing that they were together in his room.

The house seemed so empty now without Richard around. He had filled up the space and had fit in as if he had always been here. She was sorry that their relationship had become somewhat strained towards the end but she could not condone him bringing that slave girl to sleep in his room with no respect for her or her daughters. What would his mother say if she knew, and he was betrothed at that? Had Barbados corrupted him? It had a way of doing that; to the men especially.

Now that Richard had left and the troublesome slave women were out of the house, she hoped that Thomas would bring William back home. She missed him terribly and she was sure that two years was enough of a punishment for him for no matter what Thomas had called it, she saw it as banishment for defiling his precious Deborah. He had a lot to answer for.

Deborah and Sarah looked around their house in awe. Theirs! It was a quaint little wall and wood house with a shop at the bottom and living quarters above it. There was a small kitchen with a table and four chairs, a small parlor and a living room in addition to the two bedrooms. The master had even bought some basic furniture for it.

They discussed how they could make it attractive with pretty curtains, rugs and a few cushions to add some color to the room. They would have to be quite frugal with the money the master had given them but at least they had saved a little of their own over the years that they could use. Just the freedom to decide how to spend their money was exciting.

Deborah was delighted to find a tiny enclosed yard where she could create a small garden and grow a few herbs. At the back of the shop were a storeroom and two small rooms where Jacko and Mamie, the slaves the master had given them, could sleep.

"I can't believe this Deborah. Two years ago who would have thought that we would be free and have our own house? You realize how things changed ever since Master Richard came?"

Deborah's heart ached at the mention of Richard's name and she wondered how he was and how far from Barbados he had gotten in the four days since he had left. Was he thinking about her? Was he looking forward to getting back to Carolina and would he even remember her in the months and years to come?

"I told him that I felt he was sent here on a mission but he didn't take me seriously. I miss him so much already I don't know how I will get through the next few weeks."

Sarah hugged her and said, "Time will heal your heart, girl."

Deborah knew that but it didn't make her heart hurt any less right now. With a determination that she had learned over the years, she pulled herself together and took her mind from Richard.

"Let's go in the shop and see how we can set it up," she told Sarah. Sarah quickly agreed, excited about buying material and making dresses to sell. She would earn her own money and no one would be able to own her again. Soon she would be able to pay a lawyer to prepare papers to free Mamie and Jacko. Perhaps one day they could buy Cassie's freedom as well. Hattie would have to fend for herself but she was resourceful, she would no doubt be looking to take her place with the master. Sarah felt a twinge of jealousy at the thought but she had no illusions that the master would soon be looking for someone to take to his bed; that was just the way of things.

Looking out from the window of the shop she gazed at the busy street, High Street it was called, with many shops and taverns close together. It was a little over-whelming to think that they would be living among the hustle and bustle of Town. It wasn't the peaceful coun-try life that she was accustomed to but she would rather be free in the city than a slave in the country.

Thomas was surprised at how desolate and lonely he felt without Sarah. It was not that he used to call her for every day, but somehow just knowing that she was avail-able if he called for her was a comfort. Now she was far away in Town and the house seemed empty without her.

The thought entered his mind to go in to Elizabeth but the truth was he felt a deep resentment towards her that left him cold to any attraction he may have had for her in the past. After all, if it had not been for her, Deborah and Sarah would still be there. Perhaps he would send for the newest one, Hattie, to ease his loneliness and take his mind off Sarah for a short while at least.

He missed Richard as well, for he had come to enjoy his company and their talks in his office after dinner most nights. Now that he had gone and Deborah was no longer on the plantation, he would write to William and tell him to come home. He hoped that England had civilized him and that their relationship would improve when he came back. Maybe he would be more interested in helping on the plantation.

He opened a drawer and took out a sheet of paper and dipping his quill in some ink, started the letter right away.

July 7, 1696

The Acreage
St. James

Dear William

I hope this letter finds you in good health. I know that writing is not your strength, and in that you take after me, but thankfully your aunt and your mother have been in communication, so that we have been appraised of any news concerning you and we are pleased with the good reports that we have had.

Your mother misses you a great deal, especially now that your cousin Richard has returned to Carolina. I'm sure she would have mentioned him in her letters. He spent three months with us to learn the workings of the plantation and now he has gone back to run his father's business until he gets married later in the year, after which he will take over his father-in-law's plantation. He is a fine fellow and was a great help to me these last few months.

We have had quite a few changes on the plantation, with some new additions to the slaves. Jacko lost his hand in the mill during harvest this year so I have had to buy a new boy to replace him. We also have a new house girl, Hattie, and I am looking to buy two more since Deborah and Sarah have been freed. Your mother has long desired to have them removed from the house so I recently agreed to her request. I gave Jacko and one of the women from the field to Sarah and they have settled in Town.

We had a good crop this year and profits should be up since the demand for sugar continues to increase in England. You may well be drinking sugar from our own plantation in your tea or coffee every day. The rum is also doing well and continues to expand. I will soon need someone to manage either the rum or the sugar since I can no longer do both.

I believe that the time has come for you to return home and start to apply some of what you learned in England. As I am getting older, I would like you to be more involved in the running of the plantation as it will be yours one day. I will therefore arrange passage for you on my ship at the end of October, once the hurricane season has passed. Please take this opportunity to put your affairs in order so *that you can return then. I look forward to seeing you in a few months and may you have travelling mercies.*

Your father
Thomas Edwards

He had hesitated a few minutes before signing the letter, not really sure how to sign it. What a sad testimony of his relationship with his son. He would have to make a greater effort to spend time getting to know him better when he returned, as he had with Richard.

William read his father's letter and smiled. He was being summoned home. Thank God he would be soon far from this place. The servant girls left him as cold as the miserable weather, the food was tasteless and the people unfriendly. His cousins and their friends thought that they were all above him because he had been born "in the colonies" as they said. He was as much a part of the gentry as they were, after all, his father had been born in England and was one of the elite. It was ironic that they acted so superior when his family was probably far wealthier than theirs.

He wished it was October already because he could not wait to leave. His father had hoped this stay would make him more civilized? Well he certainly knew which wines went with what meal and how to dance all kinds of reels and waltzes so if that was his idea of civilization he was, but he certainly missed the life in Barbados and he couldn't wait to get back to it.

So Sarah and Deborah had managed to persuade his father to free them. He was sure that his mother had wanted them sold rather than freed. Nevertheless, he was glad that they were gone; maybe his mother would now be spared further humiliation, but he didn't hold out much hope that his father had changed. There would soon be another Sarah to take her place. He would bet that his father had bought them the house in Town and it wouldn't be that hard to find them. He would pay them a visit to offer his regards when he got back. He was sure that Deborah was even more beautiful now than when he had left.

He glanced at the letter again. Who was this cousin of his that his father called a "fine young man"? When had he ever called him that? Even without meeting his cousin, he resented him. He had no doubt been sleeping in his bed and taking his place in his father's affections, if he ever had a place in them, he thought bitterly. For all he knew, he probably even had permission to bed Deborah when she had been forbidden to him. It was just as well that he had gone back to Carolina.

Yes, he was looking forward to returning to Barbados. He had paid his dues and he had learnt his lesson. Never again would his father hear of him gambling, drinking and whoring; he would be a lot more circumspect.

Chapter Twenty-Five

Richard's eyes eagerly drank in the sight of the Carolina coastline as the ship sailed towards Charles Town Harbor. Suddenly a feeling of homecoming came over him, nudging away the reluctance to return that he had felt on the voyage.

As the ship sailed into the Harbor he saw with new eyes the similarity between Carolina and Barbados which wasn't surprising since the first settlers had brought a lot of Barbados with them. Maybe that was why he had felt so comfortable there, as if he was home.

Thoughts of Barbados brought Deborah to his mind; not that she was ever that far away. His uncle had been right; it was hard to get Deborah out of his system. It had been a mistake to think that bedding her would have cured him. Now that he was back he needed to focus on his goals again; marry Ann and run her father's plantation.

Shouts of "Heave to" shook him from his reverie and he soon felt the boat slowing down and minutes later the anchor hit bottom. While the crew was busy throwing ropes and securing the sails, he shook the captain's hand and headed towards the gangplank that had been lowered, eager for firm land under his feet. If he didn't have to sail anywhere for a long time he would be happy, which was quite ironic since they owned five ships.

As soon as his trunks were unloaded he hailed a driver with a horse and cart to take him home. He feasted his eyes on the familiar landscape as they made their way to the house. The day was so beautiful that a feeling of wellbeing, such as he had not felt for a long time, lifted his spirits.

He looked forward to seeing his parents and his siblings and catching up on their news. Absence really did make the heart grow fonder, he smiled to himself, and felt some hope that he would feel fonder of Ann as well.

He idly wondered how Anise was and remembered his mother's disapproval of her. If she had not approved of Anise, she would probably have had a fit over Deborah. He smiled as he pictured the two of them, both strong willed, meeting each other. The realization that it would never happen quickly sobered him up.

The door opened soon after he knocked and a broad smile crossed Jackson's face as he saw who was at the door.

"Master Richard! Welcome back," he greeted taking his hat and jacket.

"Thank you Jackson. It's good to be home. Have my trunks taken up to my room. Is the family at home?"

"I'm afraid only Master Charles is here. He is in the office. Your father is out and the Mistress and Miss Charlotte are shopping for the wedding I believe."

Richard headed down the hall to the small office just as the door flew open and Charles appeared in the hallway.

"I thought I heard your voice. Welcome home." Richard hugged him, surprised at how glad he was to see his boyish face.

"It's good to see you, little brother. What has been happening while I was gone?" he asked heading into the office and throwing himself on a leather chair.

Charles spent the next few minutes bringing him up to date about the business and filling him in on the news about their parents and what was happening in town.

"And have you been looking after Ann for me?" Richard asked him. A flush came over Charles' face and he admitted that he had escorted her to a few parties when her parents were not able to go. Richard eyed him thoughtfully, wondering if that was guilt he observed. Maybe they had become closer while he was away.

"I hope you've kept your hands off my fiancée," he teased and was rewarded to see Charles flush again. Maybe something had developed between the two of them, he thought seeing Charles practically squirm under his gaze. As if he had any right to question Charles' behavior given how he'd spent the last three months.

"Of course!" he spluttered. "And what about you? Have you managed to keep your hands off the Barbadian women?" Richard grew serious.

"I wish I had," he replied enigmatically and elaborated no further, even though Charles looked at him curiously.

"And how are Charlotte's plans coming?" He asked, deliberately changing the topic. Charles saw it for what it was but obediently took his lead and filled him in on the upcoming wedding.

"Tell me about Barbados," he insisted afterwards.

"Barbados is a like a beautiful woman. She draws you in and seduces you and before you know it, she has your heart and you never want to leave her." Charles saw the faraway look in his eyes and wondered if he was really talking about Barbados.

"The island is very wealthy and much more developed than Carolina. After all, it was colonized over forty years before us. The planters live like lords. They don't deny themselves anything it seems and I've never seen people consume as much alcohol," he added with a smile, remembering the party that had been held for him.

"It's amazing how similar it is to Carolina, the buildings, the layout of the town, even some of the food. I felt as if I belonged there. Our uncle and aunt were very hospitable and made sure that I felt right at home and that all my needs were met."

"That's good to hear. And what have you learned about keeping slaves?"

"I've learned that it's not always easy," Richard said smiling reminiscently as he thought about his clashes with Deborah, earlier in their relationship. Charles was burning with curiosity. "In fact it can often be very hard," he grew serious remembering Jacko's hand being caught in the mill. "And sometimes very heart wrenching," he added as the face of the slave woman whose daughter had been wrenched from her arms flashed into his mind.

"Heart wrenching?" Charles repeated in disbelief. Surely this was not the same brother who had left Carolina three months ago.

Richard nodded. "I've discovered that slaves are more than just assets to be bought and sold. They are people with emotions and hopes and dreams."

"So does this change what you plan to do with the Carlisle's plantation? Are you still going to use slaves to cultivate rice?"

Richard thought for a long while and finally answered, "To tell the truth, Charles, I just don't know right now."

Charles was stunned. Once again he was struck by the fact that Richard had changed. He didn't know what it was that had changed him but he was going to find out.

Later that day

Richard felt much better after a good meal and a rest in his own bed. He knew that he had probably raised some questions in Charles' mind, who had barely managed to keep himself from trying to pry any information from him. He didn't feel like confiding in him anyway and it was best that he never knew about Deborah, because he would never understand their relationship and would disapprove of it. Anyway it was all in the past now.

He made his way downstairs, noting how their house, although well furnished by Carolina standards looked plain and functional compared to the grandeur of his aunt's house in Barbados. He silently stood in the doorway leading to the patio and had a few minutes to observe his family before they noticed him. They were laughing at something his sister had said and looked happy and content. He wished that he felt the same. He hadn't felt happy and content since he had left Deborah asleep in the bed in Barbados.

"Is this a private party or can anyone join it?" he asked by way of announcing his presence.

All eyes swung around towards him and his sister squealed in delight and she and his mother launched themselves at him, laughing and crying all at once. His father was more controlled but embraced him in a surprising hug that told Richard he was glad to see him.

"You're finally awake! We had to restrain ourselves from waking you up!" his mother admitted.

"I'm so glad you're back. Now I can get married," Charlotte said.

"I'm delighted to see you too, Charlotte," he replied wryly.

"How was Barbados?" His father asked.

"We were so worried about you," interrupted his mother. "We were beginning to wonder if you would make it out alive. First the stomach ailment and then being kicked by the horse and suffering from smoke inhalation. Did anything good happen while you were there?"

"Many good things happened. It may not have sounded like it but it was a wonderful trip. Life changing! Uncle Thomas and Aunt Elizabeth treated me like a son and made me feel very welcome and I learned a lot more than I thought I would. I'll share the stories with you some time, like when one of the slaves got his hand caught in the sugar mill and it had to be cut off."

"Richard! You're joking. That's not the kind of story I want to hear," his sister protested while his mother looked shocked.

"OK, that may be a bit too much for you," he agreed. "I'll tell you about the party that Aunt Elizabeth threw for me that lasted almost twelve hours. Half of Barbados must have been there. Well, at least the planters, their wives and all their delectable daughters."

"Well Ann will be glad to know that you didn't fall in love with any of them and that you're back home in one piece," his mother asserted.

Richard acknowledged that while he was indeed back home, he wasn't so sure if he had not fallen in love with a Barbadian girl after all or if he was in one piece, for he felt as if he had left an important part of himself in Barbados. He was also becoming increasingly concerned that the thought of marrying Ann, even with the incentive of her father's plantation, was now becoming most unappealing.

Richard knew that he should go and see Ann. He could not return to the country and not seek out his fiancée, even though he was reluctant to do so. His reluctance was because he didn't know how he could pretend to be delighted to see her when, in truth, he wasn't.

Putting these thoughts aside, he got into one of their boats the next day and rowed to James Island to the Carlisle's plantation. The physical exercise felt good after having very little to do on board the boat.

The servant who opened the door greeted him warmly and showed him into a small sitting room while she went to let Ann and her parents know that he was there. In minutes the door opened and Ann practically flew into the room, followed by her parents. Ben was leaning heavily on a cane and looked more frail than when he had last seen him.

"Richard!" She exclaimed in delight and threw herself in his arms. Well absence seemed to make her heart fonder for him, he thought in bemusement, and certainly less shy.

"Hello, Ann," he said, hugging her in return and trying not to compare the feel of her in his arms with holding Deborah. He released her to greet her parents who were delighted to see him back safely.

"We'll give you two a few minutes to talk alone," Ben said leaving the room and discreetly closing the door behind them.

Richard's eyes travelled over Ann's perfectly styled hair and her beautiful dress and he couldn't help but compare her to the olive skinned beauty that had turned his life upside down in the last three months. Shaking himself out of his thoughts, he tried to attend to what she was saying, even as he wondered how he would marry this woman and live with her when all he could think about was a beautiful free woman in Barbados who had somehow captured his heart.

"I'm so glad that you're back!" she exclaimed excitedly. "I was getting worried when I didn't hear from you so I was very happy to get your note. Barbados sounds like a wonderful place to visit. Maybe you can take me there some time."

That was the last thing Richard wanted so he made a noncommittal comment. Ann didn't seem to notice as she gushed on telling him about all the things she had done when he was away. He noticed that Charles' name came up quite often and he wondered if Ann had begun to develop feelings for him. The thought gave him some measure of relief although he did not examine why that was. After a while her constant chatter began to wear on him and he told her that he really had to get to work to see what had transpired in his absence.

He sensed that Ann was waiting for him to kiss her and any man would have been happy to oblige her. Any man but him, that is. This was a very disturbing turn of events; he was reluctant to kiss his fiancée! That did not bode well for the fact that they were supposed to get married before the end of the year. In the end he gave her a brief kiss on the lips and quickly headed for the door, trying not to look at her confused face.

Chapter Twenty-Six

August 10, 1696

St. Michael's Town
Barbados

Thomas knocked at the door and looked around while he waited for it to be opened. The sun was beginning to go down since he had left home in the afternoon with the plan to spend the weekend in town. Elizabeth had been less than pleased when he'd told her not to expect him back until Sunday evening.

He could see that in the month Sarah and Deborah had lived here they had done a lot of improvements to the property. Down below in the garden were barrels cut in half with small plants in them which he assumed were Deborah's herbs. They had also planted some flowers which added color to the well kept yard.

The door opened and Sarah peeped around it. Her face broke into a welcoming smile and he stepped inside as she opened the door wider to let him in. She looked as happy to see him as he was to see her.

"I missed you Sarah." He pulled her into his arms for a hug, surprised at how good it was to hold her and see her so happy and content.

"I missed you too Master Thomas," she said taking his hat and coat and the small bag that he had brought. "You spending the weekend?"

"Yes and you don't have to call me Master any more Sarah," he reminded her.

"It's hard to change, Thomas," she said deliberately, smiling again. "May I get you a drink or something to eat?"

"No, thanks Sarah, I don't want anything just yet. Only you," he said, pulling her into his arms again. The sound of someone entering the hallway stopped him and he looked over Sarah's shoulder to see Deborah looking somewhat embarrassed to see her mother in his arms.

"Hello Deborah," he greeted, releasing Sarah reluctantly. Thomas had never embraced Sarah in front of Deborah and it was strange to see.

"Hello, Master Thomas. How have you been?"

"I've been better. I missed your mother terribly," he confessed, unable to resist pulling Sarah to his side again. He realized that it was true. He had called for Hattie a couple of times in the month but she was not Sarah.

"You want to see what we did with the house?" asked Sarah excitedly.

"By all means," he said.

The ladies proudly showed him the living room, the small parlor and the kitchen which they had decorated with curtains, rugs and colorful cushions and then took him downstairs to see the shop which was only partly stocked since they were waiting for their first shipment of goods to arrive.

"Have you made contact with the merchants I suggested through my lawyer?" he asked Deborah.

"Yes, we made some orders so we're waiting for them to come in but my mother bought some material from one of the shops and has been sewing already and people are beginning to come in and buy whatever teas I have available. I also planted some herbs."

"Good, good. Where are Jacko and Mamie?"

"We gave them the evening off." Thomas looked disapprovingly at them but kept his mouth shut since he did not have the right to tell them anything anymore.

"It all looks very nice," he complimented instead. "Let me see what you did with your room," he hinted to Sarah. Deborah smiled slightly and excused herself, saying that she would go and start dinner.

A while later Sarah lay with her head on Thomas' chest, idly playing with the graying hair that liberally covered it.

"Thomas?"

"Hmm?" he responded lazily.

"I want to ask you something."

"What is it?" He waited.

"How is it that when you owned us you were so good to me and to Deborah but at the same time you could order one of the field slaves to be whipped for running away or for stealing or sell one of their children without thinking how they felt?"

Thomas was silent for such a long time that Sarah thought he wouldn't answer. Had she gone too far with her questions? She started to move from his arms but he tightened them around her, keeping her where she was.

"I don't know how to answer that Sarah. Thinking how they felt never came into it. They are just slaves. You and Deborah are different. You are more like one of us."

"We're all the same," she said quietly. "Maybe it's just that when you don't know people, when you don't mix with them, they seem like they different. But we're all the same," she repeated.

"The pain I would feel if you had taken Deborah away from me and sold her is the pain any mother would feel, whether she work in the house or in the field, whether she is pure black or she mixed with white. And the pain Deborah felt when Jethro flogged her is the same pain that the field slaves feel when they get flogged."

Thomas thought about that for a long time. Years of prejudice battled with the truth of what she was saying and finally he admitted, "I suppose you're right, Sarah."

"I know I right."

Two months later

Deborah looked around the shop with apprecia-tion. Deborah's Health and Beauty Shop and Sarah's

Sewing Emporium were doing well. She had just got a shipment of new herbal teas which she displayed in large glass jars ready to sell in smaller portions to her customers. The soaps she had made would soon need to be restocked as there were only a few bars left and she was expecting a shipment from France. She smiled at that. Who would have believed that she, who had been a slave just months ago, would now be ordering soaps and perfumes from France for her own shop?

At first they were regarded with a bit of wariness by the merchants on their street. After all it was not common for two free colored women to own a shop in Town. However one day, a distraught woman had run into the shop asking for herbs to help her daughter who was suffering from a terrible tummy ache and nothing would help her. Deborah made up a small packet of herbs and gave her instructions how to prepare the tea. The next day the woman came back to thank her and tell her that the tea had worked. After that incident the merchants' wives began to patronize their shop. They had also got to know some of the slaves of the merchants in Town and a few free colored people that they could count on one hand.

Jacko and Mamie were a tremendous help, even though Jacko only had the one hand and Deborah was glad that the master had insisted on giving them to Sarah. It was not that she liked the idea of owning slaves but she could not imagine how they would handle the heavy lifting or how she would have time to make her soaps and work in the shop as well without them.

Deborah was just about to lock the door for the day when Jacko came in from running some errands and said: "Mistress Sarah, I just heard that they having a Quaker meeting tomorrow night at the Brown's boarding house."

"It must be like the one Jethro told us about," she said.

"Yes. A man and woman named George and Margaret Baxter are staying with them and they tell me to invite you all to the meeting tomorrow night. It's to start at nine so that some of the slaves could sneak out when the masters gone to sleep."

"So late? You think it safe to go Jacko?" asked Sarah.

"Yes. I can take you all."

Deborah was curious to hear more from this group of people who were bold enough to speak out against the treatment of slaves and she was happy to know that they were being included by their new friends. She hoped they could explain more about what Jethro had told them. Now that she was free from slavery, she was more willing to hear about being free from sin.

"Let's go and hear them, ma," she urged. Sarah was reluctant since she didn't want to get into any trouble.

"Alright, we will go."

The Next Night

Jacko, Deborah, Sarah and Mamie walked quietly down the road to the Brown's boarding house. Since it was late and a day in the week the roads were fairly quiet and thankfully there was no moon to draw attention to their presence.

Deborah and Sarah were a bit nervous as they did not usually go out at night. In fact this was the first time that they had been on the streets after dark and they were glad that Jacko was with them. His size was enough to deter anyone from attacking them, even with the one hand.

Nevertheless Deborah was glad when they arrived at the boarding house and knocked. One of the Brown's servants opened the door and led them into a large parlor that was lit by several lamps and had about fifteen people already there sitting around on sofas and chairs that were pulled from the dining room while some of the slaves sat on the floor. They were a mixed group, a few whites, about ten black slaves and about four free coloreds including them.

Doreen Brown introduced them to the Baxters and Deborah and Sarah were surprised when the attractive, well dressed white couple, came and hugged them warmly in greeting.

They shared that they were on their way to America and were catching a boat the next day. Deborah wondered if they were going to Carolina. The thought brought Richard back to mind, with an ache that dulled a bit more each day. She would never forget the time that they had together but she knew that she had to move on with her life. After all he might already be married and she would probably never see him again.

After waiting a few minutes for any latecomers to arrive, they began to sing a hymn softly which Deborah and Sarah had never heard before, but felt soothed by the quiet song.

After the hymn, George began by saying: "One of the main reasons the Quakers are not welcome in Barbados is because we do not condone slavery. The Anglican Church has not done anything to help the slaves and in fact they have sought to justify it by quoting from the Bible where Noah cursed Canaan, the son of Ham."

"Who is Ham?" Sarah asked.

"Do you know anything of the Bible?" The wife asked kindly.

"Not a lot. When the master's children were taught I used to hear a little of it."

They went on to explain about Noah and that Ham was one of Noah's sons who did something that was so abominable to him that Noah cursed Ham's son, Canaan and said he would be a slave to his brothers.

"Many people believe that Ham was cursed and since Africans are one of the races that descended from Ham, they apply the curse to that race and that is what they have used to justify slavery. However Noah cursed Canaan and the African race did not descend from Canaan."

"God loves all of us, whether we are slave or free, black or white. He loves you so much that he sent his son Jesus to die for you so that you can be free."

"But I free now," insisted one woman. She was one of the few free colored women who lived in the city.

"Some of you may have been set free by your master; others may have had to sell themselves to buy their freedom and thank God, you are now free from slavery." Deborah's guilt made her feel that they were talking directly to her and inside she cringed in shame because she was one of those who had sold themselves for freedom.

"But you are only free from one master."

"What you mean?" the woman asked.

"Anyone who sins is a slave to sin." Deborah and Sarah looked at each other. That is what Jethro had told them.

"It is the masters who are slaves to sin," accused a dark skinned woman. "That is why they so evil!" she declared. There were nods of agreement all around from the other slaves.

"But it is not only them. We are all slaves to sin. In the past some of you women may have been forced to sleep with your master even if he had a wife and some of you may be doing it now." A number of women, Sarah included, lowered their eyes.

"I'm sure your conscience told you it was wrong. Before, you may not have had any choice but for those of you who are free, you do. Think about how their wives must have felt knowing that their husbands were sleeping with you. I'm sure that many of them tried to take that out on you in many horrible ways and you may have hated them for it, and understandably so, but we're supposed to love our enemies," said Margaret.

"That is a hard thing," said one man who still bore the stripes of his beatings on his back.

"Yes," agreed the husband. "But the good news is that you don't have to do it alone. God will help you."

"You said that Jesus died so that we can be free. How is that?" asked Deborah since Jethro had not been able to explain it to her satisfaction before.

"The Bible says that the wages of sin is death. But rather than us receiving the wages of our sin, Jesus died in our place and received the wages for us. This was his gift to us and if you believe that and accept his gift you will be free and sin shall no longer be your master."

They then shared a story of a woman who was caught in adultery and a crowd wanted to stone her for her sin so they brought her to Jesus to see what he would do. Jesus challenged any of them who had no sin to throw the first stone and when everyone left, recognizing that they all had sin in their lives, Jesus told her to go and sin no more. His love for her gave him compassion so rather than condemn her, he gave her the opportunity to change the way she lived.

Go and sin no more. Those words reverberated in both Deborah and Sarah as they left the meeting with much on their minds to think about.

Chapter Twenty-Seven

As Deborah locked the door behind them, Sarah headed to the kitchen where she lit the fire and put on the kettle to make some herbal tea to soothe her head. Thoughts were swirling around in it and giving her a headache. Deborah joined her and asked how she was when she saw her rubbing her temples.

"I'm real confused, child. Long ago my mother told me that she refused to sleep with an overseer and she got whipped for that and then it didn't matter if she refused or not because he took what he wanted and that is how she had me. When I first went to the plantation I was innocent so when Master Thomas told me to come to his room, I was frightened to go but I was even more frightened that he would flog me so I went."

"He was good to me and I liked to be with him. To tell the truth I never thought about how the mistress felt. Then she started to treat me bad and the worse she treated me, the gladder I was that he preferred me to her."

"Ma, you didn't have any choice. But I had a choice. Richard gave me a choice and I didn't have to take it. I didn't have to go to his bed. I knew that he was engaged and I knew that it was wrong and I still did it. I'm worse than you."

"We both sinners. There is no bad sin and worse sin, all is the same. If I want to serve Master Jesus I goin' have to stop serving Master Thomas because one of the things they said is that you can't serve two masters." Sarah sounded grieved at the thought of giving up Thomas and Deborah realized that she genuinely loved him.

Deborah could understand how she felt. For the first time she was glad that Richard had gone back to Carolina so that she would not have to make the hard decisions that her mother was now grappling with.

The water began to boil in the kettle and she got up to make them both a cup of chamomile tea which would help them to sleep. She added some skullcap to Sarah's to ease her headache which was probably caused by tension or perhaps it was guilt. Her own guilt plagued her. She had not been interested in hearing Jethro when he told them they could be free from sin. The only thing she had cared about was being free from slavery. Now as she sipped her tea her conscience reminded her of the things she had done, the hatred she had had in her heart, especially for William, choosing to sleep with Richard for her freedom and she knew that she had to deal with them if she wanted to be really free.

Sarah dreaded Thomas' next trip to town. He had not been for a few weeks now and she knew that he would soon be coming back. Although the Quakers had left, the group had taken to meeting at the Brown's and talking about some of the things they had learned and some of the ones who could read, like Deborah, read the Bible to them.

She knew that she couldn't continue to entertain Thomas in her bed, not if she wanted to do what was right. Why was this so hard? She knew that most masters in Barbados bedded their slaves and many also had free women as mistresses. These women often lived in Town and its surroundings and the men frequently came to spend time with them, as Thomas did with her. But just because everyone was doing it did not make it right. She prayed for strength to resist him even as she longed to see him again. Unless he was prepared to just visit her as a friend, she would not be able to see him anymore.

Sarah felt as if her thoughts conjured up Thomas when he appeared in the shop before noon the next day. He looked so handsome that she devoured him with her eyes even as she felt a pang in her heart that she could no longer have him in that way. He took the key to the door upstairs so that he could put down his bag before he went about his business in town and when he returned it, she could see him looking at her with anticipation.

A sudden anxiety gripped her and she could barely concentrate on dealing with her customers that day. She didn't know how she would tell him that she could no longer sleep with him. After all she had never refused him before but now she was free and she had a choice. She considered using Deborah's excuse but knew that she would only be delaying doing what she had to do. She had begun to feel peace and joy such as she never had before in her life and she didn't want to lose that so she would have to make the hard decision.

Deborah saw how distracted her mother was and knew that she was thinking about what she would tell Thomas that evening. She didn't envy her as she knew how hard it would be. Why was life always so hard? When would things ever work out for them? She would love her mother to find a free man and get married since she was still young and beautiful; someone who would love her and appreciate her and be free to do so. She knew that Jethro had a soft spot for her mother. Maybe Master Thomas would free him and they could get married. She would pray about it. She had no desire to pray for anyone for herself as her heart was still bruised from losing Richard.

By the time evening came and they closed up the shop Sarah was in turmoil. Thomas had not returned yet and for that she was glad. It gave her some time to freshen up and prepare herself to talk to him. She prayed for the right words to say and she hoped that he would understand.

When Sarah greeted Thomas later that evening and led him into the kitchen where she watched him eat the meal she had prepared she could hardly sit still and kept getting up to fix things that did not need fixing.

"What's the matter, Sarah?" asked Thomas with concern. He had never seen her so jittery.

"Let's go into the parlor so that we can talk," she suggested. Deborah had headed for her room after coming upstairs so that her mother and Thomas would have some privacy.

Thomas sat in a two-seater chair but rather than sit next to him Sarah sat in a straight backed chair close by.

"About a month ago, Deborah and I went to a Quaker meeting," she began.

"Quaker meeting? Those people are nothing but troublemakers," Thomas exclaimed.

"You may call them troublemakers but they told us the truth and they made us realize that how we were living was not right." Thomas already sensed what was coming and he braced himself.

"I never really thought about how the mistress must have felt about me and you. But I know now that it was wrong and she only treated me bad because she felt bad. I know that if you were my husband and you didn't come in to me but you called for Hattie or Cassie, I would feel real bad." The pang of conscience that stirred in Thomas as Sarah spoke became a full force by the time she had finished. He could say nothing. There was no argument for the truth.

"So what are you saying Sarah?" he asked sadly, already knowing the answer.

"I real sorry Thomas, but I can't sleep with you any-more. I know that it wrong. But you welcome to visit us whenever you in town. I can sleep with Deborah and you can have my room unless you want to stay at a boarding house."

Thomas felt a deep sadness that their almost twenty year old relationship was finished; at least the way it used to be. He knew that there was no point trying to change Sarah's mind because he could see that she was as saddened as he was and he knew that it could not have been an easy decision.

"OK, Sarah. I will have to accept that this is what you want. As long as you know that if you ever change your mind, I will be here. I would still like to come and see you and Deborah and make sure that you are alright." Sarah nodded. She couldn't speak past the lump of emotion in her throat. All she could do was pray that God would take away the pain in her heart.

October 12, 1696

Charles Town
Carolina

The Fairfax family was dining alone for a change. Richard was relieved, as he had no interest in attending another party or entertaining friends. In fact he had begged off many invitations, insisting that Charles escort Ann in his place. His mother, in particular, was less than pleased but he really did not feel like humoring her. He was surprised that rather than getting dimmer with time, he missed Deborah as acutely as the day he left and he therefore had little patience for Ann and her constant desire for social interaction.

He had been to see Anise once, and that was only to bring closure to their relationship since he had no desire for her. So here he was, being without a woman for almost three months and no desire for any other than Deborah. When he thought back to the conversation he had had with Charles months ago, when he scoffed at love, he felt that his own words had come back to taunt him.

He had thrown himself back into his work and at Ben's urging had also started investigating the equipment and manpower he would need to begin cultivating rice. They had even started to prepare the budget but it did not give him the excitement that it would have a few months before.

He did his best to avoid being alone with Ann and he hoped that she believed his hints that it was because he was tempted to pre-empt their marriage vows when in fact it was quite the opposite. He did not know how he would marry her and if the truth be told, he had recently begun to ask himself if he could marry her. The idea depressed him and he felt as if he would be giving up his freedom. But freedom to do what? He would have the freedom to run her father's plantation as he wanted, so what was it that he was really afraid of giving up?

"Richard," his mother interrupted his thoughts. "Don't you think it's time to set a date for your wedding? You have been at home almost three months now and I have not heard any talk of it from you. In fact one would think that Charles was Ann's fiancé since he seems to escort her about more than you. What has gotten into you? You have not seemed yourself since you came back from Barbados. All you do is work and skulk about in your room."

"Mother, I do not skulk about in my room. I am usually so tired after working that I prefer to go to bed early rather than go to the endless social events that you ladies seem to love to attend."

"If I didn't know better," chimed in Charlotte who was visiting with her husband of just one month, "I would say that he is heartsick."

"That would presume that he has a heart," derided Charles who resented how badly Richard had treated Ann since his return. Of course it was to his benefit since she poured out all her concerns on him and he was happy to comfort her.

"I would appreciate if you two would desist from speaking about me as if I am not present," Richard admonished them. Truth be told he did feel heartsick as Charlotte claimed, but Charles was also right when he said that he had no heart because he had left it in Barbados.

"But it's true Richard. Now that Charlotte has mentioned it, you do seem to have the symptoms of someone who is sick at heart. Tell me you didn't fall in love with a girl in Barbados as poor Ann feared."

Richard wondered what they would do if they knew the truth. What was the truth anyway? All he knew was that there was an emptiness where his heart should have been and he wondered if running the Carlisle's plantation could really fill it? Could he settle for Ann after he had been with Deborah? He didn't know what he wanted anymore. Life had been so simple before he went to Barbados. He wished for that simplicity again. Throwing down his napkin he muttered his excuses, pushed back his chair from the table and stalked away.

Even his father, who had not got drawn into the conversation, looked up from his plate in surprise and asked, "What in the world has gotten into that boy?"

"I would guess that one or more of you has hit upon the truth," offered Charlotte's husband. "I think I will go and have a man to man talk with him," he said pushing back his own chair.

Richard sat on the patio, glad for the cover of darkness to hide his face when he saw Albert coming out to join him. Although they were good friends and he knew that he was concerned about him, he didn't feel like talking. He hadn't even worked out what was going on in his head yet; far less to discuss it with someone else. Or maybe what he needed was an objective opinion.

"I must admit that I have never seen you like this, Richard, and we've known each other since we were boys. What's this about?" Albert came straight to the point. Richard had always liked that about him.

He hesitated for a few moments, debating how much to tell him and then made his decision.

"This is not even to be shared with your wife," he warned Albert who nodded, more curious than ever.

"My uncle owned a slave called Deborah. She is actually his daughter who he had with a mulatto slave so she is a quadroon. She is the most beautiful woman I know. From the time I saw her I wanted her but my uncle said that she was off limits."

"Eventually he agreed to sell her to me. I bought her for £20, which was a bargain because many planters wanted to buy her and would have paid handsomely."

"You bought her?" exclaimed Albert. Richard ignored his outburst.

"I promised her that if she came to my bed willingly I would free her when I left Barbados. I ended up freeing her a month before I left but she stayed with me, even though she was free to go."

"Why did you free her before you had to?"

"I don't know. It was her eighteenth birthday and I wanted to give her something memorable. Something that would be precious to her."

"You love her."

"What makes you say that?"

"It's obvious. No man would free a woman he still wanted, knowing she might leave, unless he loved her."

"Well if this empty feeling means that I love her, then yes I do. I never thought I would hear myself admit that."

"So that's why you're so miserable."

"Yes. Charlotte is very perceptive," Richard admitted. "So now I have to decide if I'm going to go ahead and marry Ann and run her father's plantation or if I should take a chance that Deborah will have me and go back to Barbados."

"What will you do in Barbados?"

"There are a number of options. My uncle has offered me a position on his plantation if I want it. Rather than using the agent there I can set up an agency in Barbados and expand our shipping routes and cargo, if my father does not disown me because of this," he said half-seriously, knowing that the alliance between the two families was very important to him.

"And what will you do about this Deborah? Do you plan to marry her?"

"I don't know. I do not even know what the laws are in Barbados about marriage between races, although I know that it's illegal here in most states."

"Are you sure she's still available? And does she feel the same way about you?"

"I don't know, but I need to go back to Barbados and find out."

"What will you tell Ann?" Richard paused. He hadn't thought that far ahead. He had entered into an agreement with Ann's father. He couldn't just cancel their engagement. His head hurt just from thinking about the situation. It would make things so much easier if Ann decided that she didn't want to marry him. Was that what he had been hoping by ignoring her and pushing her and Charles together? He owed it to her to talk to her.

"I don't know," he finally answered Albert's question. "But it's time I had a talk with her."

Next Day

Once his mind was made up, Richard wasted no time in seeking out Ann. He had planned to take her on a picnic but the day had turned nasty and it was pouring rain.

It perfectly fit his mood as he knocked at the Carlisle's front door. He would have preferred not to have this meeting here but it could not be helped. He needed to have this resolved today.

Ann was beautifully dressed when she joined him in the parlor. It was as if she made sure that she looked her best for him.

"You look lovely, Ann," he complimented sincerely.

"Thank you, Richard," she said sitting down on a blue velvet sofa. Richard remained standing, uncharacteristically nervous. He didn't know where to start.

"I have hardly seen you since you came back," Ann observed. "Thankfully Charles has been very good to escort me about. I have grown very fond of him." He waited for her to continue but she didn't say anything. She was not going to make this easy for him.

"I'm glad to hear that. I always felt that you two would make a better couple."

"I did not say that we were a couple. Is that what you were hoping?" Ann's voice had taken on a hard tone and he really couldn't blame her. She sounded more mature than she had before.

Rather than answer her question, he asked instead, "Do you remember when I was leaving for Barbados and you warned me not to fall in love with any Barbadian girls?" He paused, not sure how to proceed without hurting her feelings.

"I'm afraid that I did not listen to your warning. I am very sorry, Ann, I certainly did not plan on it happening and it was the furthest thing from my mind but it happened. However, I want you to know that I will not renege on our agreement."

Ann's face turned white. "Do you really expect that I would marry you, knowing that you love someone else?" she asked angrily. Pulling the ring from her finger she extended it to him. "I knew that you never really loved me, not as Charles does, but I had wanted you from the time I was a girl and I thought it would be enough but I have grown up in the last three months and I realize that it's not. I deserve more and I believe that Charles can give me that and wants to; so you can have your freedom. I just wish I hadn't wasted so much of my life pining after you. You were not worth it." Richard could not debate that. He knew that he deserved her ire for the way he had treated her.

"You are right. You deserve a lot better than me," he agreed taking the ring. "You and Charles have my blessing, not that you need it. Thank you for releasing me from our agreement." Ann did not respond so Richard bowed slightly to her before heading for the door. As he closed it behind him, a feeling of freedom that he had never before experienced came over him and he wondered if this was what Deborah had felt like when he gave her the manumission papers. He only hoped that he had not thrown away his dream to go after her, only to find that she did not return his feelings.

Chapter Twenty-Eight

October 14, 1696

Charles Town
Carolina

Dear Uncle Thomas

I hope that you are well and that all is at peace in the house now. Forgive me for taking so long to write this letter but I know that you will understand since we share the same dislike of letter writing. So you must know that I have something of utmost importance to communicate.

First of all I am long overdue in expressing my gratitude for the way you and Aunt Elizabeth welcomed me in Barbados and made my stay so enjoyable. To tell the truth, apart from learning even more than I expected, the trip completely changed the course of my life, as this letter will explain.

When you told me I would be unable to get Deborah out of my system I never considered that it would be true, but now I humbly admit that you were right. Once

I returned to Carolina and saw Ann I was reluctant to go through with our engagement but I was prepared to honor my word. Nevertheless I had to be honest with her and let her know that I had fallen in love with someone else (yes I do love Deborah) and gave her the choice to proceed with the engagement if she still wanted to. Thankfully she did not and she and Charles, to whom she became quite close when I was in Barbados, will soon be announcing their engagement, for which I am extremely grateful as it eases my conscience considerably.

Once my father recovered from the news of my broken engagement and was happy that the Fairfaxs and Carlisles would still form an alliance through the marriage of Charles and Ann, he did not disown me. I was therefore emboldened to suggest to him that I should move to Barbados and take over the agency for our shipping, with the plan to expand our routes and the cargo that we carry as I have been discontented with our agent's performance for some time now. I obviously had to explain my desire to return to Barbados so soon but I did not go into any details about Deborah and as far as all are concerned, I have fallen in love with the daughter of a plantation owner, which in fact I have.

I am therefore pleased to let you know that I will be setting sail for Barbados once again in about three weeks and I would be grateful if you could appoint an agent to identify a house in St. Michael's Town or its environs for me to rent initially or possibly buy later depending on how things turn out.

I need to see Deborah and hopefully be able to persuade her of my feelings, trusting that hers have not changed, *although she never actually said that she loved me. I do not know of the laws in Barbados concerning marriage between races but it is my deepest desire to marry her and if the laws do not permit, then I am prepared to move to England to do so; if she will have me that is. You see how this girl has bewitched me. I hope therefore that she has not met anyone else; otherwise I would have turned my whole life upside down for nothing. Fate surely cannot be that cruel.*

Please do not tell her of my plans as I would like to surprise her when I get there, hoping that I am not the one who will receive an unpleasant surprise.

Give my regards to Aunt Elizabeth and the girls and I look forward to seeing you all when I reach Barbados.

Your faithful nephew
Richard

When he had left Carolina for Barbados six months ago, he had never anticipated this. In fact if anyone had told him he would fall in love with a slave, granted that she was now a free woman, and leave everything to pursue her, he would have laughed in their face. He had only known Deborah for three months. How had she made such an impression on him that he would give up everything he was familiar with to be with her?

His mother was still lamenting the fact that he had just come home and was going to be leaving again, this time for good. Only the realization that she was not losing Ann as a daughter-in-law and that she would soon have another wedding to plan, soothed some of her distress.

Richard was happy that her attention had turned from him. As it was, he didn't want to answer too many questions about Deborah, but he could honestly say that she was the daughter of a plantation owner. That she was once a slave and Thomas' daughter, they didn't have to know yet. Needless to say, if she did agree to marry him they would eventually find out about her ancestry. He wondered what they would think of his uncle when they knew.

Now that he had written the letter to his uncle and started putting things into motion, anticipation filled him so that he could hardly contain himself. If all went according to plan, he would see Deborah in less than two months. He was taking a huge gamble and he could only pray that it would pay off.

He was not even sure what he would say to her. Suppose she did not feel the same way? Then again she could have left as soon as he had given her the manumission papers but she stayed. Surely that counted for something. But he'd been gone for more than three months. What if she thought that he was married by now and was involved with someone else, or worse yet, even married? The very thought of Deborah with another man was enough to make him ill.

What a hypocrite he was! When he was with her in Barbados, he was betrothed to Ann and Anise was still his mistress and here he was sick at the thought of her with someone else. How love had transformed him. He had no interest in Anise or any other woman; only

Deborah and he wanted to spend the rest of his life with her, if she would have him.

November 6, 1696

The Acreage
Barbados

Thomas read Richard's letter again in disbelief, then he chuckled to himself. He was happy that Richard was returning to Barbados but he wasn't sure how successful he would be in courting Deborah, given how she and Sarah had changed. There were no laws prohibiting them from getting married in Barbados and while marriage between races was rare, theirs would not be the first, if Deborah accepted him that is. He knew of at least one documented marriage between a black man and a white woman which had taken place several years before in the '80s, if he remembered rightly.

From the date of the letter he worked out that Richard should arrive in about two weeks barring any delays. William would also have set sail from England and would reach Barbados by the end of the month. He didn't hold out much hope for a close friendship between them because William would no doubt resent Richard's relationship with Deborah who had been forbidden to him and Richard probably would not forgive him for taking Deborah's innocence.

So much had changed in the last month since Sarah had ended their physical relationship. He had given much thought to what she had said about his treatment of the slaves and the way Elizabeth must have felt about their relationship. It had caused him to stop sleeping with Hattie and Cassie and instead he was now thinking about acquiring a free colored mistress near Town. The habit was hard to break, but at least Elizabeth would no longer be humiliated in her own house. He had even found the desire to visit her room one night and she had not turned him away.

As for the slaves, he would try not to separate families but he didn't see how they could get them to work without the threat of the whip. It wasn't as if they overdid it anyway, not like some of the other plantations. Surely Sarah didn't expect him to change something that had been a part of plantation life for years.

He would have to go into town next week to hire an agent to start looking for a house for Richard so he would pay a visit to Sarah and let her know the changes he had made. He would feel out Deborah as well and see if she still had any feelings for Richard or if she was seeing someone else. It was the least he could do for the poor boy.

November 13, 1696

The last business Thomas carried out in Town was with the housing agent who he gave instructions to find a few comfortable and attractive houses, either in or within a reasonable distance from Town, to show Richard when he came. Outside of Town might be better so that the lot could be of a size to allow Deborah to plant herbs and other things if they married. Maybe he was getting ahead of himself, he thought as he headed for Sarah and Deborah's shop.

He was looking forward to seeing Sarah even if there could be nothing physical between them and he enjoyed talking to Deborah who he had found to be quite an astute business woman, as he had known she could be given the opportunity. People only needed a chance to use their talents and with a little education they could do anything they put their minds to, provided they were willing to work hard. He hoped that William had found his talent and that he would use what he had learned to benefit the plantation. After all, it would be his someday.

Sarah and Deborah welcomed him warmly and he was quick to let Sarah know that he was staying at a boarding house. He was happy to see her and couldn't help but give her a hug which she returned but quickly pulled away.

"And how is business?" he asked as they all sat together in the parlor.

"It is growing steadily," reported Deborah with a pleased smile.

"I may soon need someone to help me sew because I'm getting real busy," Sarah said happily.

"That is good news indeed. You'll be glad to hear that I took what you said to heart and I will not bed any of the house slaves, out of respect for Elizabeth."

Sarah's eyes misted up to hear that Thomas actually listened to her and had acted on what she said. "I'm glad to hear that Thomas. You know the good book says that a foolish son is his father's ruin and a quarrelsome wife is like a constant dripping so the mistress should not be quarrelsome anymore."

Thomas laughed. "Thankfully the constant dripping has stopped and I don't want it to start back. William is coming back soon and that should make Elizabeth happy. I only hope that he is no longer foolish."

Deborah tensed at the news and then forced herself to relax. After all she was free now; William had no power over her.

"What about you, Deborah? Have the men in Town been accosting you?"

She smiled and said, "I'm not interested in getting into a relationship with anyone right now. Anyway any man that I get involved with will have to share my beliefs and I have not come across any of them yet." She would have liked to ask him if he had heard from Richard and if he was married yet but she could not bring herself to do it; she would rather not know.

"And you Sarah?" Thomas asked, not really wanting to hear the answer.

"I'm not interested in that kind of thing," she said. "I'm happy doing what I'm doing right now." Thomas was selfishly glad to hear that. If he couldn't have her, he didn't want anyone else to either.

He couldn't help but feel Deborah out so he casually said, "I recently got a letter from Richard." Deborah's head flew up but then she caught herself and carefully arranged a blank look on her face, seeming to brace herself for what he would say next. "He has not married as yet," he added, carefully watching her face. Although her expression did not change, her body relaxed as if that news had brought some measure of relief.

"I would have thought he would have been married by now," commented Deborah quietly.

"He didn't say but maybe they're planning a Christmas wedding," Thomas said, again watching her face closely.

Deborah forced a smile and said, "That would be nice." Thomas was sure she was lying but he said nothing; he had found out all that he needed to know. Richard appeared to be still very much in Deborah's heart but he was going to have to make some changes to his life if he wanted to stay there.

Chapter Twenty-Nine

November 16, 1696
Somewhere on the Caribbean Sea

The small cabin was lit up by a flash of lightning seconds before a crack of thunder shook the ship that was already being tossed around like driftwood on the sea. Richard sat up abruptly, disoriented and unsure what had awakened him. Before he could figure out what was happening, the boat was tossed almost on its side by a massive wave, slamming him against the wall. Pain shot down his arm from his shoulder that had taken the brunt of the impact.

Rain and sea water pelted the porthole and as another flash of lightning lit up the sky he could see the rain pouring down in sheets from the turbulent sky. Tugging on a pair of boots he lurched towards the door as the ship continued to buck and weave under the pounding of the merciless sea.

The cabin door was wrenched from his hand by the sudden roll of the ship and he had to grab the doorjamb before he fell back. He stepped out cautiously into the dark corridor and braced himself against the walls. The floor was slippery from sea water that had forced its way down the companionway as waves broke over the ship.

He struggled to keep his balance as another wave hit the ship and he had just begun to climb up the ladder when water poured down on his face. Spewing salt water from his nose and mouth, he briefly released one hand to wipe his eyes and push his now sopping hair from his face. The sway of the ship made him grab the ladder quickly and he managed to climb onto the deck which was like a cold, wet version of hell.

The men were just blurry shapes in the driving rain, struggling to batten down whatever they could without being blown overboard. As another flash illuminated the sky he could see that the masts been stripped of their sails and looked like skeletons. He could just make out the captain as he shouted orders hoarsely over the howling wind and the driving rain.

Richard strained against the wind which fought to suck him overboard, and clinging to the rigging he struggled over to the captain. Sea water surged over the side of the ship, stinging his eyes and dousing him afresh, while trying to dislodge his hold from the rigging. He shivered in his thin, saturated clothes. Who would have thought that just hours ago they were sailing under a hot Caribbean sun?

"Captain," he shouted above the wind, "What's the damage? Are all the men accounted for?"

"You shouldn't be up here, boss," he shouted. "The men are fine and we managed to get most of the sails in before it hit hard but the mizzen was ripped and the mast is broken. But if we get through this we should be alright with the rest of sails. You best go below deck. There's nothing you can do now but pray."

Richard slapped him on his back in encouragement and fought his way back to the ladder. The stairs were slippery from the sea water and as he climbed down, the ship slipped into a deep trough between two waves and the sudden drop caused Richard's hands to slip. He tried in vain to reclaim his grip on the stairs but he slid the rest of the way, landing in a painful heap at the bottom of the stairs after hitting his shoulders several times of the way down. He groaned in agony as the shoulder which had been bruised before was subjected to further injury. Pulling himself up with one hand he leaned against the side of the hallway to catch his breath before easing his way back to his cabin where he collapsed on the bed.

Was he to die on this ship? Would he ever see Deborah again? As the ship bucked and tossed from side to side, he began to pray for deliverance from the torture of the storm and for the safety of the crew and to see Deborah one more time. A picture of the first time he had seen her flitted through his mind. He had wanted her then. He still wanted her.

The boat lurched again, tossing him around and making him feel helpless and trapped. He had no control over the wind and waves that were battering the boat. Was that how Deborah felt as a slave? As if she had no control over her life? He had not really understood how she felt, until now.

He remembered how he had demanded that she get him a meal on her day off when he had found her reading by the grove. How could he have been so selfish? But then when had he not been selfish? When had he not pursued what he wanted, at all costs? He had pushed Deborah until he finally got her into his bed and he knew, initially anyway, that it was only because he had held the keys to her freedom. He had asked her if it would be so bad to be owned by him, as if she was a horse or a mule. No wonder she had hated him. He had seen nothing wrong with owning another person, as if they did not have the same soul as he did. What a detestable creature he was.

"Forgive me," he whispered to God. "Wash me thoroughly from mine iniquity and cleanse me from my sin. Create in me a clean heart and renew a right spirit in me." Parts of a psalm he had heard before came back to him as he sat on his bed, head hung in shame, drenched from the rain and from guilt. "Give me a chance to see Deborah again so that I can beg her forgiveness."

The only answer he got was the sudden illumination of the room by another bolt of lightning and a crash of thunder that felt as if it would tear the boat in pieces.

November 23, 1696

St. Michael's Town
Barbados

Thomas was glad that he had chosen to ride his horse into Town rather than take the coach or cart. The rainy season was drawing to an end and it was as if the heavens were pouring out the last rains all at once. The rain had been incessant over the last few days and the roads were muddy and impassable in some places. The only reason that he had ventured into Town was because the week before he had been told by the Fairfax's shipping agent that he was expecting a ship to come in around the 20th and according to the time that Richard had told him he would be leaving Carolina, he would probably be on that ship.

Elizabeth had been very happy to hear of Richard's plans to take over the agency in Barbados and he was wise enough not to mention the role Deborah had played in that decision. He had been quite vague in answering her questions about his fiancée and whether she would be coming as well. He had left her preparing to write a letter to Mary and no doubt she would eventually find out about Deborah.

He now rode his horse towards Carlisle Bay to see if the Adventurer had come in yet. He had been kept in town for three days now by torrential rains and there was no sign of the boat. Thankfully, the sun had broken out at last. He tried not to be anxious but even the agent had begun to look worried when the boat had not come in.

While he was still quite a distance away he saw a sloop sailing towards the Bay and heading for the Careenage. He rode his horse towards the Careenage and as the boat drew closer he could see that one of the masts was broken and it looked battered and damaged. As it turned, the name on the side became visible and he was relieved to see the word "Adventurer".

Richard feasted his eyes on the Barbadian landscape as the boat sailed closer to the shore. He had never been so glad to see land, and Barbados in particular, after the ordeal which had lasted about twelve hours before the sea had eventually returned to more comfortable swells.

He was surprised to see his uncle waving to him from the wharf and he vaguely wondered how he knew that he would be arriving today. He waved back and impatiently waited for the boat to pull up next to the dock. He almost kissed the ground when his feet touched land, so glad was he to have been delivered from a watery grave.

"Richard, my boy, it's good to see you." His uncle enfolded him in a hearty hug which he returned enthusiastically. "What happened? You're three days late and the boat looks damaged." Boats were only allowed into the Careenage for cleaning and repairs and this one was badly in need of repairs.

"We ran into a storm that made a believer out of me. I did not think I would live to make it to Barbados but I thank God that he delivered us here safely with no loss of life or limb."

"I was getting very worried when you didn't come in on the day your agent had said so I'm glad to see you here alive and well. I'll arrange for you to be taken to the boarding house that I'm staying at and if you want to, you can come out to the plantation to stay for a while when I go home tomorrow."

"Thanks Uncle but I think I'll stay in town rather than answer any awkward questions from Aunt Elizabeth right now. I don't even have any answers to give her." Thomas nodded.

They hired a carriage to take them to the boarding house while Richard's trunks were loaded on to a cart to which Thomas' horse was tied.

Once they were on their way, Thomas wasted no time in telling Richard: "In your letter you asked if it was legal for races to intermarry here," Richard unconsciously held his breath. "There's no law against it but of course it's quite rare. I do recall a black man and a white woman marrying several years ago and there may have been others since then. I personally don't have anything against you getting married and I will support you all I can. However I don't know how Deborah will be accepted by the planters' wives if you do get married."

Richard was relieved that there were no legal obstacles to their getting married. Any other issues they would deal with as they came up, provided that Deborah accepted his proposal.

"Thank you, Uncle. I'm very relieved to hear that because I really did not fancy moving to England. We'll take one step at a time."

They discussed the arrangements Thomas had made with the housing agent and Richard was eager to meet with him so that he could begin looking at houses. He wanted to know if his uncle had seen Deborah but it was almost as if he was reluctant to ask in case he heard bad news. As if sensing this Thomas took pity on him and told him that he had seen Deborah and he was pretty sure that she still had feelings for him but that he would have to talk with her himself to know for sure.

Richard wanted to go and see Deborah right away but his uncle took one look at his bloodshot eyes and unshaven face and told him in no uncertain terms that he needed to bathe, shave and rest before he approached Deborah.

Chapter Thirty

Richard slept like the dead that night since it was his first proper night of sleep since the storm and the first in a comfortable bed in over two weeks. The bath and the sumptuous meal he had in the boarding house's dining room also aided his rest but he mostly attributed it to the peace he now felt.

A feeling of vulnerability that was unfamiliar and uncomfortable came over him at the thought that Deborah had the power to bring him great joy or, he didn't even want to entertain the thought, great misery. He fervently prayed for the former.

Washing and dressing quickly Richard shrugged into a well fitted jacket, tied his hair back with a ribbon and headed out the door. He met Thomas downstairs in the dining room for a quick breakfast after which Thomas accompanied him to High Street where Deborah and Sarah lived and had their shop.

"I wish you all the best," offered his uncle, shaking his hand. "You have my blessing. Let me know how it turns out."

"Thank you, Uncle. I will."

The street was not that far from the Careenage where the boat had been pulled up. It was a bustling commercial street with many stores on both sides of the road offering everything from clothes and jewelry to furniture and household items with a few taverns in between to quench the thirst of shoppers.

He perused the shops as he made his way down the road until without warning he saw a sign a few doors down announcing "Deborah's Health and Beauty Shop and Sarah's Sewing Emporium". He stood for a moment staring at it with a slight smile and felt a surge of pride for Deborah and her mother. Who would believe that less than six months ago they were slaves and now here they were operating a business in Town. He drew in a deep breath and crossed the street.

Deborah was busy tidying her shelves and putting out some imported scented soap that had arrived the day before. It was still quite early in the morning and she didn't expect customers until a bit later. Sarah was still upstairs getting ready since she had been up quite late finishing a dress that a customer had ordered for that day.

She heard a footfall just inside the shop and quickly turned around to see who had come in so early. She felt as if the breath had been sucked out of her and as if to compensate for the lack of oxygen in her body, her heart sped up to increase the flow of blood to her vital organs. She looked in disbelief at Richard standing in her shop with a broad smile on his face. Her eyes devoured him eagerly as she reacquainted herself with the face that Hattie had sworn was more handsome that the master's and the tall, muscular body that still invaded her dreams some nights. Words deserted her.

"I can't believe I have you at a loss for words, Deborah," teased Richard even as his eyes darkened in the way that she had become so familiar with. Richard was surprised that he could form a sentence when he was so overwhelmed by the sight of Deborah wearing one of the dresses he had bought her and with her hair in a long plait over her shoulder. His fingers itched to unravel it and bury his face in it as he had done so many times in the past.

"Richard! What are you doing here?" She managed to get out, still frozen in the same position.

"I've decided to take over from our agent and expand our shipping business from Barbados," he answered as if it was a logical answer. A dozen questions poured into her mind but the one that was foremost came out before she could stop it.

"Is your wife with you?"

Richard smiled as her question gave him information that he needed. "I don't have a wife, yet." He watched her closely and was satisfied to see the blank look appear that she assumed when she wanted to hide her emotions. She turned back to the shelf to put down some bars of soap that she was still holding.

"Oh," was all she said.

"Actually Ann and I have decided not to marry."

Deborah turned back around so quickly that she knocked over the box of soap that was on a stool next to her. Richard crossed the room to help her pick up the bars that had spilled out, secretly pleased with her reaction. As he came close to her, the familiar lemony scent of the soap that she used teased his nose, causing his body to stir in response.

Without conscious thought he put his hands on her shoulders and pulled her to her feet, cupping her face with his hands and fusing his mouth to hers. There was no gentleness or hesitancy in the kiss as the full force of his long restrained passion broke free. Deborah responded eagerly, burying her fingers in his hair. Richard nudged her backwards until she was pinned between his body and the shelf without taking his lips from hers. The close proximity of his body left no doubt of the extent of his desire for her.

"Deborah! What you doing?" Sarah demanded from the doorway, making Deborah jump guiltily and push away from Richard. Richard closed his eyes in frustration before turning around to greet Sarah.

"Master Richard? What you doing in Barbados?" She asked with wide eyes.

"I've come to work here, Sarah. Deborah, we need to talk."

"I cannot talk now," Deborah told him reluctantly. "Our customers will soon be coming in."

"I'll come back this evening when you're closed. Anyway I have to go and see an agent about renting a house. See you later." He couldn't resist running his fingers down her cheek, soliciting a slight shiver from her. He nodded to Sarah, feeling her disapproval surrounding her like a dark cloud, as he passed and left the shop.

"Deborah, you forget which master you serving now?" Sarah got straight to the point. "And he ain' engaged to a girl in Carolina?"

"He said that they decided not to get married."

"So what he want with you now?"

"I don't know ma, we did not get the chance to talk."

"But you get the chance to kiss," accused Sarah. Deborah's faced reddened. She had no answer for that so she turned back to the task she was doing when Richard walked into the shop and turned her new life upside down.

Later that day

Deborah had just put on the kettle to boil when she heard a knock at the door. Her heart immediately sped up as she knew that it would be Richard. Her mother had already warned her about falling back into his bed even if he was not engaged anymore as they had left that life behind them.

Deborah was in two minds as she went to open the door. She was hungry for the sight of Richard but was not looking forward to their talk. She knew that she could no longer be with him as she had been before and that he wouldn't understand. She could now fully empathize with her mother and how she must have felt when she had to end her relationship with Thomas. Not that she had a relationship with Richard anymore, but she would like to. She had missed him so much and if she was honest with herself, she still desired him. How would she endure this?

Richard waited impatiently for Deborah to open the door. After the way she responded to him in the shop earlier, he was sure that she still had feelings for him. He couldn't help but pull her into his arms as he pushed the door closed and buried his face in her neck, where he knew she was ticklish.

"Richard!" she protested breathlessly, squirming away. "You said that you wanted to talk."

"Talking can wait," he said throatily, pulling her back to him. "I missed you. I missed being with you." His eyes fell to her lips seconds before his lips followed and this time he gently and exquisitely explored her mouth, reacquainting himself with the taste of her.

Deborah reluctantly tore herself away in case her mother came upon them and gestured towards the kitchen, where she offered him a cup of tea and some cake that Sarah had made. Richard's eyes followed her hungrily as she moved around the tiny kitchen and she was reminded of the first night that she and Cassie had served dinner when she had felt his eyes on her. This time she was not afraid; at least not in the same way. Now she was afraid that she would not be able to restrain herself from giving into the passion that simmered just below the surface when they were in close proximity of each other. She sent up a prayer for divine help.

"Richard, what are you really doing in Barbados?" she asked as she sat down, coming straight to the point. Richard hesitated. He could tell that she was still very attracted to him but there was a hesitation in her that he did not understand, especially since he had told her that he was no longer engaged and he wondered if she was involved with someone else.

He took a deep breath and decided to lay his cards on the table. He couldn't pretend that he had come on business when the main reason he was in Barbados was because of her. Before he said anything there was something he had to do first.

"Deborah, before I tell you why I'm in Barbados I need to first of all ask your forgiveness for treating you as less than a human being. I'm sorry for buying you from your uncle in the same way I would buy a horse and for telling you that many women would be happy to be owned by me. My only excuse is that I just didn't know any different at the time."

"What?" Deborah was shocked at his confession as it was the last thing she was expecting.

"On the way to Barbados we ran into a storm. I did not think that we would make it and I began to reflect on my life and the way I treated you and I asked God for forgiveness and now I'm asking you. I'm so sorry that I made your life a misery and made you pay for your freedom by sleeping with me. Will you forgive me, Deborah?"

Deborah was stunned and moved to tears at his words. What an awesome God she served who could touch Richard's heart as he had done hers. She silently thanked him for sparing Richard's life and allowing her to see him again.

"I forgive you Richard. How can I not, when God has forgiven me? You know I hated you before you even came to Barbados, and even though you were constantly provoking me, I began to see that deep down you were a good man although you had been brought up to believe that slaves were less than human."

"But why are you in Barbados and why have you and Ann decided not to marry?" she asked remembering what he had said earlier.

"When I went back to Carolina, one of the first things I did was to end my relationship with Anise, my mistress." He caught the brief look of surprise and satisfaction on her face before she schooled it once again. "Then I found myself reluctant to be with Ann and the more I was with her the less I felt that I could go through with our marriage. In the end my brother-in-law made me see that I had to talk to her and tell her the truth."

"The truth?"

"That I had fallen in love with the daughter of a plantation owner; the very thing she had warned me about."

Deborah froze with the cup half-way to her mouth. She shakily replaced it in the saucer and her eyes met Richard's.

"You mean me?"

Richard smiled indulgently and said, "No I mean Mary-Ann Newton," referring to one of the planter's daughters he had met at his party. "Of course I mean you."

He suddenly became serious and said, "I didn't expect to fall in love with you, Deborah. I thought that once I took you to my bed I would be able to get over my desire for you and go back to Carolina and marry Ann and run her father's plantation, but I was wrong. I couldn't get you out of my mind. I still can't. I want to marry you."

Deborah was stunned. Richard loved her? He had given up marrying Ann and running her father's plantation to be with her? He wanted to marry her? Joy surged in her again before she realized that it would not be fair to marry him.

"I'm sorry Richard but I can't marry you. I've heard that marriage between races is illegal in America so if we married we would never be able to go to Carolina and see your family."

"I don't need to go to Carolina, Deborah. Or I can go by myself if I need to and come back. All I need is you."

"What about here? I don't want you not to be accepted because of me."

"As I told my uncle, we'll take one step at a time. All I know is that I love you and I want to spend the rest of my life with you."

"You talked to Master Thomas about this?" she asked surprised.

"Yes. And we have his blessing. I don't know how Aunt Elizabeth will take it though, but right now I don't care. We only need to please ourselves and God."

Deborah thought about that for a few minutes. She had never imagined that she would find someone who loved her and was willing to give up everything for her. God had truly blessed her so she would trust him to work it out.

"Yes, you're right Richard. I will marry you."

He pushed over his chair in his haste to get up and pull her into his arms, hugging her to him and burying his face in her hair. The crash of the chair hitting the ground brought Sarah out of her room to find Richard passionately kissing Deborah.

"Deborah, what you doing girl?" she asked for the second time that day.

They reluctantly pulled apart and Richard answered for both of them saying, "Celebrating our upcoming wedding."

They had to laugh at the shock on Sarah's face before tears of joy flooded her eyes that her daughter had finally found someone who loved and valued her.

Chapter Thirty-One

November 30, 1696

W illiam could not contain the smile that broke out across his face as his beloved Barbados came into sight and the boat headed for Carlisle Bay. He was finally home, after two long torturous years. He had missed the island more than he had expected to and he had missed his mother and the girls, although he rarely spent much time with them. He wondered how his partner in crime, Henry, was and if he was still as wild as ever.

No one was there to meet him but he wasn't surprised since the boat was actually a bit earlier than scheduled as a brisk wind had added several knots to their speed and hustled them towards Barbados. He decided to spend a couple of nights in Town before going home. It had been a long time since he had experienced its pleasures and he didn't plan to deny himself a moment longer, just in case his father got it in his head to put him to work right away and made sure that he did not leave the plantation for a while.

As the boat dropped anchor and waited for the cockboats to come to take the passengers and cargo to shore, he went below deck to arrange for his trunks to be brought up. He would stay at his favorite boarding house and reacquaint himself with all of its delights before heading home. Anticipation hastened his feet as he remembered the beautiful mulatto girls that kept the patrons well entertained for a few coins.

That reminded him that Deborah and her mother now lived in Town. He would ask the proprietress if she knew of them since she seemed to know everything that went on in town. He would definitely have to visit them and pay his respects. And he had some unfinished business with Deborah.

William sat in the White Hare tavern a few doors up the street and across the road from Deborah's shop. The Madame at the boarding house had been very helpful in providing the information he needed. After all, two colored women running a shop in Town was not a common occurrence so he had had no trouble finding them. From his seat in a darkened corner of the tavern near the door he could see their customers coming and going. From the looks of things, the business seemed to be doing well. It certainly was well patronized. He should pay them a visit and offer his congratulations.

Tossing back the last bit of rum in his glass, he left a few coins on the table, pushed back his chair and headed down the road.

He stepped into the shop and let his eyes adjust to the dimness after being in the sunlight. Deborah was standing behind a counter serving a well dressed lady whose slave girl stood by carrying her purchases. His eyes ran hungrily over her and images of her in his bed stirred him. She was even more beautiful than he remembered. Gone were the drab slave clothes and the handkerchief. Her hair was in a simple plait over her shoulder but she wore a beautiful flowered dress that flattered her figure.

Glancing around the shop he saw a stand with clothes hanging on it but he didn't see her mother and he was glad that he would be able to talk to Deborah without her interfering presence. The lady at the counter finished her purchase and headed for the door. William nodded politely to her and moved further into the shop, watching Deborah's face as he drew closer and was gratified to see the politely welcoming smile on her face change to one of shock as she recognized him.

"William!" Her hand flew to her chest as if she was trying to hold her heart in place. Her face paled and she looked in panic towards the door as if she was gauging how easily she could escape if she needed to.

Deborah's heart began to beat a furious tattoo in her chest. She had known that William was coming back soon but she had not been prepared for the shock of seeing him. His face was somewhat thinner than before but he was still very good looking in spite of the coldness of his green eyes that revealed his cruel nature. What was he doing here? How did he find their shop and what did he want with her?

"Is that all you're going to say?" he taunted her. "Surely you're glad to see me," he mocked. "A welcome home kiss would not be amiss either," he added laughing.

Deborah drew herself up. She would not let William intimidate her any longer. She was a free woman, she no longer belonged to his family and he had no control over her life.

"May I help you with anything? Some soap as a gift for your mother and sisters perhaps?" she asked ignoring his comments.

"I'll pass on the gifts but there is something else you can help me with." A familiar predatory look entered his eyes as he drew closer to her. Deborah was glad that there was a counter between them but even so she forced herself not to retreat in fear as William leaned over the counter and caressed her plait suggestively. She pulled it from his grasp and was about to demand that he leave when a concerned voice interrupted.

"Deborah, are you alright?" She almost sagged with relief as she heard Richard's voice. She eagerly sought his gaze as he strode purposely into the shop, looking big and powerful.

"Yes, thank you Richard," she assured him, although he could see the relief on her face. He turned to look at the tall, lean man who had been leaning over the counter. He looked somewhat familiar but Richard could not place where he may have met him. Women would probably consider him handsome but his eyes were cold and flat.

"I feel as if we've met before," Richard said politely offering his hand although he instinctively wanted nothing to do with the man.

"That's unlikely since I've just returned from England after two years. I'm William Edwards of The Acreage," he added haughtily.

Richard's blood heated in his veins as he recognized the name and the anger that he had felt when Deborah told him that he had raped her threatened to erupt. This sorry excuse for a human being was his cousin. He clenched his hands at his side and barely managed to restrain himself from putting him on the floor with a well placed blow.

"I am Richard Fairfax."

So this was the favored nephew that his father had referred to as a fine young man and his mother had been so pleased to have visit when he was away. This was the one who had slept in his bed and probably bedded his slave in his absence. Hatred rose in him. He wondered what he was doing back in Barbados and why he was regarding Deborah with such possessiveness.

"Then you must be my cousin from Carolina. What a small world. I thought you had returned to America."

"Barbados had a great pull on me and I found I could not stay away. I have decided to move here and run our shipping agency."

"Wonderful!" said William, lying. "Anyway I must be off. I have not even been home as yet as I only arrived yesterday."

Turning to Deborah he said, "When I heard you had moved to town I had to come and see you. I've known Deborah all her life," he told Richard. "I know we didn't have much chance to catch up on old times before we were interrupted Deborah, but rest assured that you haven't seen the last of me." He smiled slightly at them both before heading for the door.

The promise sounded more like a threat to Richard and as he looked at Deborah's pale face he knew that she saw it as one too.

She quickly lifted up wooden partition at the end of the counter and flew into his arms, uncaring whether any customers might come in and see them. Richard held her close and was concerned to find her shaking. William's visit had served to bring back the disturbing memories of her past and left her badly shaken.

"Don't worry, he can't hurt you anymore."

Deborah nodded but she was not convinced. Her mother had told also her not to worry days before William had taken her innocence.

December 1, 1696
The Acreage Plantation

The Royal palms lining the driveway seemed to wave their greeting to William as the wind disturbed their long fronds. The welcome sight of them made him smile and he felt a new surge of appreciation for the plantation he had left two years ago. As the coach strained to get up the driveway, laden with his trunks, he looked around to see what changes had been made, but apart from some new flowers everything looked much as he had left it, even his mother sitting in her favorite rocking chair on the patio flanked by his sisters.

Elizabeth saw the coach coming up the driveway and knew that William had come home. Lifting her skirt in one hand she ran to it as it came to a halt and William hastily climbed out.

"Oh William, I'm so glad you're home. I missed you so." Tears of joy poured down her cheeks as they hugged each other.

"Mother, it's so good to be back. I never thought I would miss this place so much. I don't plan to go anywhere for a long time." He turned to hug his sisters who had joined them demanding that he tell them all about England and asking what he had brought for them.

"I'll get one of the stable boys to get your father. He's probably in the distillery."

William was not as eager to see his father. He could never seem to gain his approval and he wondered how he would measure up to the fine young man who was on the plantation just months ago.

Flopping into one of the rocking chairs he answered as many of their questions as he could, even as he soaked in his surroundings with contentment. A new slave girl brought them drinks and said, "Welcome home, Master William."

"Thank you...?"

"Hattie," she provided with a flirtatious smile.

"Thank you Hattie," he continued with a sly smile of his own. His father had not lost his taste in beautiful slave girls, he noticed. Well he certainly shouldn't have any objection to him having some fun with Hattie.

He was surprised to see his father hurrying towards the house followed by the stable boy. Could it be that he was actually glad to see him? William stood up as his father reached the patio and held out his hand to shake his father's, only to be stunned when his father ignored his outstretched hand and folded him into an embrace. Maybe he had mellowed in the two years he had been away.

"William my boy, I'm so happy to see you."

"Thank you, father," he said awkwardly.

"Sit down and rest. You must be tired."

"I'm fine. What's been happening on the plantation?" asked William.

"We had a very good crop this year and the rum is doing well too. I had some help from your cousin Richard and he's just moved back to Barbados as well. You should meet him next time we're in Town."

"I met him yesterday." Too late William realized that he should have kept that to himself.

"You did?" Thomas asked in surprise. "Where?"

"At Deborah's shop," admitted William reluctantly.

"What were you doing in her shop?" asked his mother sharply.

"I came across their shop almost by accident," he lied, "and Richard came in as I was there."

His father looked at him suspiciously and announced, "Well I'm glad you met. Richard plans to marry Deborah."

"What?" Elizabeth spluttered into her drink. William swallowed some of his the wrong way and began to cough.

"My nephew plans to marry that colored woman?" she shouted in disbelief. Now she understood why he had returned to Barbados without his fiancée and the reluctance Thomas had shown in explaining to her what was going on.

"There's no law against it, Elizabeth."

William could not believe that his cousin was planning to taint their blood lines by marrying Deborah. Why would he buy the cow when he could get the milk free?

December 15, 1696

As it grew closer to Christmas, Sarah and Deborah's shop began to get very busy with an influx of customers wanting clothes from Sarah and soap and perfume from Deborah. They took delight in decorating their house and shop with greenery and dried flowers and looked forward expectantly to Christmas day, their first as free women where they would not have to get up at the crack of dawn and serve the family. They could choose to do whatever they wanted. Such a thought gave them great joy and this year they had an even greater appreciation of Christmas since it celebrated the birth of Jesus.

It was only Williams' threat that prevented Deborah from fully enjoying the season. She kept expecting to see him appear in the shop and had become quite anxious. When she confessed her concerns to Richard, he advised her to carry a knife in her pocket and to make sure that Jacko was around as much as possible. He was spending many hours working with the agent before he left to return to England and she barely saw him except on Sundays. Sarah chaperoned them to make sure, as Richard teased her, that they stayed on the straight and narrow. They had set their wedding date for the last day of the year since they wanted to start their new life and the New Year at the same time.

Thomas came to Town and visited with them one Sunday and let them know that he had told the family about their impending marriage. Deborah said nothing about William's threat since she didn't want to cause any more trouble between them. She only hoped that now he knew that she and Richard were getting married he would leave her alone.

Nevertheless she did not intend to be caught unaware by him so the knife that was constantly in her pocket gave her comfort that she would not be defense-less if he ever tried to attack her. She was certainly not going to let him violate her again without a fight and she was prepared to use it if she had to.

December 23, 1696

William watched Sarah leave the house with her slave woman from his seat near the door of the White Hare. Good. He had spent hours in that seat since he came to Town on Friday surreptitiously watching the house up the street. His father had wasted no time in assigning him duties on the plantation and he had surprisingly found himself enjoying the challenge of taming the land and the slaves who worked on it.

Speaking of taming slaves, he was long overdue in paying a visit to the one across the street. All he could think about as he slept in his bed was that Deborah had willingly entertained his cousin on that same mattress while she had rejected him. Worse than that, his father had told him that Richard wanted to marry Deborah. Fool! Who would marry a slave, even if she had been freed? She had obviously bewitched him.

He had not seen Jacko leave the house, so he knew he was around somewhere but he had not seen him go upstairs when Sarah went out so he would most likely be in his own quarters. Anyway what could he do with only one hand?

Pushing back his chair he left the tavern and glancing up and down the street to make sure that no one was coming he walked quickly up the road and climbed the stairs leading up to the house.

Deborah heard a knock at the door and opened it a crack thinking that it must be Richard since she was expecting him. She cursed herself for not asking who it was when she saw William. She tried to pull the door closed but he yanked it from her grasp before quickly stepping over the threshold and closing it behind him. The sound of the lock turning froze her blood.

"Hello Deborah, that was rather careless of you. Don't you know that you should ask who's there before you open your door?" He smiled as she backed away. "I know I told you that I would come and visit you but I've been very busy."

"What do you want, William?" She tried to stop her voice from shaking even as she eased her hand closer to her pocket, thankful that she had gotten into the habit of keeping the knife in it even when she was at home.

"Do you really have to ask that? I believe we have some unfinished business."

"We have no unfinished business William. Please leave my house and don't come back," she ordered bravely.

"Do you think I'm just going to walk out now that I've got you alone?" he asked coming closer.

"Stop right there," she commanded slipping her hand in her pocket and feeling the comforting hilt of the knife.

"Or you'll do what?" he taunted.

Deborah pulled the knife from her pocket with a shaking hand and gestured at him with it. "You don't want to find out. Just leave now William."

He laughed and made a sudden lunge towards her. Deborah instinctively raised her hand to ward him off and the knife opened a two inch gash on his cheek. Blood sprang from the cut and began to drip down his face. William put his hand to his face in disbelief and stared at the blood that stained his fingers. Deborah froze at the fury that came over his face and she knew that only one of them would come out of this alive.

"You cut me," he said in disbelief and struck her across the face, knocking her to the ground. The knife flew from her grasp and slid across the room. She thought that he would kill her right there but he pulled her to her feet and dragged her against him. Her throat closed up in fear, cutting off her scream.

"You will regret that," he promised and dragged her into the small parlor. She closed her eyes in horror. Not again! She would prefer to die than let William violate her. She saw that the knife had landed near the doorway and wondered how she could get to it.

William pushed her to the floor and ripped the front of her dress open. The reality of what was about to happen restored her voice and she screamed for Jacko before he could silence her. Deborah fought like a wildcat as he tried to raise her skirt. There was no way she would make this easy for him; he would have to kill her first.

God where are you? Help me please, she prayed silently even as she tried to claw at his already bleeding face.

The sound of the door being broken down penetrated her consciousness seconds before William was plucked from her as if he weighed nothing and tossed aside. Looking up Deborah saw Jacko who opened his mouth to ask her if she was alright. Fear for Deborah seemed to have given him supernatural strength.

Before he could get the words out, William sprang to his feet and charged at him and the two men began to struggle. William had the advantage, having both hands, and years of being owned by the Edwards was ingrained in Jacko's head and he was reluctant to fight with William.

There was a clatter of boots on the stairs and Richard rushed into the room. He had been walking up the road when he saw Jacko running up the stairs and he had broken into a run. The sight of Deborah with the front of her dress ripped open stirred up a rage unlike anything he had ever felt before. He grabbed William who was attacking Jacko with furious blows, spun him around and did what he had wanted to from the time Deborah had told him her story; he smashed his face with his fist. William fell to the ground but managed to crawl over to the knife which was still by the door.

Springing back up he swung the knife in an arc towards Richard. Deborah screamed but Richard jumped back and the knife missed him. As William brought the knife down towards Richard, he grabbed his arm and stopped it in its motion. Years of physical work gave Richard the greater strength and he was able to twist William's hand until he dropped the knife.

Picking it up quickly, he stepped behind William and brought the knife to his throat applying just enough pressure for a thin line of blood to appear.

"Don't Richard," pleaded Deborah.

"Give me a good reason why I should not end his miserable life?" Richard asked in a deadly voice.

Go ahead, do it, urged a voice. *No son. Let him go. I will deal with him.*

Richard struggled with himself for a minute before releasing William with great reluctance and pushed him towards the door. "Barbados is too small for both of us. You better head back to England or move to some other island because I can't promise that I'll be so generous with your life next time. Now get out!"

William wasted no time in clearing out. The thin cut on his neck was burning from sweat and the gash on his cheek was aching badly but at least he had his life.

Richard dropped to his knees and hugged Deborah.

"Are you alright?" She nodded still shaking. "I'm so sorry I was not here to protect you. I will send word to my uncle about this and he'd better get him out of the island if he does not want him arrested. I'm sure that he won't try anything again but I want you and Sarah to move in with me until we get married so that I can protect you."

Deborah nodded in agreement. She could think of nothing she would like better.

Epilogue

December 31, 1696
The Residence of Richard and Deborah Fairfax

"I thought this day would never come, Mrs. Fairfax," Richard said as they entered the master bedroom of the house he had purchased and closed the door behind them. It was a pretty two storey house situated a short distance along the coast from Carlisle Bay and was close to the homes of two families called the Needhams, who had a business in the same area as his.

They had exchanged vows before the minister at St. Michael's Parish Church only hours before with Sarah and Thomas as their witnesses while Jacko and Mamie watched from the back of the church with Cassie and Jethro, who had accompanied Thomas to town as a surprise for Deborah.

Thomas had told Deborah how much he regretted William's transgression against her which he was reminded of every time he saw the scar on his face. England had obviously not improved him so rather than send him back he had said that he would be in contact with some of the planters he knew in the other islands

341

to see if one of them would employ William on their plantation.

"Deborah Fairfax. I like the sound of that," she smiled.

"So do I," he agreed. Looking into her eyes he said, "I love you with all my heart, Deborah Fairfax and I thank God every day that he brought me to Barbados."

"I told you that you were on a divine mission," she reminded him. "I can't believe that nine months ago I didn't even know you. Now I can't imagine life without you."

"I'm sorry that I forced you into my bed long before we made our vows."

"You did not force me, I chose to come. Let us not speak of that anymore. All is forgiven."

Richard gently kissed her lips in thanks and unbuttoned the cream colored wedding dress, letting it slide down her body until it formed a pool on the floor. He lifted her out of it and swung her around until she was free of the encumbrance and dressed only in a light chemise. Deborah pushed his jacket from his shoulders and quickly unbuttoned his shirt until it hung open giving her access to the contours of his chest to explore.

Bending his head, he reverently kissed her eyes and her cheek where the bruise from William's blow had now faded, before claiming her lips in a kiss that began softly but increased in intensity as she peeled off his shirt to delight her hands in the feel of the taut muscles of his shoulders.

Richard relieved her of the last of her clothing paying homage to her as she stood before him.

"Exquisite," he whispered in awe as if he were seeing her for the first time.

"One of us is wearing too many clothes," Deborah teased, fumbling with the buttons of his breeches. Richard hurriedly took over the task from her and quickly tossed them aside. He drew her into his arms and sucked in a breath at the feel of her against him and they held each other close, enjoying the differences between them; one soft, one hard and both made perfectly to complement the other.

Richard picked her up and carried her to the massive four poster bed where he gently deposited her like the precious gift she was.

"My wife," he said hoarsely, deeply affected by the sight of her hair spread across the pillow and the eagerness for him that he saw in her eyes.

"My husband," she answered and opened her arms to him in welcome.

There was no more talking save the quiet murmurs of encouragement and approval as they explored each other as if for the first time, their love creating in them a desire to give rather than take, and in the end rewarding them with exquisite pleasure that surpassed anything they had experienced before.

Richard drew Deborah back against him as they lay side by side under the thick blanket. December was always quite cold by Barbadian standards and the wind blowing off the ocean and through the bedroom window chilled Deborah who was glad for Richard's warmth against her back.

"I don't think I've ever been happier," she murmured snuggling against him. "I am now complete."

Richard dropped a kiss on the top of her head, supremely contented. "I feel the same."

"I really hope that one day my mother finds this kind of love and happiness," she confided. "I know that Jethro always had a soft spot for her so maybe they will get together if Master Thomas ever decides to free him."

"Jethro is a good carpenter so I don't know how willing my uncle would be to free him but I can ask him. I could offer to buy him and then set him free as I did with you. Maybe I can help him to start a business or he can work on our ships when they need repairs."

"That would be very good of you, Richard."

"I'm nothing but good." He teased. "Speaking of good, my uncle has generously given us £20 as a wedding gift. He's going to be escorting Aunt Elizabeth and the girls to England early in the New Year but he will come back once they are settled. I think they're hoping to find husbands for them and that they will remain in England rather than live in this corrupt society."

"He told me that he is trying to find somewhere for William to go and I will be glad when he's no longer in Barbados. Maybe living in another island, like Jamaica, will change him."

"I think only God can change him; after all look how he changed me."

"Look how he changed us," she corrected. "You're right. With God all things are possible."

These words reassured them as they contemplated the future they would face together in a world that was ruled by prejudice. But they had hope that one day people's eyes would be opened and they would realize the truth of what Sarah had said.

"We're all the same. Maybe it's just that when you don't know people, when you don't mix with them, they seem like they different. But we're all the same."

THE END

Made in the USA
Columbia, SC
02 April 2019